Expl

Bound by
Loyalty Honor Truth
Book Four

Copyright

Dedication

To all the heroes in my life: Karl, Billy, Skip, Trevor, August and Cooper.

Love you all so much.

TOC

Chapter One 6

Chapter Two 14

Chapter Three 29

Chapter Four 32

Chapter Five 48

Chapter Six 52

Chapter Seven 64

Chapter Eight 73

Chapter Nine 79

Chapter Ten 91

Chapter Eleven 107

Chapter Twelve 120

Chapter Thirteen 132

Chapter Fourteen 136

Chapter Fifteen 151

Chapter Sixteen 164

Chapter Seventeen 167

Chapter Eighteen 180

Chapter Nineteen 199

Chapter Twenty 210

Chapter Twenty-One 213

Chapter Twenty-Two 220

Chapter Twenty-Three 230

Chapter Twenty-Four 236

Chapter Twenty-Five 248

Chapter Twenty-Six 254

Chapter Twenty-Seven 264

Lethal 271

Chapter One..271

Chapter One

Ashlyn Pillar looked around, feeling a profound sense of loss as she carefully studied the remains of the house. The local fire department had already soaked everything down, so there was no chance it would rekindle.

And everyone was careful to preserve the scene when they saw the body.

God, sometimes she hated her job. She was an FBI agent specializing in criminal investigations—mainly anything involving explosives. She could count on one hand when her gut hadn't churned at the scene of a crime, and this wasn't your typical house fire. It also hit a hell of a lot closer to home for her.

A flash from another time sucked the breath momentarily out of her body. It was all she could do to control the trembling that swept over her. Yeah, she knew she looked calm and in control on the outside. On the inside was another story.

The house in front of her suddenly disappeared, replaced by another. The one in her mind was a two-story, midcentury, modern home with carefully manicured grounds. The kind of house that you'd expect of a high-powered attorney and his family.

Ashlyn grit her teeth, pulling her thoughts back to the present. She looked down at her arms, knowing that her long-sleeved shirt covered the scars. She drew in a deep breath and focused on the present, moving forward, always forward, and trying not to look back. She was afraid if she did, she might see the monster from her past.

The sturdy boots she wore protected her feet from the shards of broken glass and nails as she carefully made her way through the rubble. With each step, a lingering odor of smoke, lost memories, and death filled her nostrils.

The remains of a sofa faced what might have been a

picture window. A wooden table that had probably lasted for years, passed down from mother to daughter, was now broken and burnt beyond repair. It wasn't any of those pieces of furniture which drew her attention. Her gaze was fixed on the metal chair in the center of the living room. She knew, without a doubt, it didn't belong there.

She continued through the shell of what used to be someone's home—Kimberly Braddock's home, to be exact. If Ashlyn wasn't mistaken, what was left of Kimberly was sitting on the chair. Arms that had been reduced to bone and charred flesh stretched behind her. By the time the ties that bound her wrists burned away, it was too late for her to escape.

Kimberly had been a young woman on her own. She'd inherited her parents' farm after they'd died within a few months of each other. They'd been an older couple blessed later in life with a child they thought never to have.

Kimberly was twenty-six, engaged to be married. Her fiancé was out of state on business at the time of the fire. He wasn't a suspect. Not that Ashlyn thought he would be. When they told him, they said he broke down and cried. Who wouldn't?

Ashlyn stopped in front of the metal chair and stared at what used to be a vibrant young woman with her whole life before her…until she crossed paths with a sadistic killer.

"We've got to catch this guy," she said, voice cracking. She compressed her lips, swallowing her emotions.

"You okay?" Nolan asked.

She looked at him for a moment, then turned back to the body. "Yeah, I'm fine."

How much had Kimberly suffered before death took her? Had she thought of her fiancé, Colin, during her last moments? The life they would've shared if she hadn't stopped at the gas station that night?

Yes, he'd told them exactly where he'd abducted her.

No, that wasn't quite right. He'd specifically singled Ashlyn out. He'd always spoken directly to her, as if she was the only one who could save the victims. He told her what he was going to do and when he would do it. Clues, always clues. Taunting her. Asking her if she'd be able to save this one.

Damn, sometimes she'd wake up in the middle of the night and hear his raspy voice scraping across every fiber of her being. A cold chill ran down her spine even as moisture dotted her face from the hot Texas sun bearing down on her.

"Why the hell does he tell us everything he's going to do?" Nolan asked.

Not everything. If that were the case, he'd already be in jail. She sighed, for a moment, wishing she could turn around and just walk away. Strip off her latex gloves and drop them as she went. Except she couldn't. He was still out there. Waiting to kill again.

"He's goading us," she told him.

Nolan was new to the team, even though he was experienced in fieldwork. She knew sometimes he couldn't grasp the ugliness. She pulled her attention away from Kimberly's remains and scanned the area.

"Maybe he gets off on our reaction. Who knows what's going on in his warped brain. He didn't set the explosive device under the victim this time. He's evolving, becoming angrier, and wanting us to see more of the victim."

Taunting them. It was as though he wanted them to suffer right along with the victim. No, it was more than that. He wanted *her* to suffer, knowing the woman had died a painful death because Ashlyn couldn't stop him. He wanted *her* to figure out the clues he left.

She continued. "He started the fire first, then set off the

explosives so the outside walls would blow out. He wanted us to see what was left of the woman sitting in the chair as soon as we pulled up—framed by the jagged edges of partial walls. He planned it that way."

"That's gruesome as hell," Nolan muttered.

"I agree. What's worse, this guy is good. He knows a hell of a lot about explosives, and he's learning more as he goes. This is his third victim, but it won't be his last."

"That's why we have to catch the bastard before he can hurt anyone else."

"Agreed. Let's go back to the office," she said.

All the evidence had been collected. She'd found the explosive devices almost immediately and carefully bagged them. The photographer had taken pictures of the scene and surrounding area. The rest of the team were back at the office by now, but she'd stayed behind.

She needed to feel what had happened. She needed to get inside his head. She scanned the area one last time, making mental notes before they made their way back through the rubble.

The M.E. would collect the remains and attempt to piece together a story. They would analyze the evidence and try to figure out why the killer was stalking Ashlyn.

Could it even be called stalking? It was more as though he challenged her to a horrible game of cat and mouse, and she was the mouse. Anger began to build inside her. She was damned tired of him and his games.

"We'll catch this guy," Nolan told her after they got into the black SUV and drove away. "Waylon said he's bringing in someone to help."

"So I heard," she mumbled and looked out the window. Yes, she knew a fresh set of eyes might help solve the case, but she didn't like feeling that she'd somehow failed. All the clues were there. She just hadn't been able to pull them together.

It was an hour back to the office and already mid-afternoon. As soon as she walked in, she sensed something was different. "What's going on?" she asked as she sat at her desk.

The team had their own desk and computer, but they were near enough they could discuss whatever came up. There were five on the team, each with their own specialty. She was the explosives expert and the youngest on the team at thirty. Leah and Nolan were thirty-four, Ginny was thirty-two, and Brad was thirty-six. Together, they were damned good—most of the time.

"New guy is here," Leah told her in a whisper. "My God, he's hot. I'd leave Gerald for him if he crooked a finger in my direction."

That's what she liked about Leah. No matter what, she always made Ashlyn smile. Gerald wasn't bad looking himself. They'd been married ten years. Leah had bright red hair and freckles across her nose. There was no way she'd ever leave her husband. She talked a good game, though.

Ashlyn nodded toward Waylon's office on the open second floor. "Is he in with the boss?"

"No, they went to the conference room. I figure they'll be calling us in next to make the introductions, and so we can review the new evidence. God, that was grisly this morning. Sometimes I wish I'd chosen a different career—like school teacher or something." She was thoughtful for a moment. "No, I think I'll stick with the serial killers."

Ashlyn laughed, and some of the tension eased.

At least, until the door to the conference room opened and Waylon stepped out. He was in his early fifties, slender, with salt and pepper hair. He might be older than them, but he was in great shape. He'd become a cop at eighteen, and from there, college, where he'd gotten his degree in crime scene investigation, then FBI, before settling in the San Antonio area. He was damned good, but this one even had him stumped.

"If you join me in the conference room, we'll see what we can do to catch this killer," he said, then turned and went back inside, leaving the door open. He was a man of few words. Rarely did he show emotion, but this case was getting to all of them and putting them on edge.

Ashlyn followed the others up the stairs. As soon as she stepped into the office, she felt his presence. She studied the new guy for a moment before moving to a chair. She guessed him to be in his mid-thirties, at least six feet, two inches of pure muscle. He wore a black pull-on shirt and low-riding jeans. He looked relaxed as he leaned against the windowsill, arms crossed. Hot was an understatement.

Their gazes locked. His intense green eyes slowly moved over her in a way that made her body grow hot and started a fluttering in her stomach. When his gaze shifted back to her face, there was a knowing look in his eyes and a slight curving of his lips, as if he knew exactly what kind of reaction her body had to him.

Her eyes immediately narrowed as she jerked on the back of the chair and took her seat. She didn't care what he thought about her or what he might've thought she felt. Nothing was going to happen between them. She didn't do office romances or sex with a co-worker or whatever he had on his mind. She was good with a one-nighter if she wanted release, as long as she never had to see the person again.

"I want to introduce Dylan Rowley. His qualifications are impeccable. Ex-Special Ops who works for the government with a team of other operatives. He's agreed to look at the evidence we have so far to see if he can help us catch the killer." Waylon nodded toward Ashlyn. "He'll be working directly with you since you know more about explosives than the rest of us."

She caught her groan before it escaped. When she met his

gaze, his smirk had become a full-out smile. Yeah, nothing else will be happening, buddy, she silently told him. He didn't seem fazed by the hard glitter she knew was in her eyes.

She pulled her attention away from him as Waylon introduced the rest of the team. They brought out the evidence from the last crime scene and immediately began going over everything. They were still waiting on the M.E.'s official report from the last scene. She quickly noticed Dylan didn't say a lot. If he was going to help, he didn't offer much of an opinion.

He suddenly turned to her. "How do you think it went down?"

She was surprised. For a while, she didn't think he knew how to talk. She looked away from one of the pictures. Okay, he wanted to know her thoughts, she'd tell him.

"I think he's a psychopath. He wants us to find him, but only when he's ready. That is, unless he has a change of heart and crawls into a hole somewhere. That's why his clues are cryptic. He's giving us just enough that it's more frustrating than anything."

He pointed toward the picture of the farmhouse from this morning. "And this particular scene?"

She looked at the pictures pinned on the board. Three innocent women whose lives were cut too short. Her gaze moved to the burned-out farmhouse. "I think he doused her with an accelerant, then struck a match. Maybe he gave her something to knock her out, or maybe he killed her first, then set her body on fire. I like to think she didn't feel any pain, but I know that's not always the case." There were evil people in the world who liked nothing better than to feed off someone's misery.

"And then what?"

"He probably had the explosive device set in advance. He wanted to watch her burn. Then, when he couldn't recognize her, he walked away. One push of a button was all it took to blow out most of the walls. He set the stage to showcase what he'd done. Framed his masterpiece for the media to report so the world would see his brilliance."

Dylan turned to Ginny. "Is that what you think?"

"Mostly." Ginny carefully studied the pictures. She was good at figuring out how someone's mind worked. "He definitely wants to showcase his work. He enjoys the media attention." She looked across the table and met Ashlyn's gaze. "But I'm still not sure if he's trying to impress Ashlyn or drive her crazy. The killer is fixated on her for some reason."

"Could he know you?" Dylan asked.

"Doubtful," Ashlyn said. "I'm originally from up North. Other than moving here a few years ago, I have no ties in Texas."

"Maybe he followed you down."

She'd wondered the same thing but then dismissed it.

"I'd like to look at the evidence from the other two cases, especially the explosive devices." Dylan walked closer to the wallboard, studying the pictures of the crime scenes. "I want to know about all his correspondence and any recordings of when he called. I think the key will be finding out why he feels this connection with Ashlyn." He looked at Ashlyn. "I'll need to look into your past."

She felt the color drain from her face. She didn't want anyone digging into her past and resurrecting memories better left buried. Memories that she still couldn't face.

How the hell was she going to tell a stranger what happened when she refused to think about it herself?

Chapter Two

Dylan wondered about the sudden change in Ashlyn. She immediately busied herself looking at the evidence on the table, but he'd seen how her face lost a little bit of color, and her eyes skirted away from his. When she rubbed her arms, he couldn't help but wonder if she realized what she was doing. The signs were there, telling him that she was hiding something.

Why was she wearing a long-sleeved shirt in the middle of June in Texas? He was pretty sure there was something she wasn't saying. Just a feeling he had, and he was rarely wrong. He'd think about it later, see what he could find out about her. Maybe get in touch with Ethan and see what he could dig up. The guy was a genius with a computer. Right now, he'd focus on catching a killer.

The team of agents went through all the evidence with Dylan, and there was quite a lot that they'd gathered. He could see why they were stumped. There was nothing cohesive enough to point in one direction. The guy was all over the place. Maybe he hadn't perfected his game yet.

"How long does he keep the victim alive?" he asked.

"We don't know for sure. I'd say this last one less than twenty-four hours," Waylon told him. "The first female was an introvert, according to all her neighbors. He took her to an abandoned warehouse, then set an explosive device under her chair. The local police department didn't realize there was a victim and figured it was a random incident until the fire department found a partial leg bone. That's when they started digging a little deeper and finally discovered the rest of what was left of her and, eventually, her identity. When they questioned her neighbors, they didn't know she was missing. According to her mail, she'd been gone about eight days, but we don't know how often she picked it up."

"I got the first phone call a few days later," Ashlyn told

him. "The suspect wanted to know why the locals hadn't contacted the FBI, namely me. It was shortly after that when I got the first note. It was in an envelope with my name scrawled across the front. It showed up on my desk one day." Her lips pressed together. "He had access to our offices."

"Or he paid someone to drop it off," Dylan said. "Or maybe someone found it in their suit pocket after he slipped it inside. It wouldn't be hard to do if he accidentally bumped into someone. No one ever thinks about the person after they give a mumbled apology. The man or woman might wonder about it, but they'd see your name, and put the note on your desk. He'd be careful he didn't get caught this early in the game."

"We figured the same thing," Brad said. "So far, everyone we've interviewed hasn't seen anyone lurking around. No strangers, no new tenets. We keep running up against a brick wall."

Dylan studied him for a moment. Brad was tall, about six feet, broad shoulders, and keenly alert, dark brown eyes. "So, we'll find a way around the wall," Dylan told him. "Do we have a timeline on the second victim?"

"The same. She'd returned to college. She let her parents know she'd made it back okay. When they called the following week to check-in, she didn't answer her phone. We know she was in class the day before he killed her."

"What about her roommate?"

Leah shook her head. "Private room. Her family donates a lot to the university. At least, they did until their daughter went missing and then turned up dead."

"Brad and I are going back to the gas station where he abducted Kimberly. Maybe someone will have remembered something," Ginny told them. "Their damn cameras weren't working."

Leah came to her feet. "I'm going through what's left of

Kimberly's computer. At least it wasn't completely destroyed. Maybe I'll find an e-mail that will give us a clue." She looked at Nolan. "You up for scanning through her social media accounts?"

Nolan grimaced. "Yeah, sure."

Before everyone left to go their separate ways, Brad spoke, "It's good to have a new set of eyes on this case. I have a bad feeling about this one."

Dylan nodded.

After everyone left, Waylon looked at Dylan. "Brad's damned good at his job, but he always has a bad feeling about cases. We're glad you're here, though." His deep sigh was pained. "I've got a meeting that I'm dreading. They always want to know why we can't solve the case immediately, and then I have to explain everything to them…again."

"I hope I can help," Dylan told him.

"You're in good hands with Ashlyn," Waylon said. "I'll leave you to it."

As soon as the door closed, Dylan turned to Ashlyn. "Let's start with the obvious since you're the one being targeted by the perp. Could it be an old boyfriend who's angry because you dumped him?"

She shook her head. Tendrils of pale blonde hair escaped the low ponytail and brushed across her face. She reached up and tucked the strands behind one ear. There was something about the way she did it. Her hands were delicate, with long fingers. He wondered if she played the piano. The movement had been graceful. He only drew his attention back to the matter at hand when she began talking.

"No. That's not a possibility."

Maybe he'd misread her and she wasn't into guys. She had certainly shot daggers in his direction when he'd let his gaze roam over her. But damn, she was beautiful. If he was wrong about her, he was losing his touch. Heaven help him if the guys on his team ever discovered he had. They'd never let him live it down.

Not that he'd ever be a playboy like Ethan. Women practically burst into flames when he looked at them. He had some kind of crazy-ass pheromones that drove women wild. As far as Dylan knew, no woman had ever been able to resist Ethan.

"Okay, what about old girlfriends?" He left no doubt about what he was thinking.

She cocked an eyebrow. "If you think I'm gay, I'm not. I have nothing against anyone living their life the way they want as long as it doesn't harm anyone else, but that's not me."

"Then why do you think it couldn't be an old boyfriend?"

She crossed her arms in front of her and propped one hip against the table. "In my line of work, it's not good to have long-term relationships."

"How long is long-term?"

He noticed she was starting to look frustrated as hell. He was already pushing the wrong buttons. He had a feeling by the time all this was over, she wouldn't like him very much. Not that he was here to make friends. He was here to catch a killer.

"One night. That's it. I'm fine if I never see the guy again. It's better that way." Her cold gaze met his and didn't waiver even an inch.

Damn, she could freeze his balls with that one look. Had he really been thinking she looked angelic, kind of fragile? He might've underestimated her.

And he knew exactly what she was saying. She went out with a guy one time for sex. She probably left immediately afterward. There would be no point in staying the night. He had a feeling Ashlyn carried a lot of baggage. It would be interesting seeing what she'd packed away.

"Okay," he began. "It's not an old boyfriend. What about girlfriends? Maybe one of them got jealous because her boyfriend flirted with you." She was already shaking her head before he finished the sentence.

"I don't have girlfriends."

He slowly nodded. No girlfriends, no boyfriends. He would have to look deeper. He didn't think she was going to like it. He looked at her sleeves again. She was hiding something. But what? He had a feeling that was the key to her past that she wasn't willing to unlock. She was going to hate him for his next question, but it had to be asked.

"What scars are you hiding?"

She visibly flinched. "None of your business." She rubbed her arms.

"Even if it'll help catch a killer?"

"This has nothing to do with my scars."

"How do you know?"

"Because I know for a fact the man who caused them is still in prison."

"You checked?"

She raised her chin and glared at him. "It was the first thing I did when I started getting the notes. The man will never see the light of day outside the prison walls. Now, since we're past all those questions, what other flashes of insight do you have to help us catch this killer before he strikes again?"

"Are you sure you want to catch him?"

Her mouth dropped open, then snapped closed. "Of course I want to catch him. He's a killer. I want to lock him away for the rest of his life."

"Then I have to know everything about the case," he

quietly told her.

He admitted to himself that he wouldn't want someone digging into his past. Not that he had a lot to hide. Great family. No skeletons in the closet, except for a great-great-uncle that was a bootlegger during prohibition. He was more of a character than a criminal. Maybe he could take it a little easier on her, though.

He continued, "I'm not your enemy. I'm only here to help. A fresh set of eyes. That's all. If it means ripping apart your life to catch him, then I'll do it."

She took a deep breath, turning away from him, and stared down at the table littered with evidence. They'd sectioned off the long table into three areas. Each one numbered one, two, or three to differentiate between explosions.

Her shoulders rose and fell as she tried to rein in her emotions. After a moment, she turned back and faced him.

"You're right. We're here to catch a killer by any means. You'll have to trust me when I tell you it has nothing to do with my past. For some reason, the killer is enamored with me. Maybe we met on the street and I smiled at him. Or maybe he dislikes me enough that he doesn't want us to solve the case. I don't know."

He glanced down at the table. "I want to see the notes he sent you."

She frowned as she looked down at the evidence. "Waylon must have them. I'll be right back."

He watched her leave. She moved with a natural grace as if she'd gone to finishing school or something. So, she probably came from money. He didn't doubt that some sick bastard could just have a crush on her and that it had nothing to do with a past relationship. Not that he wouldn't keep digging. She didn't want to talk about something, but it could still be a key to unlocking a clue.

She returned a few minutes later with a file and laid the notes on the table. "This is the first one." She pointed to one, then moved down. "And this is the last."

He picked up the first one. It had been bagged in clear plastic as evidence.

Sweet Ashlyn, I miss you. Have you missed me?

Dylan looked at her. "He knows you. Someone who hadn't met you wouldn't write this."

"That's what we thought, but then he called."

"How did he sound on the phone?"

"Angry. As though he was mad we weren't connecting the dots."

"But yet, his notes are almost flowery, poetic. A man in love."

"Or just a sick son of a bitch. He didn't give us anything definitive. Nothing from my past. Nothing current. I don't think he does know me. He wants me to think he does. Look at the second note."

Dylan picked up the second bag. They were all written on stationary with flowers. Daisies or something at the top of the page. Not exactly what a man would use. He began to read the note.

If only we'd met at a different time or place. This was the only way I could get your attention. I had to make you see we're meant to be together. Do you see it yet?

"Do you see it *yet*," Dylan repeated. "This is one sick bastard. It's as though he's leaving you some kind of hint at the scene, and he wants you to figure it out." He went to the board again and studied the pictures of the last scene. Nothing he saw stood out, other than it was a brutal murder.

"Our thoughts exactly," Ashlyn told him. "We've been

over everything a dozen times, and we haven't figured it out. I don't think there is anything at the scene we're supposed to find. He's taunting us."

"And you may be right about him not knowing you. I'm leaning more toward someone you casually met on the street or in a coffee house. What's your daily routine like?"

She shrugged. "Early morning jog, I work out at the gym twice a week, sometimes I go to the firing range. I go home afterward, shower, and get ready for work."

He glanced at the cup she'd brought into the conference room. "Coffee?"

"From the vendor right outside the office building. The guy is probably in his late sixties. He's not a suspect. Don't you think I've thought about everyone I've ever met?"

"You've missed something."

She blew out a frustrated breath. "Apparently, but I don't know who or what it could be."

"Why is the guy who caused your scars in prison? What did he do?" He knew he was throwing the question at her and completely changing directions. He wanted to see how she would react. She didn't disappoint him.

Her eyebrows drew together, but then almost immediately, she relaxed. "It happened a long time ago. The guy who's now in prison had a beef with my father. My father was a high-powered defense attorney who decided he was tired of getting rich criminals off with little more than a slap on the wrist. He switched to prosecuting them, rich and poor, instead. He pissed off one of the criminals. Albert Duncan was on his way to prison but broke out and decided to blow up our house. There, are you satisfied?"

"No, not really, but it will do for now." He glanced out the window. The sun had already gone down, and his stomach was rumbling. "It's late, and I'm starving. Let's call it a day and catch a bite of dinner. I'll buy."

She took a step back, reaching for the Styrofoam cup that was probably empty by now, and dropping it in the trashcan. "No, thank you. I have enough leftovers in my refrigerator, so I'll have that."

"I don't know the area. Are you just going to leave me on my own my first night in town?"

When she hesitated, he pressed his point across.

"We can talk more about the case." Now how did he know that would be the deciding factor? Because he'd already figured out she was all work and no play? It wasn't hard to see she shied away from close relationships. He figured it had something to do with her scars.

She hesitated. "Just dinner and talking about the case, nothing else." She said as if to warn him.

"Absolutely." He'd probably go to hell for lying, but he wanted to be in her company. There was something about her that drew him closer. She was strong but fragile at the same time. It made him want to know more about her. She was damned interesting.

Maybe the suspect had seen the same thing. She might have even rebuffed his advances at one time. If he was right, Ashlyn would be in danger at some point. He'd have to make sure the guy didn't get to her. Yeah, he had a feeling she wasn't going to like him hanging around her all the time.

She insisted they take their own vehicles and said he could follow her. That was fine by him. He got the address and put it in his phone so he could use the GPS in case they were separated. He wondered if that might have been her idea in the first place. He'd give her the benefit of the doubt—for now.

After about ten minutes of driving through San Antonio

traffic, she pulled into the parking lot of a pizza place. Nothing fancy. Not that he'd expected her to go to a restaurant with flowers and candles on every table. He had no problem with pizza, though.

She didn't wait for him to walk inside with her. His stride was longer, so he easily caught up with her by the time she got to the front door.

"Great choice. I love pizza," he told her as he quickly grabbed the door handle and held it open.

Her lips turned down. He wondered if she'd hoped he wouldn't care for pizza. She didn't say anything as they went inside.

It was your typical pizza place—booths down both sides and the back, tables in the center. The young man behind the counter looked up as they entered.

"Just sit wherever you want and someone will be out to take your order."

Ashlyn chose a booth and slid into the seat. When he sat across from her, he wondered if she'd suddenly realized how intimate it was sitting in a booth rather than a table because she frowned, but other than her change in expression, she didn't say anything.

She reached for one of the menus behind the napkin dispenser. He reached for the other and glanced at the options.

"Do you have any recommendations?" he asked.

"No. I've only been here a couple of times."

Away from the office, she wasn't very talkative. He frowned. All she talked about was the case. What kind of life was that?

The waiter came over about that time anyway. "Do you know what you want to order?"

"A Coke, a slice of sausage pizza, the house salad, and ranch dressing on the side." She looked across the table at him expectantly.

"I'll have the same, but with two more slices of pizza."

The waiter nodded and then left.

"You don't look like the salad kind of guy."

A real conversation? He was surprised. "There's a guy on our team who lives on salads with grilled chicken. He's into eating healthy food. I guess some of it rubbed off on us."

Curiosity must've gotten the better of her because she continued. "What's it like working with your team? I mean, Waylon said you were special ops, and you worked with a group of guys."

He leaned back against the seat. "We're ex-special ops, actually. They're a great bunch of guys. We're more like brothers. Do you have siblings?"

The closed look was back in her eyes. "A younger sister."

"Are you close to her?"

"Yes."

He could immediately tell that was all she was going to say about her sister. More secrets, he guessed.

"Tell me about the guys you work with," she said.

He knew she was changing the subject, but that was okay with him. He had a feeling he would have plenty of time to get to know her better. "Well, there's Carter. He's a senator's son and probably has more money than Midas. Breaker is Cajun and lives down in Louisiana. He has his own bar. Samson reminds me of a grizzly bear. He's big and will take anyone down in a heartbeat if someone he cares about is threatened. Ty is the health nut..."

"The one who eats a lot of salad?"

"That would be him. Then there's Ethan."

"What's his specialty?"

Dylan wondered what she would think if he told her that Ethan's specialty was picking up women, but he chose to stick with what Ethan brought to the team. "Computers. The guy is a genius."

"Same with Leah."

"What's it like working with your team?" he asked. Right now, he had to think anybody could be a suspect. He'd noticed Brad had kept looking at Ashlyn, and he wondered what their connection was, but Ashlyn had said she made it a point not to get romantically involved with a coworker.

"I don't know. We all get along if that's what you want to know."

"Tell me about Brad?"

One eyebrow cocked. Then she did the unexpected. She started to laugh. He liked the sound. It was light, almost musical, and washed over him in rippling waves.

"Did I say something funny?" he asked as soon as he recovered his wits.

"If you're asking if he might have a crush on me and possibly be the suspect, you're way off base. Brad has been like a brother to me."

"Are you sure it's just brotherly affection?"

"Yes, I am. Brad has a boyfriend, and they're very much in love."

"Okay, I was wrong about him." He shrugged it off.

"I thought you were supposed to be good at profiling people," she goaded.

"Usually, I am. My specialty is explosives, though."

"Don't sweat it. He's a great guy. Definitely not a suspect, though."

"What about Ginny?"

"She's not gay."

There was just the hint of a smile playing about her lips. "That's not what I was asking. Tell me about her." She'd known exactly what he meant. At least she could tease and let her guard down just a little. The smile was quickly gone, and the serious side returned.

"Ginny's good at profiling. She hasn't been able to get a clear picture of this guy. I think it bothers her a lot."

"And Leah?"

"Devoted to her husband, Gerald. They've been married ten years. Madly in love. She may look like a bubbly housewife, but she has some mad skills when it comes to taking down a suspect or cracking a computer."

"What's the story on Nolan?"

"I'm not sure he'll last in the field. I think he's better suited for the office. He's smart and devoted to the job, though."

"Why do you think he's better suited for a desk job?"

"Every time we go to the scene, it affects him."

"He hasn't learned to swallow his emotions."

"I'm not sure he ever will. Sometimes this job gets to all of us."

He tilted his head and looked at her. "What about you? Does it get to you?"

"Yeah, sometimes. You?"

"I'm no different from anyone else. Some cases bother me more than others, but I know someone has to do it."

Their food arrived, and they concentrated on that for now. Not that he'd learned a whole lot about her. She'd kept the conversation pretty generic. That wasn't going to help him solve the case. She'd told him she had a sister, and some guy had blown up their house and he was still in prison. It was time to learn more about Ashlyn.

"Did everyone make it out of the house?" he asked.

"Excuse me?" She looked up, a forkful of salad halfway to her mouth.

"You said the man blew up your house. Did everyone make it out alive?" There was the slightest hesitation before she spoke.

"Yes."

"Good."

Every time he tried to ask a personal question after that, she steered the topic back to something else. After a while, he decided to let the matter drop…for now.

"I guess I'll see you in the morning," she said after they paid out and were walking toward their vehicles.

He stopped at her car. "I'll be there."

Dylan waited until she was driving away before he started toward his pickup. The hairs on the back of his neck began to tingle. He stopped at the door and slowly scanned the area. Someone had been watching them. He'd stake his life on it. His training in special ops had sharpened his senses.

Nothing moved. Not even a leaf on the nearby oak. His gaze landed on the used car dealership just over from the pizza place. It would be easy to hide there. All anyone would have to do is blend in with the other vehicles. Nothing moved there either.

A carload of teens pulled up, and suddenly the feeling

was gone.

The perp would be back. Dylan was certain of it.

Chapter Three

Elijah stepped behind the brick building. When the man opened the door for Ashlyn as she went inside the pizza place, he'd assumed they didn't know each other. They'd come in different vehicles. Just in case, he'd crept closer and glanced through the window.

When she'd turned his way, he quickly moved back. That had been close. He would have to be more careful in the future. But he'd seen what he needed to see.

Anger slowly built inside him until he thought he would explode. This wasn't like him. He was always, *always* in control of his emotions.

"No, you belong to me!" he fumed as he moved away from the pizza place. What was she doing with that man? Sitting in the same booth as if…as if…they were dating.

His limp was more pronounced as he moved to the safety of the used car place once again. He'd followed her. She didn't come here very often, but as soon as she turned off thirty-five, he was pretty sure he knew where she was going.

That's how well he knew her! No one else knew her like he did! He understood what she'd gone through. Him! No one else!

His laugh was bitter as he remembered thinking that he might go in and order a pizza so that he could sit and watch her. She was so beautiful, so fragile, like an angel. It didn't matter that she had scars. He had his own scars.

Now this new man had entered the picture. No, no, no! He drew in deep gulps of air as he tried to calm himself.

He'd already planned to speak to her this time. He hadn't spoken to her yet. He'd been told he had a nice voice and wasn't bad looking. After parking farther away, even though his leg bothered him more than usual tonight, he'd started toward the pizza place. But then he'd seen the man hold the door open for Ashlyn, and he decided to wait. Now, he was glad he had. Who was the stranger? *Were* they dating?

Sometimes she went out with a man. He didn't like it, but he knew she had needs. Someday, she would be his and his alone. That day hadn't come yet. He had to prepare her. Ashlyn needed to realize he was the only man who would accept her as she was. That would take time, and he had to be patient.

His heart skipped a beat when she came out of the pizza place. The man walked her to her car and his anger returned, stronger now. He studied the stranger. He was big and would be hard to take down. Better to put a bullet in his brain. Quick and easy. No, he couldn't shoot someone, could he?

What if he was caught? That was a distinct possibility. Guns were loud. All his plans would be ruined because this man chose to interfere.

No, he was too careful for that. He'd never gotten caught. Not that any of it was his fault. But people saw a cripple and immediately thought he was weak. They always got it wrong.

Kimberly had. She'd been pretty like Ashlyn. He'd hated to say goodbye to her. He hadn't wanted her to die. It wasn't his fault!

Elijah frowned. He didn't like when they cried and begged. Even when he tried to explain that she would go to Heaven because she was so nice. But he'd felt sorry for her, and there'd been no reason to make her suffer. He'd at least made sure she wouldn't. She'd never been mean to him.

They'd always talked when he went into the library where she worked. It never failed that she would ask how he was doing. That's why it was so easy to tell her that he would give her a ride home when her car had a flat tire. And that was all he planned to do. He even promised to pick her up the next morning, and they could get her tire changed. He knew she was saving money for her upcoming wedding. So, no, he hadn't wanted her to suffer. He'd made that perfectly clear.

He was thoughtful for a moment. He might be reading more into the situation with Ashlyn and the stranger. They didn't ride in the same vehicle to the pizza place, he reminded himself. Maybe she wasn't dating him.

He drew his attention back to the present when the stranger stopped at his pickup and looked around. Did he sense someone watching? Maybe this was another FBI agent.

He blended farther into the shadows and then hurried to his vehicle. Best not to hang around. By the time he unlocked the car door and crawled inside, his ragged breathing filled the small space, and his leg had begun to ache. He rubbed the heel of his hand down the side, trying to ease the pain.

For a moment, he sat there with his eyes closed as he thought about Ashlyn. That always helped. He'd known for a long time that she was meant for him. She was like an angel opening her arms and welcoming him. He knew she'd only been stretching before her morning run, but he didn't care.

Elijah sighed as the pain in his leg subsided.

Someday, they would be together. Maybe then the nightmares would stop, too.

Chapter Four

Ashlyn didn't mind going to the crime scene with Dylan the following day. It was her routine to visit it several times during an investigation.

Did he have to look so good, though? He hadn't bothered to shave, so he had a little bit of five o'clock shadow. He'd dressed casually: jeans, boots, and a black T-shirt. The cotton material hugged his muscles and she caught just a bit of tattoo peeking out from under his sleeve.

And damn, the man smelled sinfully delicious.

She really needed to get her head screwed on straight. Okay, right, she could do this. He was just a man, after all, a man who happened to look hot and smell sinfully delicious. Dylan probably had a lot of bad habits that would irritate the hell out of her if she ever got to know him better—which wasn't going to happen. As soon as they solved the case, he'd be out of here, and her life would return to normal.

They went to the scene of the first crime. He pulled up alongside the warehouse, almost destroyed by the explosion.

"There's not much left," she said as they got out and walked closer.

"I can see that. I wonder if he meant to do this much damage."

"I wondered the same thing. I don't think he did. He wanted us to know what he was capable of doing, but I think he planned for someone to find the victim sooner. It probably frustrated the hell out of him when she wasn't."

"So, he called to make sure you knew," Dylan said.

"Yes, but by the time he did, the fire department had already found a partial leg and called us. That's when we got involved. The first note landed on my desk a day later."

"And what do you know about the victim?"

"Not much. She was an introvert and lived in an apartment complex. She worked two jobs just to make ends meet. No family. We figure he got her as she was leaving the second job. She would've been exhausted and not as careful." Ashlyn closed her eyes for a moment as she pictured what probably happened.

The girl wouldn't have been frightened at first. Had he forced her into his car? That's when the fear would've set in. The cold dread of knowing she was going to die.

"You okay?"

She opened her eyes and looked at him. "Yes, I just want to catch him."

"That's two of us."

She drew in a deep breath and then exhaled. "He went into more detail with the second victim, the college student, when he called. That's when I got the second note as well. He let me know what was going to happen."

"Did he give you a timeline?"

"No, when I began questioning him, he ended the conversation. He took her to an vacant house and was more careful with this one. She'd struggled against the ties that bound her wrists. There were ligature marks on her neck as well where he strangled her. Afterward, he set his explosions, but again, he did more damage than he wanted and almost obliterated that scene. It's still roped off. There's not much to see. The third scene was more staged. He finally got it right, in his mind, at least."

"Let's go to that one."

They climbed inside his pickup, and she gave him the directions.

"And this is the one he took from the gas station," Dylan

said.

She nodded. "Yes, Kimberly Braddock. Ginny and Brad questioned the clerk, but the perp took her at night, and there was only one attendant on duty."

"And he didn't see anything," Dylan guessed.

"Apparently not. He was watching a movie and wasn't aware of his surroundings. He did remember her coming inside the store and buying a soda. When she went back out, she only drove a few feet before the tire went flat. They towed her car in and checked it out. So far, it's clean, but they're still going through it." She doubted he would be careless enough to leave fingerprints.

"No signs of a struggle?"

She shook her head. "No."

"Even if he'd seen the abduction, he might not have thought anything about it. Not if Kimberly knew this man," Dylan continued. "Maybe he offered her a ride home and promised to have someone fix the flat. She wouldn't have known what was going to happen."

She nodded. "I agree. We think he probably used an icepick to let the air out of her tire. The place where she stopped for the soda didn't fix tires, so she pulled to the side, thinking she would have it towed the next day or have someone come out and fix it. She didn't have a spare. We figured that's when the perp came up and offered her a ride home."

"We need to question all of her friends and her fiancé to see if they might know anything that could help us."

"They're coming in this afternoon."

"And you've ruled out the fiancé?"

"Yes, he was out of town on business."

Talk about the crimes ended as they got closer to the

scene. She pointed to each road he needed to take. Kimberly had lived out in the boonies.

"This is the road to her house," she finally told him.

"Pretty isolated," he mumbled.

She froze when she saw a car she didn't recognize.

Dylan looked across the seat. "You know that vehicle?"

"No." She could see someone sitting behind the wheel, a man.

He slammed his foot on the brake, put it in park, and they jumped out, pulling their guns out of the holsters at the same time.

"Get out of the car and raise your hands," Dylan's voice boomed.

The man inside didn't move.

"Now!"

The door slowly opened, and a man got out, arms raised as he faced them—probably mid-thirties, nice looking, clean-cut.

"Who are you?" Ashlyn asked, voice firm.

He raised his head and looked directly at her. She'd never seen so much grief on one person's face. She had a feeling she knew who this was without asking.

"You're Colin, the fiancé," she said as she moved closer.

"He tied her to the chair, didn't he?" Tears began to run down his face. "They said she was burned beyond recognition." He drew in a ragged breath. "She was so beautiful, kind of fragile looking. She wasn't fragile, though."

Ashlyn holstered her gun and walked nearer. "Identification." She needed to be certain. Dylan still had his gun trained on the subject.

He reached into his back pocket and pulled out a wallet, flipping it open to his driver's license. She glanced at it, then nodded at Dylan.

"What are you doing out here?" Ashlyn asked as Dylan looked inside at the front seat.

Colin hesitated, wiping his hand across his face. "I needed to see where it happened, but I didn't disturb anything. I wanted to leave her some flowers. She always liked carnations. The red ones. Said they smelled better than roses and lasted longer." His voice hitched.

"And the gun?" Dylan quietly asked.

Ashlyn drew in a sharp breath.

Colin began to shake his head. "I can't live without her. She was my whole world." He dropped to his knees, sobbing, hands covering his face. "Oh my God, oh my God, she was everything good in this world. I just want her back. I don't want her to be dead. I want to hold her in my arms and never let her go."

Dylan holstered his gun, then squeezed Colin's shoulder. "From everything we know about Kimberly, she wouldn't want this. We'll get you some help."

Ashlyn pulled out her phone, punched one number, and spoke to Waylon, telling him what was happening. He said they would send a car out for Colin. When she turned around, Dylan had helped Colin to his feet, and they were talking. She couldn't hear what they were saying, but Colin nodded a few times.

That was the trouble when someone was taken from this earth in a violent way. Not only was the person who died a victim, but everyone they'd touched was affected. They would have to live with it for the rest of their lives, and it would be damned hard.

She let Dylan talk to him while she slowly walked around

the house. She stopped at one end, focusing on the chair. In a flash, it was as though the house was whole once again, and she stood behind the chair. Kimberly would've been crying, begging for her life.

The remnants of a wooden chair once sat in front of the metal chair. What had he thought as he stared at her? Had he felt remorse that he was about to take a life? Someone he probably knew. The M.E.'s report had come back this morning and there were drugs in her system. Enough to knock her out permanently. She was probably dead before he doused her in gasoline.

Yes, he'd felt remorse, but not enough to stop what he was about to do. Then why did he kill her? What point was he trying to make?

And why did he want Ashlyn to figure everything out? What connection did he have to her? She ran a hand across her forehead. She'd checked on Albert Duncan, who was still in prison for the attempted murder of her and her father. He'd been in isolation for the past four months because he didn't play well with others. Before that, the guards said everyone kept their distance. The guy was crazy.

Even so, she'd made sure he'd had no contact with the outside world in case he tried to get revenge on her family. The guy didn't even use the computer. No, she didn't think there was a connection.

When an unmarked pulled up to the scene, she froze, hand on her gun, only relaxing when she recognized the man getting out. He worked with social services. Colin would be in good hands. Bill spoke with him for a few minutes, and Colin nodded. Before he left, he placed the flowers near the house and bowed his head for a moment, shoulders shaking. After a moment, they left together.

It would be hard for Colin to recover from this. He would have to work through the stages of grief. It wouldn't be easy, but he could do it. From what she'd read in Kimberly's file, she would want him to continue living his life.

Her gaze moved to Dylan, taking in his reaction to the scene. The blown-out walls, the rubble of what used to be someone's home...and the metal chair in the center of it all.

She squared her shoulders and tried not to let her feelings take over. It was like this every time. She had to close off her emotions when things started getting too much for her. It had gotten easier over the years and that scared the hell out of her. When her grandmother passed a few years ago, she realized how well she'd gotten at closing everything off. The woman had practically raised her, and she couldn't feel anything.

Even now, ice surrounded her heart. She'd tried to feel, but somewhere along the way, she'd forgotten how.

So how could Dylan, this stranger, bring out the worst in her? And why did he set her pulse beating faster?

She needed to get out more.

She drew in a shaky breath and circled back around to meet up with Dylan. His expression was grim.

"This is one sick bastard," he said when she joined him. His gaze scanned the area. "What about that wooded area? Did anyone walk the property?"

She looked toward the thick growth of oak and cedar trees and the bushes tangling beneath them. She slowly shook her head. "I don't know for sure. That's awfully far away. What do you think? Would someone actually watch from that distance?"

He glanced down at her hiking boots and the black uniform pants she wore. "We won't know until we check it out. You up for a walk?"

It was a good distance to get to the trees, but it was open pasture between that and the crime scene. Had the perp hung around to watch what was going on? Damn! She should've already thought about the possibility. He would've wanted to witness the chaos he'd created.

She pressed her lips together. "Let's go."

It was farther than it looked, but she was in good shape, so by the time they arrived at the edge, she wasn't even breathing hard. She noticed he wasn't either, but then, she had already figured out that he went to the gym. The guy had some serious muscles.

"He would've used binoculars to watch everything," Dylan said as he looked toward the scene. He glanced her way. "Or to gauge your reaction."

A shiver ran down her spine. It was all she could do to keep from rubbing the goosebumps that popped up on her arms. *Had* he been watching her? Was he watching them now? No, he wouldn't have stuck around when they started walking toward the trees. He would know they were coming and be long gone before they got there.

"I'll go in first," Dylan said.

She raised her chin and glared at him. Did he think she was incapable of taking down a murderer? Before she could say anything, he began to speak again.

"My jeans are thicker than your uniform pants, and the bushes growing around the bottom of the trees have some pretty wicked thorns."

With just a couple of sentences, he'd taken away her bluster. He was right, of course. She probably hated that more than anything. She didn't want him to be right.

Her feelings were unjustifiable. He was only here to help. For some strange reason, it didn't take much for him to get on her last nerve.

But she knew she was wrong. "You're right, of course. Thanks."

He chuckled softly under his breath.

"What?" she asked as she followed him into the shadows of the trees, where only patches of light managed to escape past the branches covered with leaves. She had no idea what she'd said that amused him.

"I'd wondered if you were capable of accepting my help."

She frowned. "Why wouldn't I?"

He suddenly turned. They were only a breath apart. Even though she was five feet seven inches, she had to look up at him. He was way too close, but she refused to back up and admit that he was invading her space.

She drew in a deep breath and caught his scent again. The woods, pine trees, the earth, the muskiness of his cologne. She found herself wanting to lean the rest of the way in, rest her head against his chest, and just inhale.

Instead, she took a step back. Let him think what he wanted.

"You're fighting me every step of the way," he continued. "At least, that's what it feels like. I'm only here to catch this guy. We have to start working together."

"I followed you out to the woods, didn't I?"

He suddenly grinned. The kind of half-smile that only lifted one side of his mouth. It was sexy as hell and sent a different kind of shiver over her body.

"I'll have to remember that if I ever want to take you to the woods for a different reason."

Now he was flirting. She frowned. "Can we just get back to the matter at hand?"

Without another word, he turned around, but she felt as though she'd lost this round with him. The guy had an ego problem. She was pretty good at deflating men's egos. Dylan might just be the exception.

"Look over there," he said, pointing to an area to his left.

She looked where he was pointing. "I don't see anything."

He stepped nearer, then squatted. "The branches on that bush are broken."

She shook her head. "A small animal?" She moved closer. Her eyes widened. "That's a partial boot print."

"Very good. It's hard to spot. You had to be looking for it. I bet if we looked around, we might find a full print. It could give us an indication of his size."

"Do you really think it was him?" Her heart was already thumping madly inside her chest. The more they knew about him, the closer they would be to catching him.

"He was probably watching everyone at the scene," Dylan said. "Even if they decided to investigate this area, he would have plenty of time to make his escape."

"You're right that he probably used binoculars. He was watching us the whole time." Her shoulders squared, but before the angry emotions could bubble to the surface, she tamped them back down. He might've even been out here watching Colin. Did he derive satisfaction from Colin's pain? Yeah, she was going to catch this guy. She wouldn't stop until she did.

"We need to get someone out here to make a casting of the shoe print," Dylan told her.

She was already pulling her phone out of her pocket. She talked to Waylon, and he was sending someone out.

"Do you think we might find a better set of footprints?" she asked.

"I don't know. This guy seems to be pretty careful about leaving anything behind. They always screw up at some point, though."

"If we recognize the signs."

"Exactly. But we'll find him."

She studied him for a moment. "Will we?"

"I'm about ninety-nine percent positive."

Yeah, well, it was the other one percent that worried her.

After marking the boot print, they scoured the rest of the area but didn't find anything. There was a nearby road where he probably left his car, but this one was paved, so there were no tire marks. Not even where he might've moved off to the side. He'd probably pulled back onto the road, then stopped long enough to brush the ground with a broom so they wouldn't find any tire marks. He was good, but he'd slipped when he left the boot print. He would slip again.

Ashlyn was dusty, sweaty, and tired when they finally made it back to the office. She hadn't slept well last night. Another nightmare. Yeah, they had to catch this man before he drove her crazy.

But what about the next perp? And the one who would follow him? She quickly shook off the knowledge that it might not get any better. Instead, she concentrated on this serial killer.

They went over all the evidence again from the last scene, Nolan and Leah were still going through Kimberly's social media accounts and the laptop, but they hadn't found anything yet. The same with Brad and Ginny. They were also coming up empty-handed.

They had to hope Kimberly's contacts might be able to tell them something. When Kimberly's friend came in, she and Dylan went to the interview room. She was around the same age as Kimberly, with short, light brown hair and a scattering of freckles across her nose, red from the fresh tears she'd shed.

"I can't believe she's gone," Jill whispered.

Ashlyn handed her the box of tissues. "I know this is difficult, but can you tell us about the last time you spoke with Kimberly. Was she feeling anxious about anything?"

She shook her head. "I met her for lunch and she seemed incredibly happy." Her words broke as she dabbed at her eyes.

"Did she happen to mention anyone harassing her or maybe following her?"

"No, she was the type of person who was always willing to help people. Sometimes I thought she was a little too gullible, but she believed people were good. She loved working at the library. She also volunteered at the food bank. I don't know why anyone would want to hurt her."

They continued questioning her, but Jill couldn't give them anything more than they already knew.

Jill dabbed at her eyes. "I haven't been much help, have I?"

"It's okay. Kimberly was lucky to have you as a friend. Call me if you think of anyone who seemed overly friendly or anything, no matter how insignificant you think it is." Ashlyn reached into her pocket and brought out a card with her name and extension.

"You handled her very well," Dylan said after Jill left.

"I wish she'd known more." She sighed. If the others were like Jill, it would be a long day.

Ashlyn wondered if she might have jinxed herself as the rest of the day continued about the same. The head librarian came in and voiced Jill's statement. Kimberly had been a sweet girl who wouldn't hurt anyone. Colin came into the office with his tearful parents. Thank goodness they were there to give him support. No one knew anything, though.

The day drug out, and they were still no closer to a suspect. When Waylon called Dylan into his office, she glanced at the clock. It was already after six. She was going to call it a day and get a fresh start tomorrow. She walked past Waylon's office with barely a glance.

At least he wouldn't guilt her into going to dinner with him. She didn't know whether she could handle a few more hours in his company. He exuded too much confidence. No, it wasn't that exactly. The guy was confident, but not overly so, and he was intelligent.

She was starting to enjoy his company, though. Maybe that was it. She enjoyed his company a little too much. That was after only one full day. What would it be like after a week? No, she wasn't going to think about it.

Whatever the reason, she was going home to take a hot shower, grab a ready-made chef salad out of the refrigerator, and pour herself a glass of wine. Maybe she would call Mindy. She hadn't talked to her this week. She always liked to make sure her little sister was doing okay.

By the time she got home and took a shower, she could already feel herself relaxing. She slipped on her favorite nightgown with spaghetti straps and shoved her feet into fuzzy slippers.

When she caught sight of herself in the full-length mirror, she drew in a sharp breath. Instead of walking away like she usually did, she studied her arms with a critical eye. The scars weren't that bad. Not like in the beginning. Surgery had helped.

But the memories of that day flooded her mind every time she saw her reflection. Closing her eyes tight didn't stop them. Nothing ever stopped the memories. She quickly walked past the mirror.

She hurried to the kitchen and grabbed a salad with chunks of ham out of the refrigerator, club crackers, a fork, and the ranch dressing before carrying everything to the small table next to the window. She went back, poured herself a glass of wine, and took it to the table before calling Mindy.

When the phone started ringing on the other end, she put it on speaker and set it down. Warmth flowed over her when she heard her little sister's voice.

"Before you ask, I'm doing fine, I'm still in college, and I broke up with Michael," Mindy blurted.

"Hey, I'm your big sister. I'm supposed to worry about you." But she was smiling as she spoke the words.

A deep sigh followed by, "I know, I know. You do realize, though, I worry about you, too."

Now she was confused. "Why do you worry about me?"

"Duh, your job? You take down murderers. The scum of society. Why wouldn't I worry about you? Me, on the other hand, I'm just going to college. I only have to deal with horny men."

She sat forward just a little. "What do you mean, horny men? Did Michael do something? Is that why you broke up with him? I'll make him regret it if he did." She'd met him once and didn't care that much for the guy.

Mindy's laughter came across the line. "You know, I've used that on occasion, don't you?"

Her eyebrows drew together. "Used what?"

"The fact that you're in the FBI. If a guy starts to act like a dick, I just casually mention what you do for a living. It works every time. They don't want the FBI breathing down their necks. Just FYI, Michael and I had different interests. He wanted to party all the time, and I didn't. Breaking up was a mutual decision. We're still friends. Now, how's work going with you?"

She should've known her little sister would be resourceful. Mindy wasn't like her. She didn't have any real hang-ups. What happened the day of the explosions didn't affect her as much.

Mindy had only been eight when it happened and only remembered bits and pieces of what their grandmother told her. Sure, she knew about Ashlyn's scars and their…their father, but thank God, she'd been with Grandmother that day. Mindy had been spared.

"You still there?" Mindy asked. "Is this a bad one?"

Ashlyn always talked a little about her job without going into great detail. She didn't want Mindy's innocence tainted. Like this one, some of the cases could be gruesome.

"Yes, I'm still here. Just the usual at work."

"It must be bad if you're unwilling to talk about it."

Mindy would make a great lawyer. "A serial killer, if you must know. We'll catch him, though." She bit her bottom lip. "Be a little more cautious, though. For some reason, this creep has been sending me notes. Sort of singling me out."

There was a pause before Mindy began to talk. "You don't think it might have anything to do with Dad or—"

"No," Ashlyn quickly interjected. "The guy is just crazy. I only told you because I want you to be more careful. Albert Duncan is still in prison. He'll never be released."

"You'll be careful, won't you?"

For just a moment, Ashlyn was reminded of the little girl Mindy used to be. She'd been so unaware of what happened that day. She didn't know all the details, and Ashlyn would make sure she never did.

"Of course I'll be okay. I'm always okay."

"Well, just make sure you are. You're the only sister I have." She hesitated.

She always knew when Mindy needed something. This time was no different. "What?"

"How's Dad?"

Ashlyn closed her eyes, and an immediate picture formed in her mind of a robust man who would throw Mindy in the air, then catch her, everyone laughing. All that changed when Albert Duncan came into their lives. The image quickly disappeared, and a deep shudder wracked her body.

"About the same, but the doctor is trying something new. We're hoping this will help."

"Me, too."

They spoke for a while longer and then promised to talk again next week before their call ended.

They were closer than most sisters. She wanted to keep it that way. She tried to protect Mindy from the evil side of life, and if anyone ever threatened her little sister, she'd go after them locked and loaded. She wouldn't hesitate to pull the trigger on anyone who threatened Mindy.

Maybe she was a *little* over-protective. She had good reason.

She continued to sit at the table, drinking her wine. Immediately, thoughts of Dylan filled her mind. Purely related to the case. Nothing more. She pushed everything else out of the way.

Would he be able to help find this psychopath? Or just get in her way?

Chapter Five

Ashlyn's apartment was on the second floor. From where Elijah stood, he had a perfect view into her window, where she sat at the table. She'd been talking on the phone while she ate her dinner. He should've brought his binoculars so he would have a better view, but this was enough…for now.

There were dark patches on her upper arm. He couldn't see them that well from where he stood, but he knew they were scars from the fire. They'd mostly healed—which he thought was a shame. Then she'd had surgeries to get rid of them even more, but some scars remained.

Ashlyn always kept her arms covered, but she shouldn't. She should display them like badges of honor. She'd faced the battle and won. She was so strong that sometimes it scared him. He wasn't worthy of her affection. At least, not right now. But soon, she would realize they were meant to be together.

Unless someone got in his way. His eyes narrowed. Who'd she been talking to on the phone? The man she'd been with at the pizza place?

His frown deepened. He didn't like that man. He'd managed to discover his name. It was Dylan, and he was working with the FBI to find the serial killer. He laughed. That was never going to happen.

He didn't think it was Dylan on the phone with her. She was too relaxed, and from what he'd seen when they were together, she didn't care for him. That was the way it should be.

Maybe she was talking to her little sister, Mindy. He'd seen them together once. Mindy was a cute little thing with short, dark hair rather than the long, blonde tresses that Ashlyn kept pulled back.

Ashlyn was more like a princess in need of a kingdom. Only he could provide that for her. They were meant to be together. Why hadn't she seen that by now? Maybe the clues he was leaving were too obscure. That might be it. She was smart, but she would need more to go on. Yes, that was it. She was the only one who could stop him.

They were both survivors. He remembered the day he first saw her. It had been a warm summer day with only a few clouds in the sky, but his leg had been bothering him, so he'd stayed inside that day. He was bored and flipping through the channels when he saw the news report of the fire, followed by the explosions. The news footage showed her kneeling beside an unconscious man. The reporter said she'd pulled her father to safety. Even though she'd only been fourteen at the time, she'd managed to get him out.

She had strength. Even more than he had at the time because she'd had a gentler upbringing. That day she'd discovered how strong she really was. She'd rose to the occasion. That wasn't easy to do.

Elijah was made to be strong, to find that strength inside himself that told him he had to survive. His head suddenly started to pound. He pressed his fingers to his temples, trying to block the memories, but they flooded his brain with unwanted images.

"Go to the closet!" his father ordered.

"Please, no. I don't like the dark," he whimpered.

His father grabbed him by the shirt, lifting him off the floor and dragging him toward the closet. He slammed him against the door, laughed, then opened the door and threw him inside. Elijah bounced off the wall as the door closed, and a cloak of darkness draped over him.

The images faded, and he opened his eyes, body trembling. It hadn't taken him long to realize the darkness was his friend. When his father shoved him inside the tiny closet, they couldn't put their cigarettes out on him. They couldn't hit him with the belt.

The tiny closet became his refuge. They'd leave him there for days without food and only one jug of water. A bucket sat in the corner to relieve himself. He'd found strength in the closet by praying. He'd read about the trials people in the Bible had to go through to get strong. Every time he was mocked and laughed at, he became stronger.

That's why they were meant to be together. They'd both faced the odds and overcame them, but that's not where the connection ended. No, that's just where it began.

When she turned and looked out the window, he stepped a little farther into the shadows, although he was pretty sure she couldn't see him. God, she was so beautiful with her long blonde hair loose, and when she moved her hands, it was like the fluttering of a delicate butterfly.

He laughed at his poetic thoughts. That's how she made him feel, though.

He casually glanced at the pickup that drove past. As soon as he recognized the man inside, he hugged the wall just inside the inky blackness of the alleyway.

Anger flared inside him. What the hell was Dylan doing here? Instead of driving into the parking garage, the man continued past.

Maybe it had been a coincidence.

No, he didn't think so. He was checking up on her.

When he saw the same vehicle return, he slunk deeper into the alley, knowing he could exit out the back if he had to. He always made sure he had a way to escape. The car stopped, but the man didn't get out. He looked up at the window.

Fury rose inside of him. How dare Dylan think that he could take care of her. She wasn't his to take care of. Maybe he would teach him a lesson. Yes. He needed to know that she didn't belong to him.

Elijah scraped his fingers through his hair. He wasn't the angry one. He was usually calm and accepting, but Dylan pushed him beyond the limits of what he would tolerate. Yes, he should teach him a lesson—a warning for him to back off.

He was more relaxed, smiling even, as he turned and left the alley.

Chapter Six

The hairs on the back of Dylan's neck tingled. He had a feeling he was being watched again. Nothing new. Came with the job. When he looked around, he didn't see anyone, but there was a dark alleyway not far from where he was parked. If someone was there watching him, they would probably be long gone before he could even get out of the pickup.

He rubbed the back of his neck. Maybe his feeling was wrong. He glanced up at the window one last time. Ashlyn was moving past the window. She was safe—for now.

The apartment complex she lived in was secure enough, definitely upscale for an FBI agent. It had a sound security system, so he felt confident she would be okay. After one last glance, he pulled away from the curb and drove back to the apartment the bureau had provided for him, only stopping long enough to grab some takeout food.

He smiled. Ty would tell him he was going to an early grave eating burgers and fries. It was a staple part of his diet, though. Man could not live on salads with grilled chicken all the time. When he told Ty that, his friend had only shook his head and sighed.

The team he worked with was a great bunch of guys. He'd known them for a long time. They were more like brothers, and if one of them needed something, they all dropped what they were doing to help. Usually, they worked government jobs together, but they would take the occasional side hustle. It kept them from going stale.

As he parked the pickup and went inside, he knew this was one case that wouldn't be easy. The guy was sick. He didn't like that Ashlyn was involved so much—the notes, the phone calls. It put her in a precarious position. She wanted to solve the case but couldn't get too close. The guy had zeroed in on her for some reason. Yeah, he had a feeling she'd jump in with both feet if it came right down to it.

He stepped into the elevator and rode it to the fourth floor. It was a short walk down a well-lit hallway to his door. The security wasn't bad. Not as good as the security at Ashlyn's complex, though. He unlocked the door and went inside, closing and locking it behind him.

There had to be something about her that triggered this guy. There was always a clue somewhere. He just needed to find it.

He set his food on the coffee table and reached for his laptop as he made himself comfortable on the sofa.

"Who are you, Ashlyn Pillar?"

He took a bite of his cheeseburger, flattened the bag, and then set it on top. After wiping the grease off his fingers, he typed her name into the search engine. He would never have imagined there were this many Pillar's to look through.

He finally found a brief article in the paper when she graduated from Quantico. It mentioned her as the daughter of prosecuting attorney Joseph Pillar, a younger sister, Mindy, a grandmother—and a very wealthy one at that. The cream-of-society type rich. The kind of woman who sets the standard rather than following one.

He continued reading. Ashlyn's mother died in a car wreck when Ashlyn was very young. There wasn't a lot about her.

Dylan supposed if he wanted to find out about Ashlyn's past, the best place to start would be with her father.

He put his name in the search engine and began to wade through all the articles about him. Dylan whistled under his breath when he saw the high-profile cases he'd handled. He'd been a defense attorney, commanding a fortune, but then switched to prosecuting criminals. Dylan figured he got tired of getting his wealthy clientele off when they were guilty and decided to put them behind bars instead. No wonder he was a target for some really bad men.

The man was brilliant and had written quite a few articles on criminal law. He came from old money and didn't have to work. There was a picture of him with his two daughters. Ashlyn would've been about twelve, maybe. He studied the picture for a moment.

Her blonde hair was in pigtails, and she had a toothy grin that showed sparkling braces. She looked as though she didn't have a care in the world. An innocent who hadn't been dealt the blows the darker side of life had to offer. Quite different from the woman she had become.

Her little sister was the complete opposite. Where Ashlyn was light like her father, Mindy had dark hair with a mischievous twinkle in her eyes. Maybe five or six years younger than Ashlyn. They looked happy. It was definitely before the home invasion occurred.

He skimmed more articles until he ran across the one he was looking for. It went into detail about how someone had broken into their home. Ashlyn and her father were the only two there. The intruder had tied them up and then set fires around the inside of the house.

A young Ashlyn had tearfully told the reporters as she lay in a hospital bed that the man had set explosives that would start to go off when they were triggered by the heat from the fire. Then he laughed and walked away, knowing they would die, knowing he was causing Ashlyn's father more pain than anyone could be expected to bear.

Except it hadn't happened that way. The man who'd broken in hadn't expected Ashlyn to break free of the ties that bound her, rubbing her wrists almost raw from the knobby cup towel he'd used. She ran through the smoke and fire to get a knife out of the kitchen. She wasn't about to leave her father behind.

The smoke had started billowing into the dining room, where they'd been tied to the chairs. The article said she crawled along the floor and cut the zip tie. Her father had shielded Ashlyn as much as possible, but the first explosion went off before they could escape. A heavy beam hit him in the head, knocking him unconscious.

Choking and coughing, Ashlyn managed to drag him almost out of the house when the second explosion sent tremors over the ground around her. The article ended by saying he was still in a coma.

Dylan searched but couldn't find any more articles. It seemed that everything stopped that day, until Ashlyn graduated from the FBI. So, where was her father now? She hadn't lied when she said everyone had made it out alive. Had he later died?

The article listed the name of the man who tried to kill Joseph Pillar and his daughter. Albert Duncan was eventually caught and sent to prison, where he still resided. There wasn't anything about a family, no wife, children…nothing.

Most men liked to brag to someone about the crimes they'd committed. From what little he learned about him, Dylan doubted he'd been a loner on the outside. No, there was someone in Albert Duncan's life who could shed more light on his past. He was determined to find them, but with a little help from a friend.

He reached into his pocket and pulled out his phone. After only the second ring, Ethan answered, clearly out of breath.

"What's up?" Ethan asked.

Dylan grimaced. "Is this a bad time?" It was nearly always a bad time to call Ethan. He was usually with a woman when he wasn't on a mission. His good looks and charm had them jumping into his bed in no time at all.

"It's not what you're thinking," Ethan said.

"Oh, really? And what am I thinking?"

Ethan chuckled. "I'm working out."

"Is that what you're calling it now?"

"I'm at the gym, smart ass. I was just about to hit the showers. So, are you happy now?"

Dylan grinned. "You must be losing your touch."

"Not a chance. I just have to keep my stamina up. I don't want to disappoint the ladies."

"Do you think you might have time to do some research for me?"

"I always have time for one of my brothers. Give me the info, and I'll get back to you as soon as possible."

He quickly gave Ethan what little information he knew. He wanted him to look into Albert Duncan's background and see what he could find. The guy had to have visitors when he went to jail. That would be a good place to start.

After they talked and caught each other up on what was happening in their lives, they ended the call. Dylan reached for his burger and realized he'd polished it off. One lonely limp French fry lay on the bag. He picked it up and shoved it into his mouth before crumbling the bag, then glanced at his watch. It was getting late, and it was going to be a long day tomorrow. He stripped off his clothes as he made his way to the shower.

By the time he crawled into bed and his head hit the pillow, all he could think about was Ashlyn. He couldn't stop his smile. Until she'd known it was the victim's fiancé at the crime scene, she was already jumping out of the pickup with gun drawn. He liked that she didn't take chances.

She'd missed the boot print, though. Not that he could blame her. Most FBI agents were more analytical, getting inside the perpetrator's head kind of stuff, and analyzing the evidence, than actually tracking someone.

He'd learned a lot when he was in special ops, but Breaker had taught him more than anyone. He'd grown up in the Louisiana bayou until he was fourteen and then ran away from home. He didn't know much more of Breaker's history, but the guy had scars on his back that he never talked about, and no one questioned him. In one way or another, all of them had scars.

Breaker had once told him there was beauty in the bayou, but it was also dangerous if you didn't look for the signs. Like the log in the water. It just might pop up and snatch off your arm. Breaker said he used to hunt alligators with his family. Dylan didn't doubt that for one minute.

He yawned and closed his eyes.

The next thing Dylan knew, it was morning, and his alarm was going off. He'd slept hard and didn't think he'd even dreamed, which might not be a bad thing because he probably would've dreamt about Ashlyn.

Not that it would've been a bad thing to dream about Ashlyn, except he didn't want to wake up and be horny for the rest of the day. He yawned as he sat on the side of the bed, combing his fingers through his hair. Coffee. He needed it. After turning the pot on, he dressed.

He needed more caffeine than just the cup he grabbed and took with him, but figured he'd grab another cup from the vendor where Ashlyn got her morning coffee. He wanted to check the guy out for himself.

Dylan had just stepped out of the elevator and was on his way to the garage, but the closer he got to his pickup, the more his step slowed.

The hairs on the back of his neck tingled. He quickly glanced around. Not that he thought someone was going to jump out and attack him. He studied the pickup as he walked closer. It leaned slightly to one side. He discovered why when he stood beside it. The pickup had a flat tire.

Yeah, he didn't think the guy who knifed his tire was still hanging around. No, this was the work of a coward. Someone who might take an unsuspecting woman and convince her to get into his vehicle, right before he killed her.

The knife was still in the tire. He knelt beside it, examining what was left of the radial. Whoever did this had been furious with him. There were several stab wounds on the rubber. He doubted he would get any fingerprints off the knife, but he opened the back door and brought out an evidence bag. After slipping on a pair of gloves, he carefully removed the knife and put it inside the bag. Then he got busy changing the tire.

It was almost nine by the time he parked at the agency, grabbing a cup of coffee on his way by the vendor. Right now, he needed a lot more than one cup, but he'd settle for a tall, double shot.

"You're new around here, aren't you?" The vendor asked.

He shrugged. "I'm Dylan, just doing a little consulting work. And you are?"

"Abe Willis."

Abe was probably in his sixties with a little bit of a paunch, hair mostly gray. "Well, Abe, if you see anyone around here that doesn't look like they belong, I'd appreciate a heads up."

"Lots of people coming and going. New, like you, or just passing by. So, what's it to you?"

"He's been bothering Ashlyn." He took the coffee Abe handed him.

Abe slowly nodded. "I like that girl. She always appreciates a good cup of coffee. I'll tell you if I see anything different or out of the ordinary. Me and my wife raised three girls. I made sure when they started dating the boys knew if they hurt one of them, they'd have to answer to me."

"Don't approach this one, though. He's dangerous."

"Like that, is it?"

Dylan hesitated for a moment. "Yes, it's like that."

"I'll keep a watchful eye out for anyone lurking about."

As he went inside the building, Dylan knew Ashlyn was right about Abe. He didn't think this man had anything to do with the murders or the notes that Ashlyn had been receiving. His instincts were usually pretty good.

After dropping off the knife to have it checked for fingerprints, he made his way to the main office. Ashlyn immediately looked up, then arched one eyebrow.

"Late night?" she asked with more than a little sarcasm.

"No, not really. I had to remove a knife from my tire and change the flat." He casually took a drink of his coffee as he watched her eyes widen. He didn't think she would be very good at poker. He couldn't help but wonder if she would be up for a game of strip poker. Nah, he had a feeling she wouldn't.

Brad came out of his chair and leaned against his desk. "Was it our guy?" He crossed his arms in front of him.

Ashlyn was shaking her head. "But why would he?"

Ginny was slowly nodding her head. "I think I might know. You two have been working together. Going to the scene of the crimes. Have you been together after work?"

"We went out for pizza and to talk over the case a little more," Dylan told her. "As we left and went to our vehicles, I had a feeling someone was watching us."

"This is getting out of hand," Waylon said as he came up, hearing part of their conversation. "I won't have one of my agents put in jeopardy. I want you off this case now," he said, looking directly at Ashlyn.

She jumped to her feet. "If I leave this case, it'll only make the perp more furious. I won't be any safer than I am right now trying to find him."

"She's right," Dylan said. "It might even make her an easier target."

Waylon's lips compressed, and he didn't say anything for a moment. "Okay, you're probably right. The killer has apparently been following you. I want an agent with you at all times."

She cocked an eyebrow. "I don't need a babysitter."

"It's either that or protective custody."

Her eyes narrowed as she weighed her options. "Okay, fine." As if something just occurred to her, she quickly continued. "My apartment complex is secure."

Waylon was hesitant for a moment as though he was thinking, then continued. "Dylan, since you two are working together anyway, do you have a problem shadowing Ashlyn when she's *not* at home?"

Her gaze met his. Hers eyes immediately flared with anger that she quickly hid. "No, I don't have a problem." He had a feeling she would do anything to stay on the case. Even if it meant having him as a bodyguard. She was a loner. It hadn't taken him long to figure that one out. She could work with a team of other agents, but that was where it ended. Once she left the office, he doubted she interacted much with anyone.

Because of the explosion? Probably. That day, the perpetrator had stolen her innocence. It wasn't the first time he'd seen it happen. He'd seen it in the eyes of children caught in the web of human trafficking. With some, the fear was evident in the way they shied away from those trying to help them. But then you had the ones resigned to their lot in life—the ones who had given up.

Some could live with it for the rest of their lives, forcing themselves not to think about what happened to them. But every once in a while, something would trigger them when they weren't expecting it. They would feel as if they were drowning in the memories of what had happened, and it would be all they could do to fight their way to the surface. Some didn't make it.

He was almost certain Ashlyn had been struggling with what had happened for a very long time. Her grandmother would've made sure she received counseling, but had it been enough?

Of course, he was only guessing. She might just not like people. She could be an introvert. He had a cousin who was fine around crowds or at a party for about an hour or two. The longer she stayed in that environment, the more agitated she became.

There could be another explanation. He grimaced. It might be him that she didn't like. He thought about that for a moment. Nah, he was likable enough. He'd never had a problem until now.

After everyone went to their respective jobs, and it was just the two of them, he turned back to Ashlyn. She was studying him. He wondered what was going through her mind. He didn't have long to wait before finding out.

"You think it was our guy?" she finally asked, still looking unsure.

"Yes, I do. I think he's obsessed with you. Why else would he direct the notes to you and not to everyone on the team? Why does he want to speak to you when he calls? You crossed paths with this man at some point in your life. We just have to figure out when and where."

She arched an eyebrow and crossed her arms in front of her. "I don't need a babysitter. I'm quite capable of taking care of myself."

"I'm sure you are, or you wouldn't be an FBI agent."

Her frown only darkened. "Then why didn't you say something to Waylon? You could've told him that you didn't think I needed anyone shadowing me." Her eyes widened. "Oh, wait, you've been analyzing me."

When he didn't say anything, she continued.

"You've probably looked into my past," she said. "It wouldn't be hard to find out about the explosion and the fire. Did you discover I was the one who pulled my father out of the house and that he was unconscious? No, don't answer that. I can tell by the look in your eyes that you did."

"I wanted to know who I was working with. Did you look into my background? It wouldn't be that difficult since you're with the bureau."

"No, I wasn't that interested."

Ouch, ego-buster. He wanted to ask why but decided she'd probably laugh in his face. They had to work together, though. He had to smooth things over ASAP.

He took a deep breath and exhaled. "Look at it this way, the perp's going to be so ticked off that we're together all the time he's going to get careless and screw up. It might just be how we catch him."

She opened her mouth and then closed it. He could almost see the wheels turning inside her head. He was right about her, she wanted to catch this guy bad enough that she was willing to put up with him.

"So you think if this guy has any inkling that we might be dating, he'll get careless?"

"It's a possibility." Damn, she was fighting this all the way.

"You might be right," she finally conceded. "If he got angry enough to slash your tire, then if he thinks we're dating, he might show his face or at least slip up."

"He didn't just slash my tire. He stabbed it several times. Only someone who doesn't have control of their emotions, at least when it comes to you, would do that. I think he'll very likely make a mistake if he thinks we're an item."

When she closed her eyes, Dylan had a feeling she was counting to ten. She opened her eyes and glared at him. "Don't try anything funny, or I'll make your life miserable. Got it."

It was all he could do to keep from smiling. He didn't think she realized just how tempting she was right now. Her lips were slightly puckered, and there was a rosiness in her cheeks. He wanted to pull her into his arms and kiss her soundly, but that would only have her running away as fast as she could, putting her in more danger.

"Yeah, I get it," he told her.

"I have parameters."

"Was that a challenge?" he asked before he had time to think about what he was saying.

"No, it wasn't. Now, if you'll excuse me." She turned and began walking away.

He straightened. "Where are you going?"

She glanced over her shoulder. "To the ladies' room. I don't believe I'll require your assistance."

His smile was slow. The lady didn't know, but she was already making his life miserable, and his jeans uncomfortably tight. It was like being in a candy store surrounded by sweets and unable to open any of the jars.

Chapter Seven

As soon as Ashlyn entered one of the stalls in the ladies' room, she rested her head against the cool surface of the door and expelled a frustrated breath. How the hell was she going to manage being constantly in Dylan's company? He irritated the hell out of her!

She struggled to bring her emotions under control. She was an FBI agent, trained to control her emotions. She could do this.

Oh God, she didn't know whether she could or not. Something about Dylan set her on edge the moment he came near.

She closed her eyes as she tried to pull her thoughts together. After all, he was just a man. No, that wasn't quite right. He made her feel things that she didn't want to feel. He made her want...

She didn't know what he made her want.

Her eyes flew open. Oh, hell, she knew exactly what it was. She was attracted to him. But why? He had a huge ego problem. The man was insufferable.

She blew out an aggravated breath. It wasn't difficult to figure out why she was like a moth to his flame. The guy was tanned, muscled, and off the charts hot. He had a delicious body with muscles that rippled every time he moved.

She nibbled her bottom lip. He would probably be fantastic in bed. She hadn't had fantastic in a very long time. She'd had mediocre. There was something about Dylan that said, I can satisfy all your needs. Yeah, she didn't doubt that.

But it wasn't going to happen. At least, not while they were trying to catch a serial killer. She needed to get her head screwed on straight.

That was enough thinking about Dylan. Hell, she'd been fantasizing about the guy. She quickly used the facilities, then left the stall. She took one look at herself in the mirror and saw just how frazzled she looked. After washing her hands, she splashed water on her face and was patting it dry when Ginny came into the ladies' room.

"You okay?" she asked after taking a long look at her.

"Yes, I'll be fine."

Ginny leaned against the counter and studied Ashlyn. "I don't blame you for not wanting Dylan to shadow you. I know you're a bit of a loner after you leave work. Think about it this way, it could be worse."

"Really?" She expelled a short, bitter laugh. "How do you figure it could be worse than having someone with me constantly?"

"He could be a toad. He's not. I mean, the guy is seriously buff. Where some guys are a ten, Dylan is at least a solid fifteen."

"As you said, I don't like anyone shadowing me. I can take care of myself." She wasn't about to admit to Ginny that she agreed with her about Dylan being hot. She might even go higher on the guy chart.

"Well, I wouldn't mind trading places with you." She frowned. "Not the part about having a serial killer obsessed with me, but having someone like Dylan hanging out with me practically twenty-four hours a day. Once a guy finds out I'm with the FBI, our relationship takes a nosedive."

Ashlyn had to admit that she knew exactly what Ginny meant.

"If you ever decide to take it personal," Ginny continued. "You'll have to let me know how he is."

The door suddenly opened and Leah came in. She looked between them. "Did I miss the meeting?"

"We were talking about Dylan and how he'll be shadowing Ashlyn until we catch this guy."

Leah walked over to the counter and scooted up on the surface. Her expression turned dreamy. "Dylan is every woman's sex fantasy come to life. I love how his T-shirt practically molds to all those muscles." She sighed. "And not many men can pull off wearing snug-fitting, low-riding jeans." She bit her bottom lip.

"Do you want a piece of the action, too?"

It took a moment for Ashlyn's words to sink in. Leah snapped out of her daze. "What? No! I'm quite happy with Gerald. He more than satisfies me." She tossed them a saucy grin. "Looking only increases my appetite, but I always eat at home."

Ginny laughed. "Come to think about it, I don't think it would work for us, either. Dylan smiles a lot, but I have a feeling he's an alpha male."

Now it was Ashlyn's turn to be confused. "What do you mean? Alpha male?"

Ginny shrugged one shoulder. "You know, hot guys who take care of and protect their women. All that testosterone can consume a female. Just swallow them right up."

She was starting to get a little insight into Ginny's personality. Interesting. "So you want men you can control."

"Sure, why not? It doesn't say anywhere in any rule books that a man has to wear the pants."

"You're right."

"I am?"

"Yes, and I can't see Dylan wearing a skirt." Ashlyn stared at her reflection, then redid her low ponytail.

Ginny began to laugh. Leah quit trying to stifle hers.

"Okay, maybe I want to find an alpha man who can still be gentle and work as a partner," Ginny said. "I wonder if they make them like that?"

"They do." The dreamy expression was back on Leah's face. "Gerald would take down any man who threatened me."

"That doesn't make you feel less in control of your future?" Ginny was genuinely puzzled.

"Not at all. I know I can hold my own. I mean, I am an FBI agent. It's just nice to know he's got my back, too."

"Maybe we'll find out what category Dylan is in someday." Ashlyn tossed the towels into the trash. "I'll let you know how it goes."

"Do that," Ginny said.

"Hey, we never get together after work," Leah said. "Why don't we have a ladies' night out or something?"

Ashlyn started to tell her she didn't think that was a good idea but then wondered why it wouldn't be. She'd kept herself isolated far too long. "I'd like that. After we catch this guy, of course."

"Then it's a date," Ginny agreed.

Ashlyn left the ladies' room calmer than when she went inside. Ginny and Leah had made her laugh.

Maybe that had been what they were trying to do. Ashlyn didn't socialize much with the team after work, but they were still a close-knit bunch. They would always have the other ones back. She sort of liked that feeling, even though it went against her current habit of staying home alone. Don't get close to anyone. That had always been her motto. Maybe it was time she changed a little. Stopped living her life in a bubble.

Ashlyn joined the others. The rest of the day went by reasonably smooth. She and Dylan reassembled the bombs from each crime scene, or at least what was left of them.

"The first two look amateurish," she said. "But when you get to the third one, it's a little more sophisticated. More like something a professional would make." She turned it over in her hands as she studied it.

"He was definitely a beginner with the first two. This guy isn't stupid. He's learning fast, but I don't think he started out reading from a how-to book. I think he's been around bombs for a while."

She looked at him. "Why do you think that?"

He shook his head. "Just a hunch I have. The first two are almost like he's copying someone. Maybe he's trying to prove he's as good as the one he's copying. But the third one, I think he's saying look at me, I'm better than you. And look," he pointed to a mark on a portion of the metal casing that hadn't been destroyed. "Doesn't this look out of place? It looks like a star."

She leaned in to look a little closer, automatically closing her eyes and inhaling the scent of his cologne. Damn, he smelled sexy. She quickly straightened and focused once again. She knew the mark.

"It's like a signature. Yes, I noticed the star on the other devices as well. Almost hidden from view, but I haven't figured out what it might represent." She studied all the parts they'd assembled from the three crime scenes. "So, you're saying that someone from his past might've made bombs and used that same symbol."

"Maybe. I don't know. I'm just guessing at this point. We need to look at this from every angle. Anyone involved with explosives."

He was right, of course, but it wasn't doable. "We'd be looking at all the bombers with the same MO and their family members—brothers, sons, possibly daughters as well, even though I think a man is committing the crimes. That's a lot of suspects."

"He thinks there's a connection between you and him, so we'd only be looking at the cases you've worked," Dylan told her.

She grimaced. "You still think it's somehow connected to the guy who bombed our home. It's not. He was a loner. No wife, no kids, no visitors. He stays isolated in prison. He doesn't even use the internet, so he doesn't have anyone on the outside. There is no connection between Albert Duncan and me. Not anymore."

"Are you sure? Maybe we can speak with your father. He might know more about the man's relationships since he was the one sending him to prison."

She was already shaking her head. Dammit, she didn't want to go through this, not now, not ever. "We can't."

"Even if it might catch a killer?"

"I'm not bringing my father into this. End of discussion."

She turned away from him, looking out the window, but not really seeing the cars whizzing by. She thought back to the man her father used to be. Vibrant, energetic, and so damned smart. Because their mother had died not long after Mindy was born, their father had tried to be both mother and father.

On the other hand, she had become a little hellion after losing her mother. She'd been angry that she was gone. Mothers weren't supposed to leave their children, even if it wasn't their fault.

Late one night, she'd crept downstairs to raid the cookie jar and heard her father softly crying in the other room. She'd crept to the doorway and looked inside. She'd never forget the image of a broken man hugging the framed picture of his wife. He'd lost the love of his life. They'd been teenage sweethearts as well as best friends. She suddenly realized just how much her father had lost as well.

She'd silently moved across the carpet and crawled up on

the sofa next to him, wrapping her arms around his neck and holding him close as though she was the mother now. She told him everything would be okay. They had each other.

That night, she and her father bonded, and she grew up. She didn't act out anymore after that. She became the woman of the house, even though they had a housekeeper who took care of a lot of things. She took it upon herself to take care of Mindy, sheltering her little sister from the monsters in the world.

Then after the accident, her burdens became heavier. She would protect Mindy and her father at all costs.

"It's getting late," Dylan said, bringing her out of the past. "Why don't I walk you to your car and then pick you up and take you out to dinner, say, in about an hour. Will that work for you?"

She was glad he wasn't pressuring her about her father, but she didn't want to go to dinner with him either. She started to tell him no, she was going to heat a frozen dinner but then realized they were supposed to pretend they were dating. Okay, fine. She only hoped it wouldn't take long to catch this guy.

"Make it an hour and a half. I want to take a shower when I get home."

"I'll let you know when I get to your complex. Don't come down by yourself until I get there."

She almost snapped back that she could take care of herself but changed her mind at the last moment. "Yes, that will be okay."

He walked her to her car. She ground her teeth with every step she took. This was going to get old in a hurry.

"Seven-thirty," he reminded her.

She grit her teeth and then looked at him with a smile pasted on her face. "Yes, I remember." There was no way he would let her forget. He was quickly becoming a tyrant. She pushed the button on her key fob that unlocked the door and got inside. He was still standing in the same spot as she drove away.

She didn't care that her pulse sped up whenever he walked into a room. She didn't even care that he was devilishly attractive. The man was still an ass. She didn't need a babysitter.

She nibbled her bottom lip. She didn't like the idea of someone slashing his tire either. He was right. Only a psychopath would do something like that. Someone obsessed with her. She would have to be more cautious in the future.

Her apartment complex had a guard on duty twenty-four hours a day, so no one could get inside the parking garage unless they lived there or had a temporary pass from one of the apartment tenants. She'd chosen this particular complex for that very reason. She always felt safe and secure when she was home.

She'd also made sure that Mindy's off-campus apartment was just as secure. Where her father lived was equally safe. She didn't think she would ever get over the fear Albert Duncan created when he broke into their home. All because her father was the prosecuting attorney.

She parked her car and then got out, locking the door behind her. It was only a short walk to the elevator.

Albert Duncan had been accused of robbing an older couple and beating them both. They'd identified him in court. They'd been so scared of Albert that they packed all their belongings and moved to Florida to be close to family.

Ashlyn was pretty sure he would've taken out his anger on her father anyway. Albert was that damned mean and crazy as hell. If that weren't enough, he'd shanked two men, killing them, as soon as he got to prison.

Now, rather than going to jail for a few months for the robbery, then a few years for what he did to her and her father, he would spend the rest of his life in prison. It was good enough for him. Her father was in a different kind of prison since the accident.

She got off the elevator and walked down the hall to her apartment. After unlocking the door, she stepped inside, feeling a moment of peace before she turned and locked the doors, dropping the keys into a bowl on the side table.

Damn, she was tired. She didn't want to go anywhere tonight. She'd much rather have her TV dinner, a glass of wine, and then later, curl up with a good book.

But when she thought about Dylan, her heart betrayed her, skipping a beat again.

Chapter Eight

There she was. His angel. The most beautiful woman on earth. And she was all his. Or at least, she soon would be. He'd brought his binoculars this time so he could gaze upon her beauty.

Elijah knew her routine. She would go into her bedroom to change into her nightgown. She didn't like wearing the black slacks and long-sleeved shirt, along with hiking boots, any longer than she had to. He brought the binoculars down to his side and closed his eyes for a moment as he envisioned Ashlyn unbuttoning her shirt and then tossing it on a chair in her bedroom.

Next, she would take off her socks and boots, tossing her socks into the hamper. She'd probably slide her shoes under the chair. She would unfasten the belt at her waist and then unbutton her slacks, sliding the zipper down. After she removed her slacks, she would toss them onto the chair as well.

He swallowed hard. He was only guessing, but he was almost certain this was what she'd do. He knew her better than anyone. He'd studied everything about her.

His angel.

She would stretch, getting the kinks out of her body from a long day at work, then pad over to the dresser and grab her nightgown.

Sometimes she would take a shower. She was taking longer than usual, so he imagined her standing naked beneath the spray with the water cascading over her breasts and down to her slender waist before making a path over her gently rounded hips.

No! He couldn't think about earthly pleasures. What he was doing was more important than his needs. Soon, they would be together. She would beg him to love her forever. He opened his eyes, taking in deep gulps of air as he brought his emotions under control.

He looked up at her apartment again. A frown immediately formed when she walked in front of the window. He quickly brought the binoculars up to his eyes, but she'd moved out of his line of vision. She hadn't been wearing her nightgown. What was going on?

She returned to the table, just off the kitchen, setting a glass of wine down and then taking a seat. She took a sip of the wine and then glanced at her watch.

Was she going out with someone? She was wearing one of the dresses she wore when she went out. She looked great in it. It was black with three-quarter length sleeves to hide the scars. A black belt sparkled at the waist, making the dress flare just a little. The dress was short enough to show off her long, shapely legs. She was probably wearing her strappy black heels with it.

She didn't date very often. So why now? Was it that mustached Romeo again? God, the guy was a weasel with thin, narrow lips. She could've waited until *they* were together. Most of the men she dated were losers.

Elijah stood a little straighter when a vehicle pulled up in front of her building. No, it couldn't be Dylan. He was probably only checking up on her like he had last night. Dylan should know by now that *he* was taking care of her. *He* wouldn't let any harm come to Ashlyn.

He scooted back into the shadows a little farther and raised the binoculars. He watched as she picked up her phone and, after only a moment, came to her feet. Then she walked out of his line of vision again. He practically held his breath while waiting for her to come downstairs, hoping she wouldn't get into Dylan's pickup.

But a few minutes later, that's precisely what she did. Fury rose inside him. He began to pace back and forth across the narrow alleyway. No, no, no! This wasn't happening. She never dated coworkers.

Elijah quickly looked up. Dylan was getting into the vehicle once again. He had to follow them. He needed to know where they were going.

His leg began to ache. He stumbled once and had to lean against the wall to catch his breath. He rubbed the side of his leg and continued toward his car. His breathing was ragged as he got inside and started it. By the time he drove around to her apartment, they'd already left. He stepped on the gas and made his way to the corner, stopping at the stop sign and looking both ways.

Nothing.

He slammed his fist against the steering wheel. She was making a big mistake. Dylan wasn't for her. She better be careful or he was going to make her pay.

No, it wasn't her fault. He didn't blame her for giving in to temptation. She wasn't as strong as him. He took a few calming breaths, then began driving around the city, going to all her favorite places. After about an hour, he finally gave up looking for them and went home. At least, by then, he'd calmed down. It didn't matter what happened, Ashlyn still belonged to him.

He pulled into the driveway and turned the key. The house was small, with only two bedrooms. He studied it for a moment. It was in a middle-class neighborhood. Most of the homeowners were retired. No one bothered anyone else. He liked it that way. Although, he did help the woman next door get her cat out of a tree once. She called him her savior. He smiled at the thought. He would be Ashlyn's savior as well.

Except Dylan was getting in his way.

His pulse sped up. He was anything but calm as he unlocked the front door and went inside. He stood just inside the living room for a moment, slowly inhaling and then exhaling as he brought his emotions under control again.

What could Dylan give her? Nothing, while he'd be giving her a mansion. Of course, he would have to explain everything to her so she would understand. His pulse slowed to a normal rate, so he put the keys on the hook by the front door. When he turned around, he looked at the room with a critical eye.

This house was similar to the place he'd inherited when his mother died, except that one had been in a bad part of town. His forehead creased. He missed his mother sometimes.

She'd stayed strung out on drugs. The men who visited always brought her drugs. She'd taught him how to give her the injections that would send the heroin into her bloodstream. That was about the only time there was any warmth in her. She would call him her beautiful baby boy.

Once, he'd almost asked her if he was her beautiful baby boy, then why had she thought it was funny when the men put their cigarettes out on him or beat him?

That was his mother's problem. She had an open-door policy. She didn't care what else they did if they supplied her with drugs, including abusing her beautiful baby boy.

His father had been worse than them all. He was the one who forced him into the dark closet. He was the one who'd beaten him with the buckle end of his belt. He was the one who left scars on his back and the reason he walked with a limp. It was a blessing he wasn't around very often. Usually, he only showed up when he was broke, and then he'd pimp Elijah's mother out so he could have a little extra cash. Then he'd move on to the next woman.

That's why so many men came around. They all wanted a piece of her. Not that she cared for any of them. No, the drugs were all that mattered.

It hadn't been that difficult to add a lethal dose of heroin to his mother's needle. She'd been smiling when he injected it into her vein. His beautiful mother. They'd looked a lot alike. Both with pale blue eyes and black as coal hair. He'd always thought she was attractive enough to be a model. He'd sat with her, holding her hand until she took her last breath. He'd waited until morning to call the police.

As much as he hated to, he had to let her go. If she continued down the path she was on, she would've ended up in Hell. He couldn't let that happen. It was much easier for her to go to sleep in her drug-induced state.

He'd wept. She was, after all, his mother.

He walked through the rooms. There was an old sofa he'd gotten from Goodwill, along with a few odds and ends pieces. There was a new TV on the wall. He liked keeping up with the news. Occasionally, he would see Ashlyn working a crime scene. He'd bought a computer for his study. He had a job, but mostly worked from home. He liked it that way.

He went into the kitchen and got himself a soda out of the refrigerator. He didn't drink alcohol or do drugs. He'd had enough of that growing up. He wasn't going to end up like his mother and ruin his life. No, he knew his purpose. Like a bright light shining down upon him, God told him what he had to do.

He suddenly smiled when he pictured Ashlyn at the sink. She would turn as soon as he walked inside the kitchen. Her smile would be slow, but her eyes would already be sparkling with the excitement that he was finally home. She would dry her hands on a cup towel, walk over to him, and put her arms around his neck.

"I've missed you, darling," she'd say.

She'd be wearing a dress belted at the waist with a frilly white apron. Her makeup would be perfect for him and her hair would be down. The sun would be streaming in through the window, kissing her face. They would have the ideal life. No one would ever hurt them again.

And she wouldn't care about his scars because she had scars of her own.

"Soon, my beautiful angel, and we'll be together. Forever."

Chapter Nine

"Do you think he's following us?" Ashlyn asked.

Dylan glanced in his rearview mirror before looking across the seat where at Ashlyn. God, she was even more beautiful wearing the black dress and heels with her hair free from the low ponytail she usually wore.

It took a moment for his brain to start functioning again. When it did, he cleared his throat and began to speak. "I don't think so. I'm sure he's been watching your apartment from the alleyway across the street. He wouldn't have had time to get in his car and follow us."

"Then you can take me home. It's not like this is a real date or anything. It's only for show." She brushed strands of hair behind her ear.

Well, that hadn't worked out like he thought it would. "But I can't be sure," he quickly continued. "He still could be out there somewhere, watching us. There's a lot of traffic tonight."

She glanced into the side mirror. "Maybe." She sat a little straighter in her seat. "Okay then, let's get this over with."

He laughed. He couldn't help it. Now she was frowning at him. "You act as if you're going to your execution. Is the thought of having dinner with me so repugnant to you?"

"I didn't mean it that way." She rolled her eyes, clearly exasperated. "I just meant that the only reason we're going out together is to try to catch this guy."

"Is it?"

She cocked an eyebrow. "Yes, it is."

"Maybe you should try loosening up just a little. You might enjoy my company."

"It's doubtful." She crossed her arms in front of her as he

pulled into the restaurant's parking lot. There was a little bump, so she had to uncross her arms and grab the dash to steady herself, losing a bit of her haughtiness.

He pulled into the first available parking space and shut off the engine before looking at her again. "What's doubtful?"

"That I'll enjoy myself tonight."

He studied her for a moment. "Why do you dislike me so much? What have I done that's so terrible?"

Her mouth opened, then snapped closed. Finally, she spoke. "You were born."

He laughed outright at that. "Well, don't tell my parents because they were pretty excited when the nurse placed me in their arms, or so I've been told a million times. Be honest with me, what's really bothering you?"

She nibbled her bottom lip, and it was almost his undoing. He had a strong desire to lean across the seat and kiss those delectable lips. It was all he could do to keep control of himself.

"I'm sorry," she finally said on a whispery sigh. "I guess I'm just on edge about this case. It's as though he's trying to involve me in his criminal activities. Making me just as guilty. I don't like the feeling. It's nothing that you've said or done."

"That's good to know."

"I admit I was a little irritated that we had to bring in an outsider to work on the case. I don't like feeling inadequate."

"That wasn't my intention at all."

"I know, but if we're being honest with each other, that's how I felt, and I couldn't help it. I'm glad that we have more eyes on the case. I don't want another woman to die."

Finally, they were starting to make a connection. "Let's not think about anything tonight except maybe getting to know each other. If we work together, we can solve this case."

She nodded as they unfastened their seatbelts and got out.

"I hope you like Italian food," he said.

"I love it. I've never been to this restaurant before, though."

"It had some good reviews." He put a hand on the small of her back and felt the tremble that rippled over her. He had a feeling he knew what bothered her about him more than anything. It was the effect he had on her senses. She liked being in control, and her attraction to him kicked into gear when he was around. He knew the feeling. She affected him in the same way. He wasn't immune to her charms.

Damn, she smelled good, too. There was something about the smooth, sultry blend that tugged at every one of his senses. It was a rich, sweet, earthy scent that he couldn't quite describe, but he knew he liked it.

They went inside the restaurant. He'd made the reservations earlier, so they shouldn't have to wait. The hostess standing behind the pedestal glanced up as the door opened, and they gave her their names. If he had to describe her in one word, he'd say snooty, but then her face broke into a warm smile when her gaze met his.

"Welcome To Giordano's."

"Reservation for Rowley, party of two."

"Of course." After glancing at her list, she nodded toward a waiter, and he hurried over.

"Please, follow me," he said.

"The restaurant is beautiful," Ashlyn said as they followed the waiter. "I love the Italian touches like the stone wall and the fountain. It looks like old-world Italy."

The waiter seated them and handed them a menu, taking their drink order.

"Have you ever been to Italy?" he asked after the waiter left.

She opened her menu, but he noticed a wistful look in her eyes. "A very long time ago. My parents took my sister and me there. My mother is Italian, although as far as I know, we don't have any relatives living in Italy. If we do, they're very distant."

"You must take after your father."

Her smile was soft and seemed to light up the room.

"I do take after my father. His ancestors were Nordic. Blond hair and blue eyes."

"You love him very much, don't you?"

She seemed to tighten right before his eyes. "Of course, I love him. He's my father."

Dylan quickly learned that her father was a touchy subject with her and that she was very protective of him. He couldn't help but wonder why. Because of the break-in when she was a kid? Possibly. For now, he would play it safe and talk about something else. "Yeah, that's the way I am with my father. He's pretty cool."

She relaxed. "And what does he do?"

"He blows up things."

She cocked an eyebrow. "Why does that not surprise me?"

He laughed. That's what he liked about Ashlyn. She made him laugh. "It's my family's business. Demolition. I learned my art from an early age. What about you?"

She started to fidget just a little. The waiter chose that moment to bring their glasses of wine. She took a couple of quick swallows. Liquid courage? Maybe.

She looked him straight in the eye. "I didn't become

interested in bombs or explosives of any kind until Duncan blew up our house." She leaned against the back of her seat. "Until then, I had thought about being an interior decorator."

"Really?"

"Yes, really. What? Do you not think I would've made a great interior decorator? You don't know me well enough to make that judgment call."

He shrugged. "I don't know. I just think you make a pretty damn good FBI agent."

Now she looked surprised. "You do?"

"Yes, why wouldn't I? You seem to know your job from what I've observed."

"Even though it wasn't what I imagined I'd be doing one day, I have to admit, I like putting bad guys behind bars so they can't hurt anyone. When did you become fascinated with blowing things up?"

"I was eleven."

"Eleven years old? Did I understand you correctly?"

He chuckled. "Yeah, I blew up the doghouse."

Her eyebrows shot upward. "I hope the dog wasn't inside."

"No, but he wouldn't come to me for the next few weeks. My father made me build Rex another doghouse. After that, my father said I couldn't blow up anything else unless I was with him."

"I bet that took some of the fun out of it."

He took a drink of his wine, then set his glass back down. "It did, until he let me blow up a building they were hired to demolish. I have a certain knack with explosives. Along with a healthy respect for the damage they can do."

"I know what you mean." She closed her menu and laid it on the table.

He did the same, and the waiter came over and took their orders. A moment later, their salads arrived in chilled bowls.

"This dressing is delicious," she said after a moment of silence.

"I agree. I love salads. That wasn't always the case, though."

"Ty, right?"

He looked up. He was pretty sure his expression was confused. "Excuse me?"

"Ty, isn't he the health nut? The one that got you eating salads?"

He grinned. "Yes, he did. I love them. Usually paired with pizza, though."

She laughed, and the sound washed over him in gentle waves.

"You should do that more often."

It was her turn to look confused. "Do what?"

"Laugh. You're way too serious."

"It comes with the job." She shrugged.

"But sometimes, just for your sanity, you have to leave your work at the office."

"Easier said than done when my work is stalking me."

"You're right, of course. At least for tonight, let's forget about the serial killer. Tell me about your sister instead."

Her expression softened, and she smiled. "Mindy is a sweetheart. After our mother died, she was so lost and confused. I took her under my wing, and she began to blossom. She's in college, and she's going to be a lawyer."

"Just like your father, right?"

She hesitated for just a moment. "Yes, just like my father."

"And how old is she?"

"She's twenty-four. She looks more like our mother. Dark hair and bright green eyes. She was on the Dean's list last semester. She's going to make a great lawyer." She laughed again. "She loves to argue. She's always telling me my job is too dangerous."

"She's right about your job being dangerous, but I bet she'll make a great lawyer if she's anything like you." He watched as she blushed. He marveled at how many facets there were about this woman sitting across the table from him. She was intriguing. Like no other woman he'd ever met. The more he was around her, the more he wanted to know about everything in her life.

Their food arrived, and they concentrated on eating for the next few minutes. He had to admit, it was the best Italian meal he'd ever had. That included the time he'd gone to Italy on a mission. By the time their meal was over and they were leaving, Dylan felt he knew Ashlyn a little better.

As they got into his pickup, he looked across the seat. "See, that wasn't so bad, was it."

"I suppose I managed to suffer through our pretend date."

He studied her for a moment but then saw her eyes twinkle. Okay, so the woman could tease. Maybe he liked her even more now.

"Yeah, I know what you mean." He sighed deeply as though going out with her had been an ordeal.

"Excuse me?"

"It was a dirty job, but someone had to do it."

"Now you're teasing."

He smiled. "I can usually give as good as I get."

"I guess I had it coming." She smiled.

He started the pickup and pulled out of the parking place. "You did." He looked both ways before pulling into traffic.

"I did have a good time. You surprised me."

"Not like your other dates?"

"Definitely not, thank goodness. Most of the time, they're duds."

"Then I'm glad I wasn't a dud. So, besides work, what's on the agenda for tomorrow?"

"Early morning jog, then after work, home."

"What time?"

"Jogging?"

"Yes."

"I usually like to get out early on the trail, say six."

"I'll pick you up at a quarter till."

When she opened her mouth, he thought she would argue, but she closed it without saying anything, only nodding.

The rest of the ride back to her apartment building was made in comfortable silence. He liked it, unlike many of his dates where the woman chattered the whole time. Once he pulled in front of her building, they both got out, and he walked her to the door.

"Thank you for a lovely dinner," she said.

"I guess we should make this a legitimate date."

Her eyebrows shot up. "What exactly do you mean?"

Before she could say anything else, his lips lowered to

hers. At first, hers were tight, but they quickly softened, and he slipped his tongue inside. She tasted a little bit like wine and a little bit like the desert they had after their meal, and she tasted just like he'd imagined she would. A little sweet, a little spicy. He pressed closer to her as her arms went around his neck. Her body was soft, with curves in all the right places. By the time they broke apart, they were breathing hard.

"I think I'd better go inside," she told him breathlessly. "Alone."

"Are you sure?" he asked. She'd created a need in him that was hard to ignore.

She slowly shook her head. "No, I'm not, but I am anyway. Goodnight, Dylan."

She opened the main entrance with her key card and slipped inside. He watched her go inside the building and disappear around a corner. Right then, he knew damn well he wasn't going to let anyone harm her. He went to his pickup and got inside, but before he did, he looked around. Dylan didn't think the killer was nearby. He looked toward the alleyway. He damn sure didn't want the guy watching Ashlyn. He would take care of that in the morning.

He drove back to his apartment complex, lost in thought about their *pretend* date. His forehead bunched in thought. Funny, it hadn't felt as if they were pretending. The kiss afterward had definitely been real. Ashlyn had responded to his touch. Either that, or she was a damn good actress.

He was a little surprised when he pulled into the parking garage. Dylan realized he hadn't been paying attention to his driving. If he wasn't careful, his inattentiveness would get him killed. He parked nearer one of the security cameras this time. If someone decided to slash his tire again, he'd better smile because he'd be on camera.

His phone began to ring as he went inside his apartment.

He looked at the caller ID, then answered as he locked the door behind him, tossing his keys on the side table.

"Yeah, Ethan, what's up?"

"Albert Duncan is one mean son of the bitch," he said.

"I'd already come to that conclusion." He went into the kitchen and grabbed a beer out of the refrigerator.

"From what I discovered, he tied Ashlyn and her father to chairs in the dining room and then set explosives all around the house. Damn, the kid was only fourteen at the time. Then he set fires all around the house. He orchestrated it so that each explosion would go off with the sequence he created. I have to admit, the guy was a genius when it came to explosives. If Ashlyn hadn't escaped, I don't think he would've been caught."

Dylan grimaced as he pictured a young Ashlyn desperately trying to escape her restraints. "And her father?" He twisted off the cap and tossed it into the trash before taking a long drink, trying to wash away the image of how terrified she would've been.

"From what I can tell, he's in a rehab center in Texas. He suffered some kind of brain injury. I couldn't find out the extent. I do know that he hasn't practiced law since the break-in."

"What about this Albert Duncan? Anything on him?"

"In and out of jail since he was a kid. He was pretty much a bully when he did go to school. I have the name of the last woman he shacked up with. Why anyone would have him is beyond me."

"What about her?"

"She's in prison. It might be worth paying her a visit. She's in Maryland. I'll send you the info."

"Thanks."

"So, how's it going? Is this Ashlyn woman giving you a

hard time?"

There was a pause before he answered. "No, I'm shadowing her right now. The perp is stalking her."

"Just be careful. If he's obsessed with her, he won't like having competition."

"Yeah, I figured that out on my own. I think he's been watching her from the alleyway across from her building. I'm going to have cameras installed just in case. When I took her out to eat tonight, I felt as if someone was lurking around, but I think we lost him, which wasn't my intention."

"So, how was taking her out to dinner?"

"What are you getting at?"

"She pretty?"

"I suppose."

"You suppose? She must be stunning."

He laughed. "Okay, she's stunning. She's also all business. The total opposite of me."

"Teach her how to have fun."

"I'm here to catch a killer. I'm not like you."

"Well, you're right about that. I'd probably already have her in my bed. How better to keep her safe than to sleep with her?"

"It's not like that."

"Well, be careful."

"Always."

"I'll see what else I can dig up, and if I find anything, I'll let you know."

They spoke for a few more minutes and then ended the conversation. Ethan was a good guy. He was also a ladies' man.

He had to give him credit, though. He always told the woman up front that he was not the marrying kind. If they were up for a good time, he was the guy. He'd broken a lot of hearts anyway.

He sat on the sofa and kicked his feet up on the coffee table, leaning back. He was sure it had something to do with Ethan's parents' marriage. He'd heard him talking to Carter one time. After his mother passed away, his father died shortly after that of a broken heart. Surely that couldn't be why he didn't want to fall in love.

Dylan's parents had a good marriage, and thankfully, they were both still living. He wanted to find someone like that to share his life with someday. But that was a long time off. Maybe when he turned forty, he'd start looking. That was still six years away. Until then, he liked his freedom.

He glanced at his watch. Damn, it was getting late, and he had to be up early in the morning to go jogging with Ashlyn. The thought brought a smile to his face. Maybe he should tell her he could keep her safer if he moved into her apartment. He laughed outright at that.

No, he didn't think she would go for it. That left him with a perpetual erection and a lot of cold showers in his future. Women would be the death of him, but what a way to die.

Chapter Ten

Ashlyn marched into the kitchen and opened the refrigerator door, closing it just as quickly. No, she wasn't hungry or thirsty. She was frustrated!

On second thought, opening the refrigerator was a good idea. She opened the freezer this time and began to fan the door. The cool air washed over her.

It did nothing for her raging hormones.

Why had she let Dylan kiss her?

For just a moment, she closed her eyes and remembered how it felt to have his lips pressed against hers, his body plastered to hers. His tongue exploring her mouth, sparring with hers. He'd tasted like the wine they'd had at dinner.

She began to fan the freezer door faster. Finally, she closed it and leaned her head against the cool surface. She'd never wanted a man like she did Dylan. He was everything she dreamed about or read about in one of her romance books—the kind of man who took charge but didn't invade her space.

Oh God, how was she going to face him in the morning?

She opened the refrigerator door and grabbed a bottle of wine. Maybe she did need a drink. She poured a half glass and then brought the glass to her lips.

No, she wouldn't think about him. They were colleagues. Nothing more. She would just have to deal with the situation. She'd always been strong. She could do this.

She put the bottle back into the refrigerator and then carried her glass to the living room and settled herself on the sofa.

Men like him only existed in romance books. Right? Dylan had to have a flaw. She would find it and be completely turned off. Maybe he hated animals. He *had* blown up the doghouse. She frowned. But then rebuilt it.

She didn't have a pet because of the hours she kept, but that didn't mean she didn't like animals. She'd love to have a puppy. Whatever his flaw was, she would find it, and her life would return to normal.

She glanced at her watch. Good Lord, it was getting late, and he was going to pick her up at five forty-five in the morning. She would need a good night's sleep to stay on top of her game.

A shiver of fear ran down her spine. *He* would probably be out there somewhere, watching her. Her stalker wasn't going to like that Dylan was with her. They were turning up the heat. Would it make him careless or desperate and more dangerous?

She took her glass to the kitchen and put it in the dishwasher before heading to her bedroom. Her main focus would be catching this man, who was apparently obsessed with her. That was all she was going to think about, not Dylan.

But when she woke up the following morning, Ashlyn had to fight to untangle herself from the bedclothes. She'd tossed and turned all night. She'd been dreaming about Dylan, but then he faded out, and the serial killer took his place, except he had the face of a monster. Appropriate, since he was a monster.

She couldn't get away from him. Once, she'd looked over her shoulder and thought she saw Albert Duncan, but as soon as she opened her eyes, she knew that wasn't possible. He was still in prison.

After making a trip to the bathroom, she dragged herself into the kitchen and turned on the coffeepot. She'd need a gallon this morning to wake up, but she would settle for one cup since she was going running.

She returned to her bedroom while the coffee was making and pulled on her jogging outfit, which consisted of polyester and spandex for both the pants and long-sleeved top. She had three of these outfits that she liked to wear.

This morning she chose the black and gray top with solid black pants. After dressing, she slipped on her running shoes and pulled her hair back into a low ponytail. The top was a little loose—made specifically for her. Underneath, she slipped her gun into a slim holster. Someone would have to be looking really hard to notice it was there.

She glanced at her watch. She had ten minutes. Coffee time. She poured herself a cup and curled up on the sofa. The first taste was always the best, and this time was no different. She closed her eyes, savoring the rich aroma and flavor.

Most agents she knew drank their coffee black. As if it was a rite of passage. Long hours doing surveillance work from a nearly empty apartment or vacant house. There was always coffee, but never cream or sugar. She always carried an emergency stash of cream and sugar packets.

The first time she'd pulled out the emergency kit while watching an apartment across the street, the two agents she was with had gotten snarky, but she noticed they had their own emergency supply the next time she worked with them. She'd only smiled.

The phone was ringing when she finished her coffee and rinsed her cup.

"Yes?" she asked.

"I just pulled up downstairs."

"I'll be down in a second," she told him.

Deep breath, exhale.

"You can do this," she told herself as she locked the door and walked to the elevator. She'd gone one-on-one with some of the toughest criminals without batting an eye. How hard could it be to face a man who'd kissed her the night before? She kept giving herself a pep talk as she rode the elevator to the first floor and stepped off.

She waved at Steph behind the desk as she marched out the front door…then immediately stopped. Dylan hadn't seen her yet. He was looking around, taking in his surroundings.

This wasn't going to be as easy as she thought. How could one man look so damned tempting in snug-fitting running shorts and a sleeveless top? His delicious muscles were on display, along with a very sexy tat that looked like a shield and sword.

A gust of wind suddenly picked up. Her heart skipped a beat when he absently reached up and brushed his fingers through his hair. He probably had women falling all over him wherever he went.

She squared her shoulders. Well, she was not going to be one of them. They'd shared a kiss, which wouldn't happen again. It wasn't as though they'd had sex or anything. Great, she damn sure didn't need that vision running around inside her head. Still, she took a deep breath before walking toward him.

"Are you ready?"

He turned to look at her, his gaze slowly roaming over her before returning to her face. "You look nice," he said, his raspy words scraping over her skin.

She raised her chin. "Just wait till after we finish our run. I'll be all sweaty."

He opened the door for her, and she slid into the passenger seat.

"That's how I like the women I'm with, sweaty."

She cocked an eyebrow. "Really? That's a pretty lame line, you know."

He only laughed. An equally sexy sound. It was too damn early in the morning for this. She should've gotten up an hour earlier and drunk another coffee. She needed to keep her wits about her, not only around Dylan but a possible serial killer who could be watching them this very minute.

She scanned the area as he started the pickup. Nothing looked out of the ordinary. She gave him directions to the park where she always ran. She liked going there because trees and flowers were plentiful. They used a special rubber material on the paved path that had just a little bit of a bounce, and it wasn't so hard on the knees. She always felt revitalized after her run. Now she realized the killer had probably followed her there, watching every move she made. A cold shiver ran down her spine.

"Why didn't he just grab me when I was running and be done with it?" she spoke her thoughts aloud.

"I think it's a game to him. He wants you to figure out his next move."

"But why?"

He shook his head. "That, I don't know."

He found a parking place and pulled in, shutting off the engine. Before they began their run, they stretched, but she knew they were both covertly looking around, scanning their surroundings. Two women around her age were already running the trail, but they slowed just enough to stare at Dylan, then smile.

Good Lord! She frowned when they looked her way. They quickly averted their gazes and picked up their pace. She continued scanning the area.

A maintenance man on a riding lawnmower didn't even glance their way as he continued his job. As they walked toward the trail, a young man ran past them. He took one look at her, smiled, and then winked. She hadn't seen him here before today. What if…

God, now she was looking at everyone as a suspect. Ashlyn realized she did anyway in her line of work. It was just this case hit closer to home.

"I don't think he would show himself. He's probably

hiding somewhere so he can watch you," Dylan told her.

She nodded. Now she felt even more vulnerable. "Let's go." She needed to run and expel some of this excess energy. Besides, she was damned if she would let this guy think she was scared.

Dylan stayed right with her, matching her stride. The first mile went quickly. By the time they finished the five miles she usually ran, she felt the adrenaline rush. This was why she enjoyed running. It was feeling all this energy just being alive.

Except the murderer had stolen some of that from her. Now she was constantly looking over her shoulder.

As they slowed and came to a stop, then began walking, Dylan said, "Don't worry, we'll catch him."

Was he so attuned to what she was thinking?

He looked at her and smiled. "No, I can't read your mind. It's what I would think if someone stalked me. Until we catch him, you're always going to be worried that he might be around the next corner, waiting to grab you."

She only looked at him and nodded. "Except he'll be in for a surprise. I won't go down as easy as his other victims." She glanced at her watch. "I guess we'd better head back. I need to shower before we go to the office." When she was met with silence, she looked at him. "What?"

"I thought we'd take a trip."

One eyebrow rose. "What kind of trip?" Ashlyn had a feeling she wasn't going to like whatever he was about to say.

She was right.

Three hours later, they had priority boarding and were headed to Maryland.

"How long are you going to be angry with me?" Dylan asked after she'd given him the silent treatment since he'd told her where their trip would be taking them.

She turned slightly in her seat and glared at him. "I don't know. You tell me. You've been investigating everything about my life since you arrived, as if I'm the criminal. Now we're on our way to interrogate a woman who used to sleep with the man who tried to murder my father and me sixteen years ago. I think we're wasting our time. What can she tell us that I don't already know?"

"I'm not sure. Maybe nothing," he admitted. "But I also want to look at the evidence from the explosion that almost killed you and your father. I figured we can go there first and meet with the woman tomorrow."

"Why look at the evidence from the bombing that happened so many years ago? They caught the guy. Albert is going to spend the rest of his life in prison. The prosecuting attorney saw to that."

"I've looked into what happened to you and your father. There's something vaguely familiar about that crime scene compared to the current ones."

Now she was curious, even though she hated to admit it. "What?"

He shook his head. "I don't know for sure. Just a feeling I have."

She raised an eyebrow. "A feeling?"

"You know as well as I do that sometimes you only have your gut to go on. Something that makes the hairs on the back of your neck stand up. It's at least worth checking out."

"I don't know why I had to come with you." Ashlyn knew she sounded petulant. It wasn't so much that she was in his company but that she didn't want to face her past. She didn't want to discuss it anymore either.

She turned her head toward the window and closed her

eyes, but no matter how hard she tried, her mind filled with visions of that day.

Her father was working in his study but promised to take her to the riding stables later. That was her greatest passion in the world, at least, since the year before when she'd gone riding with a girlfriend. She loved to ride one particular horse—Princess, a pretty little palomino with a sweet temperament.

Just Ashlyn and her father. Her grandmother took Mindy to visit a friend because her granddaughter was staying with her. She and Mindy were both about the same age. That was fine with Ashlyn because Mindy hated to ride. Horses scared her.

She'd just started up the stairs when the doorbell rang. Ten more minutes, and they wouldn't have been home. She hurried over and opened the door. The man on the other side wasn't tall. Maybe five feet, nine inches, but his shoulders were broad and his arms thick. As soon as she looked into Albert Duncan's face, she knew he was an evil man. He grabbed her arm and pulled her against him as he came inside, holding a gun to her head.

Her father was coming around the corner while asking who was at the door. She'd never forget the look on his face— fear that his daughter might die any second and there wouldn't be a damn thing he could do. He begged and pleaded with Albert not to hurt her, but he'd only laughed.

Then he ordered her father to sit in the dining room chair with his arms behind him.

He only had one zip tie. Ashlyn wasn't supposed to be there. No problem. An added bonus, he said, then laughed again.

Her father told her to close her eyes, no matter what happened. But Albert didn't hurt him. He had other things on his mind.

"Miss, would you like something to drink?" The flight attendant asked, breaking into her thoughts.

She shook her head and turned back to the window. No, she didn't want anything to drink. She didn't want to keep reliving what happened over and over. She tried to forget about it.

How could she? Every time she looked at her father, she knew what had happened. Pain rose inside her so strong that it threatened to engulf her.

There were things she didn't tell the police.

Get hold of yourself! You can get through this. You're a survivor.

She almost laughed. Some survivor she was. She was only fooling herself.

Dylan shifted in his seat. Even in first class, the seats were close together. She could only ignore him so long. Besides, she wanted to think about something else.

"Do you live in Texas?" she finally asked, just to break the uncomfortable silence.

"Not too far from San Antonio," he told her.

"So you've been to San Antonio before."

"Lots of times."

She crossed her arms in front of her and glared at him. *"New in town?"* She'd believed him and then took him out for pizza his first night.

"I didn't actually lie," he said with a bashful grin.

Nope, she wasn't buying that little boy with his hand caught in the cookie jar either. "So, explain."

"I haven't been to San Antonio in a long time. Things change almost overnight in a big city. You could say it was new to me."

"Or I could say you lied."

"I promise never to do it again."

"Make sure you don't."

"So, you're a transplanted Texan," he said.

"I beg your pardon?"

"You know, not from Texas originally. What do you think of our state?"

What did she think of Texas? It was big. Sometimes it felt like you were driving forever before getting to the state line. There were lots of pickups, cowboys, and livestock. The east had pine trees, and the west had wide-open spaces, the same for the panhandle region. Central was gently rolling hills and lots of deer. Then deep south, you had the Gulf of Mexico.

She had a feeling everyone owned a gun, and if they didn't, they knew someone who did. The heat was almost intolerable in the summer, but the winters were mostly mild.

There was something about Texas that made it seem right to live there. As if she'd come home. Which was crazy, of course, because she'd never lived in Texas before she moved here a few years ago.

She turned to look at him. "It's okay, I guess." She'd already discovered Texans had a lot of pride in their state. When he frowned, it was all she could do to keep a straight face.

"What don't you like about it?"

"I didn't say I didn't like it."

"You implied you didn't like it."

"No, I said it was okay."

"Same thing," he grumbled.

She began to laugh lightly. "One thing I've learned, you can get under a Texan's skin if you tell them their state is just okay."

"Now you get a sense of humor?"

"I guess you just bring it out in me."

They landed not too long after that. She grabbed her backpack, and he grabbed his.

"Where to first?" she asked.

"I thought we'd drop our luggage off at the hotel, grab a bite to eat, and then go to the evidence room. We'll go to the prison in the morning."

That sounded good to her because she was starving. She'd grabbed a stale bagel at the airport before leaving but only ate half of it.

Dylan had made all the arrangements. That was a first for her. She'd always taken care of everyone, as well as herself. She should've been irritated that he'd taken charge of the situation, but it felt nice to have someone taking care of everything—as long as it didn't become a habit. She was kind of a control freak.

He rented a gray SUV at the airport and drove them to the hotel. When they pulled under the broad canopy, she had to admit she was impressed. She knew the chain. This was at least a high four-star hotel. Not that she wasn't used to first class.

Her father had always made sure they had the best. Still, he taught them never to take money for granted. He'd inherited his wealth, but he'd still worked. He always said it was his way of giving back.

Still, she whistled beneath her breath as she stared at the three-tiered fountain with water spilling over the sides and the uniformed valets. "Wow, how did you get Waylon to spring for a hotel like this?"

"I didn't. I guess you could say I have a company card."

If the bureau agents were working a case farther from home, they stayed in, at best, in three-star hotels. She'd eventually gotten used to them, but that didn't mean she had to like the rooms. She grabbed her backpack off the floorboard and got out.

When a busboy offered to take it for her, she waved him away.

After checking in, they walked across the white marble floor and took the elevator up to their floor. His room was next to hers. Okay, she could live with that, but when she walked in, there was an open door between the rooms. After only a moment, he stood in the doorway.

"Hey, we have connecting rooms."

He was way too much temptation. She smiled sweetly. "We do!" She walked over, closed the door between them, and locked it.

"That was not funny either," was his muffled reply from the other side.

She laughed. He had a great sense of humor. When her phone began to ring, she pulled it from her pocket. Why was he calling her?

"What?"

"Do you want to grab a burger or even something at the hotel restaurant?" Dylan asked.

She had a feeling she wasn't going to get away from Dylan anytime soon. Funny, but she didn't mind being in his company that much. "A burger sounds good to me."

"A woman after my heart. Five minutes?"

"Make it ten."

"I'll knock on your door."

She ended the call without saying goodbye and looked around. The bed was huge. Bigger than just a king, with six fluffy pillows. The bathroom was spacious, with a Jacuzzi tub and a walk-in shower. The lighting was good, and the décor muted, upscale beige and off-white with bronze finishes. Yep, she'd gone into the wrong branch of law enforcement. Dylan must be damn good at his job.

She began to unpack. The one thing she'd learned over the years was how to pack light. Black leggings worked with anything, from casual to dressy. Three or four tops usually did the trick. She could wear her jeans more than once.

She always figured if she needed more, she'd buy it. If it was made out of a material that didn't wrinkle, even better. One uniform. Clean undergarments for two or three days, toiletries, sandals, a hairbrush, and she was ready to go. Besides, her backpack had a lot of pockets that stretched.

She glanced at her watch when she finished. Two minutes to spare. Yeah, she was good. She sighed. She didn't know why they were even in Maryland. As far as she was concerned, it was a wasted trip. They would've done better staying in Texas and reviewing all the evidence again. She was missing something. She just hadn't found it yet.

There was a knock on her door. She walked over and opened it. "You're a minute early," she told him.

"What can I say? I couldn't stand being away from you for another second."

"Am I going to have to put up with this the whole time we're here?"

He was thoughtful for a moment. "Probably."

She rolled her eyes as she grabbed the key card and slipped it into the back pocket of her jeans. "I bet women fall all over themselves for your charm."

"They do."

"Do the people around you have to wear wading boots?"

He wore a puzzled expression. "What do you mean?"

"To get through all the BS that you shovel out."

He laughed. "I knew you had a sense of humor."

"Well, it's beginning to wear thin. Besides, I'm hungry. Let's go." She closed her door and started walking to the elevator. She figured he'd follow, and she was right. He was like a puppy dog that had adopted her. Okay, he was kind of cute, sexy, hot...

She needed to eat something. She was starting to hallucinate.

Lunch went way too fast, though. She was getting increasingly nervous as they walked into the room where the evidence was stored. It was about the size of a large warehouse with floor-to-ceiling shelves. The officer came with them to help find the evidence.

"I wasn't too long in the area when that happened, you know," he spoke casually as they followed him. He was about sixty and wore thick glasses—which might be why he'd moved to the records department. "It was terrible what they did to that man and his little girl." He shook his head. "They should've given him the death penalty. Life in prison was too easy."

He glanced over his shoulder, studying her. "You got a personal stake in all this?"

"Yes, I'm the daughter."

He stopped in front of a shelf of boxes and stared at her. Slowly, he began to nod his head. "I'm glad you're okay now. An FBI agent, too." He smiled softly. "Put all those bastards away."

She returned his smile with one of her own. "I'm going to try."

He brought down a box from the third shelf and nodded at Dylan to grab the other one. They carried them to a table up front.

"I'll leave you with it. When you get through, I can put everything up. I hope you find what you're looking for."

"We do, too." Dylan took the lid off one of the boxes and put it to the side. He started to reach inside but then hesitated.

"Why don't you start bringing everything out?"

She nodded. She was glad he let her set everything on the wide, scarred, wooden table. When she noticed her hand was trembling slightly, she curled it into a fist and took a deep breath. When she opened her hand, it was no longer shaking.

There was a stack of pictures that she brought out first. She looked at the first one, then laid it on the table. It was a picture of their home before the crime occurred. Probably from when her father had first purchased the house.

Grandmother had always said, remember the happy memories. There had been plenty of them. But sad ones as well.

The next picture was the after photo. The fire department had gotten there quick enough to put out the blaze, so the crime scene was pretty much intact, except for what occurred during the explosions. The last one blew out a portion of the front wall.

The heavy marble table was still in place, but there were only two of the ornate chairs, and they had fallen onto their sides. If she hadn't gotten her father free, the fire or the debris from the second explosion probably would've killed them both. She wouldn't have left him. She stared at the picture for a long moment before placing it on the table.

"Are you okay?" Dylan asked.

As if she remembered he was still in the room with her, she looked his way. "Yes, of course, I'm fine. Like I told you. It was a long time ago." She quickly laid out the rest of the photos. There was even one of her on a cot about to be loaded into an ambulance. Her father had gone in the one before her.

She studied the picture as if she wasn't looking at herself. It could have been any other scared victim she'd come across in her years in law enforcement. She quickly swallowed her emotions and started going back through the box again.

There wasn't much left inside, so she moved to the other

box. This one had what was left of the explosives. She carefully brought them out and laid them on the table before moving the boxes to the floor. They sat in the chairs and began carefully going through each piece.

After a couple of hours, she was ready to give up. Nothing here could connect the crime scene to the ones in Texas. She came to her feet and stretched. That's when she noticed Dylan studying one piece closely. He reached for another part and brought the two together.

"What?" she asked. Cold chills began to run up and down her spine.

"See for yourself," he quietly told her.

She moved nearer. Her stomach began to churn. "No, no, it can't be."

Chapter Eleven

"But it can't be him," Ashlyn whispered. "I know for a fact he's in prison. It has to be a copycat or something."

Dylan could see she was upset. Who wouldn't be? Hell, they caught him a few days after the explosions and put him in jail. He still had to ask the hard questions.

"Would the public have known about his signature mark on the bombs?"

She opened her mouth, then quickly closed it. "No, they didn't know about them. They never publicized that information." She rubbed her temples. "Who could it be?"

"Maybe someone he met in prison. He might have talked about his signature on the bombs."

She shook her head. "No, I don't think so. He stays in isolation because everyone else is scared to be around him. He shanked a couple of men his first week. He doesn't get on the computer or anything. And before you ask about visitors, he doesn't have any. It's as if they're just as happy as everyone else that he'll be locked away for the rest of his life."

"Then we need to look at his life before he went to prison. Someone knows something about the bombs he used to make. The woman we're talking to tomorrow might be able to help us."

She finally nodded, reaching out to pick up all the pictures, but then paused. Her hand moved to another and then another, lightly touching them. Her frown deepened.

"What?" he asked.

"There's something oddly familiar about the picture after the explosion destroyed the room." Her eyes widened. "It almost looks like our last crime scene. I don't know why I didn't think about it until I saw these pictures. That's why it felt vaguely familiar when I first arrived on the scene of the farmhouse murder. Right here, look at how the explosion blew the wall out."

He studied the picture.

"See where the wall frames the interior of the room. If the chairs had been metal, and we hadn't made it out alive, my father and I would've been sitting at the table. Similar to how he staged Kimberly. Not the table, of course, but the way he had her near the window and tied in the chair."

"But the fire never reached the chairs," he pointed out.

"Because the fire department got there in time to put it out. It scorched the chairs where we were sitting. We lived in a very exclusive neighborhood. The fire department went en route as soon as the first explosion went off. The fire from the kitchen was spreading fast. We would have died that day if I hadn't gotten free."

"That's how you got burned. Because you weren't about to leave your father behind."

She turned her gaze away from his, staring at the picture, but he'd already seen the answer in her eyes.

"I couldn't leave him. I knew I'd never be able to live with myself. I was going to get him out or die trying." She drew in a shaky breath. "You would've done the same."

"You're right. I would've done exactly the same thing. What happened before Duncan left?"

She looked off into the distance. He knew she was reliving that day. "He didn't have anything to tie me with, so he dragged me into the kitchen and grabbed a cup towel. As soon as he…left, I began to work my hands free. Smoke was already filling the kitchen by the time I got loose. I went in anyway and grabbed a knife. I remember feeling the heat on my arms, but the fire hadn't engulfed the kitchen yet. The smoke was so thick that I crawled back to my father and used the knife to saw through the zip tie. He kept begging me to leave him behind. I couldn't. As we ran out of the house, the kitchen exploded. My father shielded me, but he was hit in the head by a wooden beam. I used my shoulder and upper arm to get it off him and pulled him the rest of the way out of the house, just before the second explosion."

He couldn't stand to hear the pain in her voice. "Let's get out of here."

Later, as they drove away, she still seemed pensive. He took her to a nearby park they'd passed on the way to the records department, rather than returning to the hotel. She looked around when he pulled into a parking place and shut off the engine. She seemed surprised at where they were, and already a little calmer. She was good at swallowing her emotions.

"Sometimes walking can relieve stress," he told her.

She frowned. "I'm not stressed. Just confused more than anything. That, and being pissed off. I should've examined the evidence before now."

"Why would you? The guy is in prison. There was no way for you to connect the bombings."

"You did."

"Because I couldn't find anything else to go on. I didn't think it would hurt to look into it. You probably would've done the same thing eventually."

"I don't think so. I don't like revisiting that time in my life. Maybe the serial killer is counting on that."

He opened his door. "Let's walk."

She reluctantly opened her door and stepped out. Neither one spoke for the first few minutes as they walked down the jogging track. Trees were plentiful, and squirrels were having fun as they darted up the trunks and down the limbs chattering to each other while birds sang from high up. Someone had recently mowed the grass, and everything smelled fresh and clean. The park had a calming effect.

"My father brought us here a few times," she said. "The trees have grown a lot, and there are more flowering plants. We would bring a picnic basket and spread out a blanket. Mindy used to try to catch butterflies. Dad would throw a Frisbee, and I'd try to catch it. Most of the time, I didn't, but it was fun anyway."

He hated to bring it up again, but he needed to know everything. "Tell me about that day. Right before Duncan got there," he said, breaking the silence. After a moment, he began to wonder if she would say anything more, but then she began to speak.

"Grandmother had taken Mindy to a friend's house, thank goodness. She was only eight and could be a real bother at times. As soon as father finished some work in his study, we were going to the stables. I used to love to ride back then."

"But not now?"

She shrugged. "I don't know. I would probably still love it. I just don't have the time anymore."

"And then what happened?"

"I was going up the stairs when the doorbell rang. I remember hoping that whoever was at the door wouldn't stay long. When I opened it, this hulking man was standing there, staring at me. He wasn't tall, but his shoulders were broad and his arms beefy."

"What else was there about him?"

"He smelled bad, like an open dumpster with rotting food or something. When he smiled, some of his teeth were missing. Before I could ask what he wanted, he grabbed me by the arm and pulled me close, then held a gun to my head. I don't think I've ever been so scared in my life."

She rubbed her hands up and down her arms as if she had a sudden chill. Dylan waited for her to continue talking.

"Father came out of his study toward the front door,

asking who'd rang the bell. He froze when he saw Duncan holding a gun to my head. I remember he turned white as a sheet. I didn't have time to warn him or I would have."

"It probably wouldn't have changed anything. What did your father do?"

"He begged him not to hurt me. Duncan only laughed. He forced my father to sit in one of the dining room chairs with his arms behind him and then made me secure his wrists. He only had one zip tie. I wasn't supposed to be there, you see. He said I was an added bonus and then laughed." Her eyes looked beyond the trees and into the past. "Don't look, father told me as he pleaded with Duncan to let us go. No matter what happens, don't look," she whispered.

They walked without talking for a short distance, and then she turned back toward the SUV.

"There wasn't anyone else with him?"

"It was just him. They sent me to therapists afterward. My grandmother insisted I go. I wasn't quite so bubbly and full of energy anymore. I think it scared her. I learned to control my emotions so she wouldn't be sad all the time. I fooled her, the therapist, everyone. She relaxed after a few weeks. Controlling my emotions helped me when I went into law enforcement."

Dylan didn't think he'd ever seen that much sadness on one person's face. It cut him to the bone. He didn't want to push her, but he had a feeling there was more to the story than the papers had reported. God help him, he wanted to kill Albert Duncan with his bare hands for what he put them through. What he'd put Ashlyn through.

"I don't want to talk about it anymore," she said. "Maybe we'll find out more tomorrow."

Ashlyn was quiet on the way back to the hotel. As they rode the elevator up to their floor, she said, "I think I'll take a shower. The warehouse was dusty, and I feel like I have a layer of grime on my skin."

He had a feeling it was an excuse to be alone for a while. Not that he could blame her. He just didn't want her to dwell on the past too much. They unlocked their doors and went into their rooms. As soon as he closed his door, he knew he couldn't leave her alone to dwell on everything. He didn't want her haunted by what had happened.

Dammit, why had he even brought the subject up? He closed his eyes for a moment and took a deep breath. If they were going to solve the current case, he needed to know everything about this guy and what happened that day. He walked to their adjoining door and knocked on it. He heard the lock click a moment later, and she opened the door.

"Did you need something?" she asked.

She'd taken the band out of her hair, and long, blonde waves hung loose down her back and over one shoulder. Ashlyn was the most beautiful woman he'd ever seen. Her eyes were such a clear, iridescent blue. Almost as if he could see inside her soul at the pain she'd suffered.

"Dylan?"

No, he didn't want to relive the past anymore today. "I thought I would order room service tonight. It's been a long day. Want to share a salad and a pizza?"

"No, I think I'll just read and then go to bed early."

"You have to eat."

She frowned. "Why do I have to eat?"

That's what he wanted to see. The woman who argued with him. The silence that had wrapped around her hadn't been natural, and it scared the hell out of him.

He smiled. "If a big gust of wind came along, it would blow you over. Besides, when we interview this woman, you'll need to be at your best. I don't want your stomach grumbling the whole time. It would throw me off my game."

She cocked an eyebrow. "Is that right?"

"Yes, that's right."

"Okay, fine. But I'm still taking a shower first."

She closed the door between them. He decided to take a quick shower himself. She was right about the warehouse being dusty.

He ordered the pizza, salads, and beer first. He didn't know whether she liked beer, but he figured it would probably relax her so she would sleep better tonight. After placing the order, he hit the shower.

Dylan felt better when he stepped out of the shower and dried off. He slipped on a pair of dark green, lightweight jogging pants, a light green T-shirt, and slippers. A few minutes later, there was a knock on his door. Food, good because he was starving.

He let in a young man pushing a cart covered in a white cloth, who then placed everything from the cart onto the small dining table. There was an ice bucket with four beers peeking out, a plate covered with a silver dome, two covered salads, dishes, and utensils.

"I hope you enjoy your meal."

"I'm sure we will." He tipped the young man before he left and then knocked on the door between his and Ashlyn's room. She opened it a moment later.

Her hair was slightly damp from the shower. He caught the aroma of jasmine as it drifted toward his nose. She wore black leggings and a long-sleeved, red pullover, and her feet were bare. As far as he was concerned, she could have stepped off the cover of a fashion magazine.

She raised her eyebrows. "I assume you knocked because dinner is here."

"Yes, it is." He realized he was blocking the doorway and quickly stepped back so she could come in. He left the door between the rooms open. "I hope you drink beer."

She sat in one of the chairs. "Are you trying to get me drunk?"

He grinned. "Could I with only two beers?"

"Probably not."

"Damn, my lascivious plan won't work then." He sat across from her. "We'll just have to enjoy the meal." He was glad she was smiling. He twisted off the cap of her beer and handed the bottle to her, and then opened his.

She poured some of the dressing onto her salad, and they ate in silence until they got to the pizza.

"I love pizza," she admitted.

"What else do you love?" he asked, curious about her likes and dislikes.

"Is this a game?"

He shrugged. "Curiosity. You intrigue me."

She laughed. "I've been called many things, but I don't think anyone has ever said I'm intriguing."

"So, what do you like?" he pressed, wanting to know more about her because she did intrigue him.

She was thoughtful for a moment. "Jogging. I love the adrenaline rush." She frowned. "I guess I never really thought about my likes or dislikes."

"What about guilty pleasure?"

She raised an eyebrow. "Exactly what are you asking?"

He laughed lightly. "Not that, unless you want to go there. I was thinking along the lines of something you love to do, but no one would guess you do."

She took a bite of her pizza and chewed for a moment. "What's your guilty pleasure?" she countered.

"Ahh, I see what you're doing. I tell you mine, and you'll tell me yours."

"That pretty much sums it up."

He could feel the warmth on his cheeks.

She began to laugh. "Oh, it's like that. I hope it's not illegal."

"No, nothing like that. Legos." Now she would probably think he was an idiot. Only kids played with Legos. "I like to build things, and it relaxes me."

"You blow stuff up, and then you want to build something with toys."

"I know, it sounds crazy."

She was shaking her head. "No, not really. It probably is relaxing."

"It is. Now, what's your guilty pleasure?"

She took a drink of beer before she answered. "Romance books. I like reading them."

Now she'd surprised him.

She leaned slightly forward in her chair. "And before you say something against them, let me just tell you that I don't care what anyone thinks. Within the pages of the book, I can go anywhere in the world or even to other worlds. I can get lost in a new adventure without thinking about anything else."

"I wasn't going to say anything. My mother devours romance books. Someday you'll have to get together and compare notes. My father's always teasing her because she has one wall that's a bookshelf that has some of her favorite authors on it, and she's always buying more."

"Then you have a very smart mother."

"Dislikes?" he asked.

"Spinach from a can. It's just nasty. I'd rather have fresh."

"Is that all?"

"Nope, not even close. I don't like to cook, so I buy a lot of throw-in-the-microwave meals. Stupid people drive me crazy. The kind when you explain something to them, they give you a blank stare as if they know you're wrong when you're not. I try never to watch the news. It's too depressing." She grabbed another slice of pizza. "And you?"

"Well, I'm not crazy about stupid people either. I enjoy cooking, but I hate washing dishes."

"That's what dishwashers are for."

"But you still have to scrape them out and sometimes rinse them before putting them in the dishwasher. Paperwork is probably at the top of my list. It's a pain in the ass."

She sat forward a little, setting her slice of pizza on the plate. "Don't you hate that? If we didn't have to do all the paperwork, we might be able to solve a few crimes."

"It's crazy how buried we can get."

"What else?"

He thought about it for a minute. "Anything too healthy."

"Like what?" She picked up her pizza and took a bite, slowly chewing.

"Cauliflower pizza. It's gross. I dated a girl once that was a health nut. She fixed me a cauliflower crust pizza once. I took one bite and spit it out. It was just nasty. You don't screw with pizza."

"What did she do?"

"Moved out the next day. She took all of her new age paraphernalia, her incense, which could sometimes be overpowering. I walked in once, and the whole apartment smelled like grape Kool-Aid. It was nauseating."

She was laughing now. He liked the sound. He was glad she was relaxing. He grabbed the other two beers and twisted off the caps, handing her one and motioning to the sofa since they were through eating. It was more the size of a loveseat. She sat on one end, pulled her legs under her, and leaned against the arm.

"What makes you angry?" he asked as he sat on the other end.

"Bullies or people who think they're better than someone else because they have money. My father inherited quite a bit, and Mindy and I both have trust funds, but Dad taught us always to give back," she told him.

"I agree with always giving back. Have you experienced bullies?"

She nodded. "In the Academy. There was one man who didn't think I should be there. He didn't have a very high opinion of women. Even less when I beat him on the wrestling mat during our training."

"No wrestling—I'll remember that."

She took a drink of beer. Her eyes were twinkling when she lowered the bottle.

"When I turned sixteen, I asked my grandmother if I could take self-defense classes, and she said yes, then she found an awesome trainer who worked my ass off. After the first week, I regretted my decision but was determined to see it through. I'm glad I did. I learned a lot, which helped when I went into law enforcement."

"You must have an awesome grandmother."

"She was. She died a few years ago." She nibbled her bottom lip.

"What are you thinking?"

She raised her gaze to his. "Do you ever have a problem with your emotions? It was hard for me to feel anything after my grandmother died. It was easier to close myself off." She began shaking her head. "Never mind, I know it sounds crazy."

"Not at all. It just takes practice. I used to be the same way. You have to be focused when you're on a mission, or it could get you or someone else killed. I finally had to put things in perspective."

"How?" She leaned slightly forward.

"At first, I tried extreme sports: rock climbing, jumping out of airplanes, scuba diving with sharks… Anything that would make me feel something. Then I realized all I would accomplish was getting myself killed if I kept it up. Ty showed me how to meditate. That helped, but I couldn't always stay focused. I started looking for other ways."

"What worked?"

"Believe it or not, comedy. Anything that would make me laugh. Not just chuckle, but sidesplitting laughter. It was like letting the steam out of a pressure cooker. Laughing released all my pent-up emotions. That's when I learned to have fun with life. Just enjoy the time you have on earth."

"It might not be that easy."

"It can if you let it."

"Maybe." She looked around. "It must be getting late. I guess I'd better get some sleep. I'm afraid we're going to have a long day tomorrow."

"And hopefully, we'll discover something new." He stood

as she came to her feet. "I enjoyed tonight. I want to do it again after the case is solved." He thought she was going to refuse for a moment, but then she nodded.

"Goodnight."

She closed the door that separated the rooms, and there was a long pause. When he'd begun to wonder if she was going to lock the door, which might've been interesting, there was a distinct click.

That might not be a bad thing because, right now, he could only think about taking her to bed. From past experience, he knew a cold shower wouldn't work. He'd just have to suffer through the night.

He was pretty sure he went to sleep the moment his head hit the pillow. Sometime during the night, something woke him. He was a light sleeper, so he laid there for a moment, listening as he blinked the sleep from his eyes.

Then he realized what he'd heard. Ashlyn was whimpering and crying. He didn't think twice as he threw the cover back and went to her door. What if the son of a bitch had followed them here? He tried the knob, but Ashlyn had locked the door. He stepped back and placed a well-aimed kick, and the door popped open.

Chapter Twelve

"No, no, no," Ashlyn whimpered, fighting the nightmare, but it smothered her. She was trying to run away from Albert Duncan, but everywhere she turned, he was right in front of her, laughing at her. He grabbed her arm and jerked her against him.

"Don't look," came her father's whispered words. "Close your eyes tight."

She heard the tears in his voice. She had to get to him. Set him free. He could save her.

"Don't hurt us," she begged.

Another voice penetrated the darkness. She stilled for a moment. This one sounded familiar.

Dylan? What was he doing here? He could save them. Couldn't he?

"Just listen to the sound of my voice, Ashlyn. You're having a nightmare. I won't let anyone hurt you."

She began to relax as she slowly emerged from the fog surrounding her. Strong arms held her, but didn't pin her down. He lightly stroked her back, telling her over and over that she would be okay, that he would protect her.

"Go back to sleep. It was just a bad dream."

"No, I don't want to go back to sleep. I want to stay awake. I can't face the monsters again, at least not tonight."

"I'll chase your monsters away, even if only for tonight," he said close to her ear.

His breath tickled against her face. "I'm sorry," she said.

"For what?"

"I woke you."

"There's no reason for you to be sorry. Everyone has

nightmares."

"I don't think they're like the ones I have." She drew in a shaky breath and realized her body was pressed against his. That should make her angry, but for some reason, it didn't. She liked the warmth coming from him and the way his fingers stroked her back.

"I guess I should leave now if you think you're okay," he said.

She closed her eyes, her brain still muddled with sleep. "No, don't leave me."

She wasn't stupid. If he stayed, they would probably make love. She could tell him that she'd changed her mind and was better now. He could return to his room. She wasn't going to do that, though. "Make love to me," she whispered into the darkness.

"You don't want to make love. You're not thinking straight. Don't worry, I won't leave until you fall asleep, and I'll make sure there are no monsters in your dreams tonight."

He was wrong. She wanted him to release the tension inside her that had been building from the first time she'd laid eyes on him. But maybe this wasn't the right time. "Promise you won't leave just yet?"

"Yes, I promise. Now go back to sleep and have sweet dreams."

With a deep sigh, she closed her eyes. He would protect her and keep her safe. She didn't have to worry about anything.

***

Morning light came streaming in from the window the next morning. Ashlyn stretched and yawned but came against a hard surface on the other side of her. What the hell?

She raised enough to glance over her shoulder to see what was snuggled against her. Dylan? What the hell was he doing in her bed? She quickly scooted away from him, pulling the cover up to her neck even though she wore a long-sleeved pajama top and bottoms.

He groaned when she dragged the cover away from him. Slowly, he opened his eyes and yawned. His hair was tousled and he looked sexy as hell. He had a still-half-asleep look, inviting her to move close and snuggle with him.

"Mornin'," he mumbled.

No, don't even go there! She cocked an eyebrow and glared at him. "Why are you in my bed?"

Had he got her drunk last night after all? No, she'd never gotten drunk after only two beers. She glanced toward the door. It was wide open and partially off the hinges.

Her eyes widened. "You broke into my room!"

"Nightmare," he mumbled and then glanced at his watch.

"I don't care if you did have a nightmare. Get the hell out of my bed."

"Do you always come alive at six o'clock in the morning?" he grumbled. "We don't even have to be at the prison until ten."

"Yes, I do, now go away!"

He frowned. "You were the one having the nightmare, not me. You didn't want me to leave. You wanted me to make love to you."

"I didn't…"

"Yes, you did."

She started to argue, but stopped when the events of last night came rushing back. She remembered having a terrible nightmare. Albert had been chasing her, and she couldn't get away. Everywhere she turned, she ran into him. And her father was there. She wanted to save him, but she couldn't.

"Okay, so I had a nightmare. It still doesn't explain why you're in my room."

He raised on one elbow. "It was either make love, as you suggested, or help you get back to sleep. I was tired. The beer we'd had didn't help. I guess I fell asleep."

Complete memory returned. Oh my God, she *had* asked him to make love to her. But he hadn't. Why not? She'd never had a problem with anyone else. Why did he turn her down?

"Don't think too long and hard about it. I only said no because I don't take advantage of women. You weren't thinking clearly last night." He rolled over and pushed the rest of the cover away, coming to his feet as he walked toward the door separating their rooms. At the doorway, he turned back and looked at her.

"Damn, you're sexy as hell first thing in the morning with your hair mussed and your lips pouty. I don't think you know just how tempting you are."

Talk about looking tempting. He wore black boxer briefs. The kind that hugged every inch of his body, and from what she could see, he had a lot of inches.

"Last night was not the time, but we'll make love at some point." He yawned again. "I hate getting up early, by the way. I'll see you in a couple of hours." He pulled the door closed behind him. At least, he did the best he could with it.

The nerve of him! Saying they were going to make love at some point. Tingles spread over her body at the thought of them having sex. Oh crap, he was probably right. Would it be so bad? No, she had a feeling it would be very good. That was the problem.

But sex was out of the question until after they solved this case. No way was she going to make love to him before, and it was still iffy she'd make love with him at all. It would also only be for one night. He would probably go back home anyway. She would never see him again—fewer complications.

Her heart skipped a beat. She closed her eyes for a moment, drew a slow, deep breath, and then smiled. He thought she looked sexy first thing in the morning, too. She crawled out of bed and glanced at her reflection as she walked past the mirror. She came to a jerky stop and stared at the mirror.

"Really?" She did not look sexy first thing in the morning. Maybe he needed glasses. She had bedhead. One side was flat, the other side sticking up. She hadn't drooled on him during the night. At least, she didn't think so. That would've been embarrassing.

She went into the bathroom, came out a few moments later and started the coffee maker in her room. She was afraid it was going to be a long day. How would she face Dylan knowing they'd been in bed together? Especially after she'd asked him to make love to her. She rolled her eyes—awkward. She'd have to bluster her way through it. She *had* been half asleep, sort of.

She'd already had breakfast by the time he knocked on the door joining their rooms. He'd been moving around for the last hour. Rather than trying to open the busted door, he just called out to her.

"Are you ready to go?"

"I'll meet you in the hallway," she told him. She wore casual black slacks and a dark blue button-down shirt. Rather than carry a purse, she'd opted for a thin wallet she carried in her back pocket with her credentials.

When she met Dylan in the hallway, she saw he was wearing black slacks and a dark green button-down shirt. He looked professional, but laid-back, and tempting as hell. No man should look that good. All she could think about was waking up with his bare skin pressed against her back, and there'd been plenty of it that she could feel through her thin pajamas.

"You okay?" he asked, sounding worried about her.

"Yes, I'm great. Why wouldn't I be? Don't worry, I don't have nightmares during the daytime. I'll be perfectly fine at the prison interviewing this woman.

"Good."

The silence stretched between them as they rode the elevator down and then walked through the hotel lobby. It continued after they were in the SUV driving toward the prison.

Dylan cleared his throat. "You don't have to be embarrassed about last night," he said.

"I wasn't." She glared at him for even bringing it up.

"That's good because you shouldn't be."

She wondered if he realized he was only making the situation more uncomfortable for her. "I had a nightmare. I have them sometimes," she said. "It's no big deal."

"That's right. I've even had nightmares."

She studied him for a moment. He didn't look the type who would have a nightmare. He just seemed too casual and laid-back. Like nothing ever really bothered him.

"When did you ever have a nightmare?"

"It was about the time I blew up the doghouse."

"You were just a kid. Kids have nightmares. It's part of their genetic makeup. Maybe we could just drop the subject. That would help immensely."

"Of course, I didn't mean to bring it up again. It's just that you seemed a little embarrassed about everything that happened."

"You do you realize you're not making this any better?"

The silence between them lingered.

"The weather is nice today," he said.

She glanced out the window at the gathering storm clouds. "Absolutely beautiful," she said sarcastically.

He began to laugh. He only laughed harder when he glanced across the seat and met her gaze.

"Now what?" she asked.

"I was just thinking, that was pretty lame to talk about the weather." He glanced out the window. "Especially when it's probably going to storm today."

She couldn't help herself, she smiled. "Yeah, it was pretty lame."

The silence that followed between them was a little more comfortable. She had to give him an A for effort.

When they got to the prison, they showed their credentials to the guard at the gate and were told where to go. It was an all-women's prison, but not as rough as some places she'd visited.

Wanda wasn't in maximum security. She'd been picked up for prostitution and shoplifting. She had too many strikes against her not to go to jail this time. She'd also been Albert's shack-up for a short time, and once reported him for domestic abuse.

They were greeted by another guard inside the building and directed to a room where they'd brought Wanda. There were no windows, only a dark metal table and three chairs. Wanda wore a bored expression as she examined her fingernails. She casually looked up, meeting Ashlyn's gaze before moving to Dylan. Her eyes widened just a fraction as she sat a little straighter. At least *he'd* grabbed her attention.

"We need to ask you a few questions if you don't mind, Wanda." Dylan's words were as smooth as a shot of good brandy.

Her grin was slow as her gaze drifted over him. "Baby, you can ask me anything you want. If you can get her to go around the block a few times, we could have a fun time. I won't even charge for it."

Wanda looked like she'd been around the block a few times herself. Her black roots were starting to show past the bad platinum-blonde dye job. Instead of going back out the door, Ashlyn pulled out a chair and took a seat.

Wanda shrugged. "You can't blame a girl for trying."

"Isn't that why you're in here in the first place? Prostitution?"

"What's it to you? A girl has to make a living. You're starting to bore me. Maybe I won't tell you what you want to know. How would you like that?"

Dylan cleared his throat. "It would be really helpful if you could." He nudged Ashlyn's leg under the table.

Okay, maybe she'd gotten a little carried away with the good cop, bad cop routine. She would keep her mouth shut and let him handle it.

"What do you want to know?" Wanda asked.

"What can you tell us about Albert Duncan?"

She sat a little straighter and began to twine her fingers nervously. "He's still in prison, isn't he? I mean, he didn't escape or nothing, did he?"

"You don't have anything to worry about," Dylan reassured her. "He's still in prison."

She visibly relaxed. "Good. That's where he belongs. It wouldn't have bothered me if he'd gotten the death penalty. Mean son of a bitch."

"We need to know about his past relationships. Does he have any family? Brothers, children? Anything you can tell us will be helpful."

Ashlyn watched the calculating gleam enter Wanda's eyes. Here it comes, she thought to herself. What kind of carrot would Dylan dangle in front of her?

"It's going to cost you," Wanda told him.

Dylan opened his hands on the table. "What do you want?"

"I've got four months left on my time here. I haven't caused any kind of ruckus. I'm sick of this place. They could let me out early on good behavior."

"I think that could be arranged. Now, can you tell us about Albert Duncan and..."

Wanda smiled sweetly. "That isn't all, sugarplum. I don't want to go to a halfway house where some old biddy is going to be watching me, hoping I make a mistake so she can get me sent back. That happened to me one time. I want an apartment. It doesn't have to be anything fancy, just decent. First and last month's rent, plus deposit, paid. And I want..."

"We can manage that," Ashlyn interrupted her. "But that's all until we know more about Albert Duncan. If you can't give us anything concrete," Ashlyn said. "Then I'll send you a calendar to mark off the next few months."

Wanda curled her lip. "Aren't you the sassy one? Yeah, well, I know a lot about Albert, and none of its good."

"Tell us what you know."

"He was evil. The kind of man that when you saw him, you would cross the street just so you didn't have to pass close to him. He'd been living with me the night he robbed that convenience store. He was bragging about it when he came home and how much stuff he took from that old couple. He pointed a gun at the old man and then told me what it would've been like to kill him."

Wanda suddenly looked worried. Ashlyn wondered what she was thinking.

"I didn't have nothing to do with the robbery," she continued, in case they might say she was an accomplice. "He was always closed mouthed, so I didn't believe him. Never shared anything he took either. I was paying the rent and buying food to feed his sorry ass."

"We know you didn't have anything to do with it," Dylan reassured her. "He always worked alone."

"Damn right, he did. Anyway, when he told me about how scared that old couple was and then wondered what it would've been like to kill them, his eyes got all glassy like he imagined every bit of what it would be like. I knew then it was time for me to get the hell out. I'd been meaning to anyway. I was tired of him using me for a punching bag. Why shouldn't I live on my own? I was paying for that rat-infested room anyway. I never saw him again after I left the next day."

"What about family? Did he have any?" Dylan prodded.

She frowned. "He never talked about any. He called me Marie a few times, though. I think he might've been with her before me. That's all I know. Now, do I get my early release? I gave you a name."

"If it wasn't fabricated," Ashlyn said.

Wanda's expression darkened. "It wasn't. A woman knows when a man calls her by another woman's name, especially when they're…busy…." Wanda cast a quick glance toward Dylan. "I mean, well, you know."

"You haven't given us much, Wanda," Dylan said. "Not enough to get an early release and an apartment."

"But if that's all I know, then that's all I know. I can't help that," she whined.

"This was a wasted trip," Ashlyn said as she came to her feet.

"Wait a minute now," Wanda pleaded, looking scared for the first time. "Let me think just a minute. You could have given me some warning about what you were going to ask and then I could've been thinking about it." She closed her eyes and rubbed her temples. After a moment, she opened them again. "I do know something. I think he had a kid. He brought him to our place once. He was kind of quiet and shy. I remember him having a lot of scars. You know, burn marks. Like someone had been putting their cigarette out on him. Lots of bruises, too. He was nice looking, though. Pretty blue eyes and dark hair. He must've taken after his mother."

A son, now they were getting somewhere. "What was his name?" Ashlyn asked.

Wanda wrinkled up her nose. "I don't remember. He was only over at our place one time and all. Albert called him his little bastard. Slapped him a couple of times because he didn't move quick enough for him. I felt sorry for the kid."

"Is there anything else you can tell us?"

Wanda shook her head. "I wish I could. I swear that's all I know. Is it good enough to get me outta here at least?"

"I'll see what I can do," Dylan told her. "You've been a lot of help."

"And the apartment. It doesn't have to be anything fancy."

He smiled. "We'll try for the apartment."

Wanda relaxed as they came to their feet. They had just reached the door when she began to talk again.

"Oh, and there was something else. He kind of dragged his leg a little. Like there was something wrong with it. There was something strange about the kid, too."

"What do you mean—strange?" Dylan asked.

"He kept muttering all the time. When Albert went to the bathroom, I asked the kid what he was saying. He told me verses out of the Bible. Said they made him stronger."

"That might get you the apartment," Dylan told her.

Before Ashlyn left the room, she turned back around and looked at Wanda. "Did you happen to call child services about an abused child?"

She looked genuinely puzzled. "Wasn't my place to rat out someone."

Yeah, that was the problem. Most people looked the other way.

As soon as they were leaving the prison, Ashlyn turned to him. "Do you think this is our guy?"

"It's a good possibility. It's the best lead we've had so far. Duncan's kid would've been around bombs his whole life."

"Do you think that's the connection? He feels there's some sort of bond between us because his father tried to kill me?" A shiver ran down her spine. Great, there were two Duncan's out there. Albert had wanted her dead, but what did his son want? To finish the job his father started? Some of the fear she'd felt all those years ago returned.

"You'll have someone with you at all times," Dylan said, his gaze meeting hers across the seat. "We won't let him get to you. If this is our guy, we'll catch him."

"How? We don't even have his name. I doubt he married the kid's mother. He probably has a different surname."

"We have a description and possibly his mother's first name. He won't be able to hide for very long."

"I just hope you're right."

As Dylan drove back to the hotel, she stared out the window at the gathering storm clouds. It felt like her life right now. There was a storm coming. She only hoped she survived it.

Chapter Thirteen

Where did Dylan take her? Elijah marched up the sidewalk in front of her building, keeping the baseball cap pulled low on his forehead. There were cameras in the alleyway now.

His hands fisted into tight balls. Dylan thought he could catch him. His laugh was bitter. That would never happen. He had a mission to complete, and nothing would stop him.

Yesterday, he'd followed Ashlyn back to her apartment and watched as Dylan dropped her off. She would get ready for work now, except Dylan didn't leave, and when she came back down, she carried a bag. No, this wasn't supposed to happen. She was supposed to go to work!

He hurried to his car. It faced the same way they were going, but by the time he maneuvered into traffic, his heart was pounding, and a fine sheen of perspiration dotted his forehead.

He was able to tail them from a distance. Dylan took the exit to the airport, then to the parking area. Why was he taking her to the airport? A lovers' rendezvous? He choked the steering wheel.

How could Ashlyn be taken in by his charm? They were all liars. Not good enough for her. He was the only one. He knew what she'd gone through.

But she'd left anyway.

Elijah had come back today, hoping he might have been wrong. No lights. She would've been up by now. Dammit! She still wasn't home!

His gaze moved to her apartment again, wishing for some sign that she might've returned during the night or early morning. There was no movement.

With a growl of rage, he made his way around the corner of her street, where he'd parked his car. After he got in, he had to rub his leg. It was aching more than usual. He sat there for a moment, rubbing the heel of his hand down the side and tried to think about him and Ashlyn being together one day, but the vision didn't come.

It was all Dylan's fault!

He started the car and drove home. Once inside the house, he threw his keys on the floor and went to the kitchen. His life had started to crumble all around him. Why was this happening? He opened the refrigerator, then shut it and moved to the sink. After filling a glass with water, he gulped it down, then slamming the glass into the sink. It shattered from the impact. He flinched when a flying shard cut his arm.

For a moment, he stared at the blood trickling toward his wrist. He dragged his finger through the bright red, marking his skin with the letter A.

"You belong to me," he said. "Only me."

"Do you really think she's going to have you?" David said.

Elijah whirled around, raising his chin in defiance. "What are you doing here?"

"You can't get rid of me that easily."

"You know she's supposed to be mine," Elijah whimpered.

David laughed. "She can't love you. Look at you. You've got scars all over your body…"

"Our father put them there! He's the reason we limp! Or have you forgotten?"

David leaned against the counter, anger blazing in his eyes. "I'll never forget." He looked up. "But I protected you the best I could."

"I know." He sighed. "I could never stand up to him. I

still have nightmares. They won't stop."

"Then go to your safe place."

The closet. Yes, he had to go to the closet. That was his only refuge. He rushed to the hall and opened the door, closing it tightly behind him. He sat down, scooting into the corner. With a deep sigh, he began to relax.

"We'll be together, Ashlyn," he mumbled.

There was laughter right outside his door. He glared toward it. Sometimes David could be such an ass. He closed his eyes, picturing her.

"Why would a beautiful woman have you? Have you thought this through?" David asked.

"We're bonded together. You should know that." David had always been the strong one, but sometimes he was so stupid. He didn't understand anything. Elijah rubbed his aching leg.

"She likes Dylan."

"She only thinks she does."

"Your mother lived in a fantasy world, and you take after her."

David could be cruel, too. They had different mothers, so he didn't understand. David's mother could be cruel. "My mother was beautiful, warm, and loving until she met our father. He got her hooked on drugs."

"But at least he didn't kill her." His words were silky. "You did that."

He pressed against the back of the closet, closing his eyes against the pain. "I had to," he mumbled. "Do you think I wanted to kill my mother? I loved her. I wanted her to go to Heaven. That's where she is, and no one can hurt her anymore."

"Do you think you're going to Heaven? How many

women have you murdered? Three? Yeah, that's right. You've killed three innocent women *and* your mother."

He covered his ears with his hands and began to rock back and forth. "No, no, no! Go away! You were the one who killed them! Leave me alone."

"You were there, too. You could've stopped me."

"I never wanted you to hurt Kimberly. She was nice to me."

"Only on the surface. Deep down, no one likes us. We only have each other."

He wouldn't listen to him. "Go away, go away, go away," he whispered. "I'm in the closet. I'm safe here."

Chapter Fourteen

"We'll go over everything in the conference room," Waylon said, then glanced at his watch. Without another word, he walked up the stairs and down the hall to his office.

His somber words worried her. Ashlyn looked at the others, wondering what was up. "We don't have another victim, do we?" she asked with dread.

Ginny shook her head. "Not that I know of, but if our killer saw you and Dylan going off together, he's going to be furious. He might decide to take another woman sooner rather than wait a few weeks this time."

"We may have hit on something while you were both gone," Nolan spoke up.

"Waylon will go over everything," Brad said.

There was only one way they would find out what had changed. She grabbed her coffee that she'd gotten on the way in this morning and headed for the conference room. Dylan was behind her, but she was trying not to look at him too much. They'd gotten in late last night, and then he'd brought her to work.

The silence between them hadn't been what she would say was awkward, just…different. You didn't sleep with a man and not expect there to be a change.

She grimaced. Not that they'd actually done anything *but* sleep. A delicious shiver ran down her spine at the thought of Dylan snuggled against her back. She quickly pulled her focus back to the here and now. She couldn't lose her concentration. Not when someone's life might depend on it.

She moved to the end of the table and took a seat. Without even looking, she knew when Dylan took the chair next to her. She took a deep breath to calm her nerves. Big mistake! His cologne wrapped around her, begging her to move closer.

Waylon came in a moment later. At least now she had something else to concentrate on.

"We had a few new developments since you've been gone. It may or may not be anything." His gaze moved to Leah. "Do you want to fill them in?"

"Nolan and I were looking through Kimberly's social media and he found something that he thought was interesting. Nolan, do you want to tell them what you found."

Nolan cleared his throat. "The guy we're looking for might be disabled in some way. Kimberly wrote something about how we need to take care of people. She spoke about this man who came into the library looking lost. When she befriended him, she discovered he'd come from an abusive home. The man had no friends, and she was trying to help him. She said he always talked about the Bible and read a lot of the library's religious books. He told her how it got him through a bad time."

Ashlyn's pulse skipped a beat. This had to be the same guy, their serial killer—Albert Duncan's son.

"That's when Brad and I stepped in," Ginny said. "We went back to the library to question the employees again. We hadn't been able to speak to one of the librarians because she was on vacation, a Lucy Clairmont, but she was back now. She vaguely remembered the guy. Kimberly seemed to like him. She just thought he was kind of weird. It wasn't anything specific Lucy could put her finger on, something about his eyes. He had dark hair and pale, blue eyes. He was thin, and she'd noticed some scars on his arms. Small circular ones. Oh, and he also walked with a limp."

Ashlyn looked at Dylan. This had to be their guy. It was too much of a coincidence.

"Tell them what we found out," Dylan told her.

"We spoke to a woman who used to live with Albert Duncan."

"And Albert Duncan is who?" Brad asked with a puzzled expression.

She drew in a deep breath and told herself this was the only way to solve the case. "My father was a prosecuting attorney in Maryland. One of the men my father prosecuted was about to go to prison, except he escaped. I was fourteen. He…he came to our house and…"

She looked down at her hands in her lap as cold chills of fear swept over her. She'd never been able to talk about what happened that day, and now, here she was, surrounded by people and about to tell them her story. Except when she tried to get the words out, they stuck in her throat. She looked at Dylan.

He cleared his throat. "Albert Duncan wanted to get revenge. He tied Ashlyn and her father up in the dining room and then set bombs around the house that would be triggered by heat. After Albert left, Ashlyn made it to the kitchen and got a knife. She cut through her father's zip tie, and they were both able to escape."

"Oh my God. I can't believe that happened to you," Leah said, tears filling her eyes.

Dylan continued as if she hadn't said anything. "We flew to Maryland to talk to one of the women who used to live with him. Albert brought his kid to the apartment one day. She said he had scars all over his arms. It looked like someone had put their cigarettes out on him, and bruises covered his thin body. When she asked him what he mumbled about all the time, he said Bible verses. They made him strong. He also walked with a limp."

"This has got to be our guy." Ashlyn looked around the room and could see by the expression on their faces that they thought so, too. She looked at Waylon for confirmation.

He grimly nodded his head. "You know, sometimes we wonder how someone can be so evil that they would take another person's life, but when you look at what this man went through as a child, you can almost understand why he snapped and started killing people. Why he fixated on Ashlyn. She became a sort of ally."

"But I had a good childhood," Ashlyn said.

"In his eyes, he probably sees you as having suffered at the hands of his father. I think that's our connection."

She drew in a ragged breath. "The only thing we have to wonder about is what he's going to do now."

"He'll keep killing until he satisfies whatever need he's looking to fill." Waylon looked at Ginny. "Do we have anything on him?"

"That's the problem," Ginny told him. "He didn't check out any books. He only read them when he was at the library. Lucy's description wasn't that detailed, but we still might be able to have a sketch artist talk with her."

"Let's do that," Waylon said. "We're still looking for a needle in a haystack. Has anyone questioned this Albert Duncan guy?"

"He's still in prison," Ashlyn said.

"Good, then we won't have to hunt for him. What prison?"

"ADX."

Waylon whistled under his breath. "Colorado. They only house the most violent criminals." He studied her for a moment. "Why this guy?"

"His first week in prison, he killed two prisoners and threatened to kill more. After that, they transferred him to Colorado."

Waylon nodded. "Ashlyn, you and Dylan go up there. See if he'll talk. Be careful, though. Leave as soon as possible. I'll have my assistant make the arrangements. Call me when you're on the way to the airport."

Great, they were going on another trip. This was one that she didn't want to make. She reminded herself why she was going. She damn sure didn't have to like it, though.

They didn't stop at their apartments but went straight to the airport. In less than two hours, they were in the air.

The problem wasn't traveling so soon after their last trip, she was used to that. The problem was who she was going to see. Would her nightmares get worse? That was what she was afraid of the most. Albert had haunted her dreams long enough. Every time she went to see her father, she saw Albert Duncan in the background, laughing that evil laugh that sent shivers of fear over her.

She knew he couldn't hurt her again, but it didn't stop her from feeling the way she did. He'd kept her prisoner all these years. Standing on the fringes of her life.

"Are you going to be able to do this?" Dylan asked from the seat beside her.

She jumped. "Of course I'm going to be able to do it. I'm an FBI agent. We always face things that make us uncomfortable, but we do our job anyway." When he continued to study her, she turned her head toward the window.

"But most agents don't have to interview the man who tried to kill them. Waylon is asking too much of you. He wasn't thinking about that when he told you to go with me."

"Maybe he thought I would shake him up so he'd tell us more." She didn't know what Waylon was thinking, but he was a smart man.

"Maybe," Dylan said but didn't sound convinced.

"I didn't get much sleep last night after we got in. I'm going to close my eyes until the plane lands," she said, shutting off any more talk about what had happened to her and her father.

As soon as she closed her eyes, flashes of the past filled

her mind. When she'd opened the door and Albert had been standing there. His evil grin and the maniacal gleam in his eyes. Her hands curled into fists as she mentally tried to block the image.

She had to think about something else. Her father. No, he only added to the stress. She'd saved him when she cut the ties, but then he tried to protect her. If he hadn't, he would've still been the same.

How was she going to look into the face of the man who'd ruined their lives? She wanted to kill him. Put a bullet in his gut and watch as he died a slow and painful death. She wanted him to suffer as her family had suffered.

Oh God, was she any better than their serial killer? She couldn't help the feelings inside her any more than he could stop his. Both of them had been scarred by what Albert did to them.

How was she going to get through this interview without losing it? She was good at hiding her emotions, but she didn't know if she was that good.

By the time they landed and were getting off the plane, she was jumping at every little thing—someone bumped her as she moved down the aisle, a baby screamed at being awakened. She couldn't stop the trembling inside her, and her stomach churned.

"Let's get something to eat first," Dylan suggested.

She looked at him as though he'd lost his mind. "I don't think I can keep anything down right now."

"That's why we're going to get something to eat first. Just something light. It'll make you feel better."

"Or make me throw up."

"Trust me on this. I've been on enough missions that made me queasy. If I eat something light, the queasiness always goes away."

She would try anything right now. "Okay, fine." She doubted she'd be able to get anything down, though. The thought of food made her nauseous.

They picked up the rental SUV, and Dylan looked up a few places on his phone, settled on one, and put it into his GPS. She assumed he would choose someplace quiet so it wouldn't rattle her nerves.

Nope, not Dylan. He chose a sports bar. It wasn't too crowded, but sports events played semi-loudly on three televisions in different areas. When four men drinking mugs of beer groaned, she assumed their team hadn't done well.

Why a sports bar? They took a booth at the back where there wasn't quite as much noise. She wondered who Dylan was looking out for, him or her? Then, to top it off, he ordered a cheeseburger and fries. When she didn't see very many choices, she ordered the same. She doubted that she would be able to eat any of it.

"He's just a man," Dylan said as they waited for their food to arrive.

"A very evil man."

"Yes, he's very evil. And he's locked up for the rest of his life. He'll never get out of prison. It was your testimony that put him there in the first place."

"How do you know that?"

Their food came, stopping the conversation momentarily. As soon as the waiter left, Dylan took a bite of his burger. She picked up a fry and took a bite, not really tasting it. He took a drink of his soda, then began to talk again.

He shrugged. "It stands to reason. Besides, I read the transcript of the trial, remember? Your father was still in the hospital, so you had to be the one who testified against Albert. It was courageous of you."

Her eyes narrowed. "I hated him. I wanted him to go away for the rest of his life." Her laugh was short and bitter. "They only gave him twenty-five years. You and I know he would've gotten out sooner than that and returned to tormenting people."

"But he murdered two men in prison."

"And stood trial again. That cinched his life sentence without the possibility of parole. I'm glad he won't ever get out."

"Me, too. Some people can't be rehabilitated."

"And he's one of them."

"So, have you ever been to Colorado?" Dylan asked, abruptly changing the subject away from Albert Duncan.

It took a moment for her brain to catch up. As soon as it did, she smiled as good memories came back. "My father rented a cabin one summer. We fished, hiked, and sat out on the porch at night looking at the stars. I remember complaining about how boring it was going to be."

"Was it?"

"Not it all. At first, I tried to pretend I didn't care. I was thirteen and, of course, knew absolutely everything."

"What changed your mind?"

"Not a what, but a who. Trevor Richardson. His parents were staying in a cabin not too far from ours. I had such a crush on him. He was fourteen and off-the-charts cute. That summer, I experienced my first kiss. I felt like a grown woman." She laughed.

When Dylan smiled, she could feel the heat crawling up her face. Why had she told him about Trevor? She was starting to sound juvenile.

"That was probably more information than you wanted, but yes, I've been to Colorado."

His eyes were twinkling mischievously. "And Trevor Richardson?"

"I have no idea what happened to him."

Dylan glanced at his watch. "I guess we'd better go," he said.

She glanced at the time and saw they had been in the sports bar for about an hour. She'd also eaten just over half her meal. She eyed him suspiciously.

"You did this on purpose, didn't you?"

"Sort of. Are you mad?"

"No, I suppose not. I do feel better. I'm still not relishing meeting Albert face-to-face again, though."

He gave the waiter his credit card and then turned back to her. "Then don't."

"I think Waylon expects me to go in with you."

"I've interviewed felons at this prison before. They have a one-way mirror in the interview room. You can still monitor everything that's going on while I talk to him."

A reprieve—maybe. "Okay, but if things start to go south, then I'm coming in."

"Deal."

They left the restaurant and got back in the SUV. Her nerves finally settled down with Dylan's suggestion. It didn't hurt that the surrounding views were spectacular. She loved the snowcapped mountains in the background, even though it was getting close to the middle of summer. There was a freshness in the air that made her want to just breathe it all in. She was completely relaxed when they arrived at the prison gates.

They had to show their credentials several times before she was standing behind the one-way mirror with Dylan, clutching the file folder she'd grabbed before they left. They waited until the guard brought Albert to the interview room.

She stiffened slightly, the only outward sign that seeing him again bothered her. On the inside, she felt a little nauseous. She would get through this, just like all the battles she'd faced over the years.

She took a deep breath, then exhaled as she studied him. He was leaner than Ashlyn remembered. Apparently, there was no beer in prison. His sallow complexion and face lined with wrinkles told her that Albert must not be adapting to prison life very well. A slight smile lifted the corners of her mouth.

He glared at the guards, but it didn't seem to bother them. She supposed they were used to it. If Albert had hoped to intimidate them, it wasn't working.

His ankles and wrists were shackled. As soon as he sat in the chair, one of the guards fastened his wrist restraints to a U-shaped bar on his side of the table and his legs to one on the floor.

"He's all yours," the warden said. "I'll keep a guard in here as well. I doubt you'll be able to get anything out of him. You know, I've had a lot of crazy men in this prison, but nothing like Albert. He's not just crazy. He's mean."

"Thank you," Dylan said. "I'll be the one going in. Ashlyn will only come in if she thinks she can get anything else from him."

The warden nodded and then left.

Before leaving, Dylan turned to her. "Remember, no matter what happens, you don't have to come in."

"I know," she said. Her gaze moved to Albert. This man had caused her to be afraid, to wake up in a cold sweat from another nightmare. "I'll be okay."

He nodded, then reached for the door. She turned her

focus to the other room.

Albert's eyes narrowed as soon as Dylan opened the door and went inside. "Who the hell are you?"

Dylan pulled out a chair across from Albert and took a seat. "I'm Dylan Rowley, and I'm investigating a case. I think you can be of some help."

"What do you want?"

"What can you tell me about your son?"

Albert looked momentarily taken aback, then he laughed. "That sniveling little bastard? Why do you want to know about him?"

"We think he's involved in three murders."

"What's in it for me?"

"It'll look good on your record that you cooperated today."

He leaned slightly forward, but he didn't intimidate Dylan. He didn't move back even an inch. "I'm here for life, and I'll never get out. Why the fuck do I care what goes on my record?"

Dylan shrugged. "It might get you a few extra privileges. Extra time in the yard."

"I don't know nothing about that kid. I doubt that he could swat a fly. He was always a pussy. I'm the one who ran that household. His mother stayed strung out on drugs. If it wasn't for me, the kid would've ended up in foster care." His lip curled. "Look where it got me for doing a good deed. Ain't no justice in this world."

"Did you ever think that attempting to kill a prosecuting attorney and his young daughter might be why you went to prison? Or killing two men once you got to prison? And maybe that's why you're here for the rest of your life?"

Albert smiled. The same evil smile he'd worn the day he came to their house. This time, it didn't scare her like she thought it would.

"Those men needed killing. As far as the kid goes, I didn't know she would be there, but it didn't matter." He paused for a moment as if remembering that day. "I had that planned so well. Each bomb would go off when it got too hot. It was perfect."

"But you didn't count on the fire department getting there so quickly."

He frowned. "They weren't supposed to. Rich people neighborhood. Those people take care of their own. They don't care for the poor folk just trying to get by."

Ashley continued to watch from behind the mirror. As she listened to their conversation, she studied Albert. He came across as tough and a braggart. He was proud that he'd almost killed her and her father.

A slow anger began to burn inside her, replacing any lingering fear. She realized Albert would never be able to hurt her again. He was a bully, and he would always be a bully, but it was past time she took away his power to frighten her.

When she saw that Dylan wasn't making any progress after another five minutes, she opened the door and went inside. Both men looked toward her.

"Take a break, and I'll take it from here," she told Dylan.

He studied her for a moment, then nodded and left the room.

"Well, I haven't seen a sweet thing like you in a long time," Albert said.

She sat in the chair Dylan had just vacated, set the file on the table, and just looked at him for a moment. He wasn't nearly as scary up close. He was showing his age. Prison life was definitely taking its toll on him. Good, she wanted him to suffer.

"You're wrong about your son," she said. "He's not at all weak. He kidnapped three women and murdered them."

"How do you know it's Elijah? Might be somebody else," he sneered.

Her pulse immediately sped up at the mention of his son's name. She forced herself to remain calm and not give anything away. "Who else knows about the marks you put on your bombs?"

"No one knows I mark my bombs with a star. Nobody can copy me."

"You're wrong. Elijah is using the same mark. The only thing is, he's doing it better than you."

Albert tried to come to his feet but only raised a few inches. She didn't budge from her position. He was still able to slam his fist down on the table. "That sniveling little bastard couldn't blow up anything."

"Oh, but he did." She opened the file she'd laid on the table, facing the picture of the last crime scene toward him. "He placed a bomb here, here, and here. Each of them had your mark on them."

He leaned slightly forward in his chair, staring at the photo of the last crime scene. "What's that chair doing in the center?"

"That's where the body was. It was absolute perfection."

Her stomach churned when she bragged about what the serial killer had done to those poor victims. She wanted Albert to take a back seat to the current bombings, to feel inferior in the hopes he'd give her more information about Elijah.

She continued, "He blew out the surrounding walls leaving only the victim sitting on the chair in the middle, as though he was framing his work. Wasn't that what you were trying to do, but couldn't?" She laughed lightly. "It didn't work.

The prosecutor and his daughter foiled your weak attempt and escaped. I bet that made you mad."

His lips pressed to a fine line. "My bombs were perfect. They always went off how they were supposed to, and if that fire department hadn't shown up when it did, it would've been perfect that time, too."

"Don't worry, your son will do the job you couldn't. I'm through here." She came to her feet but paused. "Elijah is better at it than you, and when we catch him, we'll make sure the world knows that he was the better bomber."

He hit the table with his fist again. "No, he's not better than me. If he learned anything, he learned it from watching me." His lip curled. "Besides, how do you know it was Elijah. I got other kids, too. A lot tougher than him."

She couldn't tell if he was lying or telling the truth. At least they had one name. If they had to, they would find the others as well. "I'm sure Elijah learned a lot from you, as did any other kid you might have created, but no matter what, that child still perfected your style. You saw that from the picture. That's what you wanted to accomplish with the attorney and his daughter. They're living a wonderful life. So is your son. I'm not sure we'll even catch him because he's that good," she goaded him.

"His mama owned a house."

"What was her name?"

"Marie Moore. His name is Elijah Moore. He thinks he's a little smartass and can best his daddy. No, I'll always win."

She laughed lightly and looked around. "You call this winning? You're a loser and will always be a loser."

"Tell them to unfasten these chains, and I'll show you who's a loser, baby. You ever fucked a prisoner before? I haven't had a woman in a long time. I can show you a real good time."

She turned and stepped closer to the table and then leaned slightly forward. She kept her voice low so no one on the other side of the mirror would hear. "You don't remember me, do you?"

He looked confused for a moment. "Who are you?"

"I'm that prosecuting attorney's daughter. Remember? You put your filthy hands on me, but then you got scared when the neighbor's dog started barking. I'm the one who put you in prison for what you did to us. How does it feel to know a kid had you locked away?"

His eyes widened.

"We both know you're not a man. You're a coward. Have a nice life while you're in prison, and then you can go to Hell."

She casually turned, picked up her file off the table, and left the room as he began screaming and calling her names.

Dylan looked at her with a question in his eyes. "What did you say to him?"

"Nothing much. We have a name now, though. Let's go catch a serial killer." For the first time in a long time, she felt free. Albert had been occupying space in her mind for far too long. It was time to kick him out.

Chapter Fifteen

What the hell had Ashlyn said to Albert before she left the prison interrogation room? Whatever it was, she'd pissed him off. Dylan liked that side of her, too.

There was something different about her now. She seemed stronger. Maybe facing Albert had been a way of exorcising the past.

"You did good in there," he told her.

"And now we have a name." She reached into her pocket for her phone. As they left the prison, she called Waylon. She gave him the name of Elijah and his mother, then ended the conversation and turned to Dylan. Her eyes were twinkling and she was smiling.

Dylan hated to burst her bubble. "This still might not be our guy," he warned her. "Albert said he had more than one kid."

"But he might have lied because he was angry. You think it's him just as much as I do."

"I think it's a good possibility this could be our man. We'll know more once we locate Elijah and bring him in for questioning."

"He'll probably have an arrest record if his father is anything to go by."

"It's quite possible," Dylan agreed with her.

"What will you do when we solve the case?" she suddenly asked.

He wouldn't remind her that not all cases got solved. This was her moment, and he wouldn't spoil it for her. "I'm not sure. As far as I know, there's nothing pressing. Maybe I'll take a vacation and go down to the coast. Get in a little deep-sea fishing."

"That sounds nice," she said.

He looked across the seat and met her gaze. "What about you? Do you have any plans?"

She shook her head. "No, not really. I guess I hadn't thought about it."

"Where do you usually go on vacations?"

"I stay at home, read, just relax, I guess."

"That doesn't sound very exciting."

"After some of the cases we've solved, all I'm looking for is peace and quiet."

"That's why I like to go to the coast. Just walking on the beach and looking at the ocean has a way of grounding me. It makes me realize not everything in our world is bad."

"Who knows, maybe I'll take off and go down there one day just to see if you're right."

"I am."

The rest of the drive was quiet, and he wondered what she was thinking. He also wondered what she'd whispered to Albert that agitated him before she left the room. Whatever she'd said, Albert hadn't liked it.

He pulled into the car rental company, and they turned in the SUV. It wasn't a very far walk to catch the plane back to Texas. Still, they had to hurry, so the plane didn't leave without them. He finally settled into his seat with a deep sigh.

"Tired?" she asked.

"Yeah, I didn't get a lot of sleep last night. I think I'll just doze on the trip home." He wasn't about to tell her that she was the reason he hadn't slept well. When he'd closed his eyes, he thought about her. When he dreamed, she was there to torment him. He'd known the minute he saw her that she would be the death of him.

As soon as the plane took off, he put his seat back and closed his eyes. He didn't wake up until someone jostled his shoulder. He immediately opened his eyes and grabbed her wrist. The flight attendant was momentarily startled. He immediately released her and apologized.

"It happens from time to time," she said. "I just wanted to let you know we're about to land, and I need you to raise your seat to the upright position."

"Of course," he said and then glanced down at the blonde head resting on his other shoulder.

Damn, he could get used to this. Neither one of them had lowered the arm between them, and, right now, she was snuggled against him. He hated to wake her.

He shook her shoulder just a little. She drowsily raised her head and gazed at him with sleep-heavy eyes. He had a strong urge to lean down and brush his lips across hers. The way she was staring back at him made him wonder if she was thinking the same thing.

Apparently, the thought of him kissing her was like having a bucket of ice water dumped over her head because she immediately sat up, pushing her hair out of her face.

"Are we about to land?"

"We are."

"I'm sorry I fell asleep on you. I guess I was more tired than I thought.

"I didn't even know you were there. I think I fell asleep as soon as the plane took off. The flight attendant woke me and asked me to put my seat in the upright position."

"Okay, but I still didn't mean to fall asleep on you." She raised her arms above her head and stretched.

Dylan couldn't look away. Did she even know how damned sexy she was? No, he didn't think so. He would've pulled her into his arms and kissed her soundly if they weren't on a crowded plane. He wondered what she would do if he did.

Probably knock the hell out of him. Okay, maybe he wouldn't pull her into his arms and kiss her soundly. At least, not right now, but he'd leave the option on the table for later.

Since they didn't have any luggage, it didn't take them long to disembark the plane. They went straight to where he'd parked the pickup and got in.

"Back to the office?" he asked.

"Yes, I want to see if they've unearthed anything on this guy."

Dylan felt the excitement in the air as soon as they walked into the main room at headquarters. It always happened when they picked up a new lead that might solve a case. Before they could ask any questions, Waylon came to the upstairs rail.

"Good, you're back. Let's go over everything in the conference room." He turned on his heel and made his way there.

Ashley went straight to Leah. "Have you found anything yet?"

"I'm making headway." She grabbed her tablet to take with her. "Come on, and I'll tell you more when we get upstairs. I think this is a good lead, though."

Dylan only hoped so as he followed everyone into the conference room, and they took a seat.

"Excellent work to both of you when you were in Colorado." He turned serious. "I know that must have been hard for you, Ashlyn."

"I managed, and it was worth it."

Waylon turned to Leah. "What have you found?"

Leah glanced up from her tablet. "Marie Moore was thirty-two when she overdosed on heroin leaving behind her fourteen-year-old son. He was the one who found her, by the way. That had to have been hard on him." She looked down at the tablet once more. "He continued to live in the same house with his on-again, off-again father. Although, no father's name was listed on his birth certificate. I guess it kept him out of foster care."

Dylan didn't know that foster care might have been better. If Elijah turned out to be their killer, Albert had driven him in that direction.

"The only school records I could find were up to the third grade," Leah continued. "There were some questions about the possibility of child abuse in the home, but it doesn't look as if it went very far with the social workers. After that, the record stated he was homeschooled."

"By a drug addict of a mother," Ginny said. "Yeah, I doubt that she taught him much of anything. His mother didn't want the state to question them about the boy's bruises and scars."

Brad grimaced. "They dropped the ball with this one. It makes you wonder if he would've turned out differently had he gotten a better upbringing."

"We still don't know this is the perp," Waylon said. "Right now, he's just a person of interest, and we'll treat him as such. What else do you have, Leah."

"Nolan has a little more than I do. Do you want to tell them?"

Nolan nodded. "I found a school picture of Elijah Moore from the third grade. I'll have the picture age-enhanced and compare it to the sketch artist's rendering that the librarian gave of the man Kimberly befriended. I think they'll be similar."

"How long will that take?" Waylon asked.

"I can have it by tomorrow morning."

"Good."

"But why did he move from Maryland down to Texas? If he even did." Ashlyn asked.

Dylan already knew the answer. "If he's our guy, you're why he moved to Texas. You're the link. We just don't know what he plans to do about it."

"I don't think I want to know," Ashlyn said.

No, Dylan didn't want to know either. He looked at Waylon. "Do we have an address or anything on Elijah?"

"I can answer that," Ginny said. "We have absolutely nothing on this guy. We haven't been able to find a paper trail of any kind, but that doesn't mean we're through looking. We've only been at this for a few hours."

"Someone out there must know something about him," Waylon said. "Let's shake things up a little. As soon as you get the picture back, Nolan, let's get it out to the public. He must have a neighbor or someone who will tell us where he's living."

Dylan only hoped Elijah didn't go underground until everything died down and resurface when he thought it would be safe to come up for air.

"My gut tells me this is our man, but so that everyone knows, Albert said he had other kids."

"Good to know," Brad said. "But even if he isn't, maybe he could give us more information on his siblings."

"It's been a long day," Waylon said. "Go home and get some rest. We'll get started again first thing in the morning."

"Where do you want to have dinner?" Dylan asked as they walked out to his pickup.

"How do you feel about microwave meals? I'd love to sit

at home, put my feet up, and have dinner."

After they climbed inside his pickup, he turned to face her. "Is that an invitation?"

"If you want. I figured you might be as tired as I am eating every meal in a restaurant."

"You're right, I am. I have a better idea, though. I can make the best damn omelet you've ever tasted. How about I cook us dinner tonight, but at your place. I don't have the necessary cookware."

Her sigh was audible. "A home-cooked meal? My mouth is already watering. I'm afraid I don't cook very often. Well, at all, if you must know. I've got everything to cook with, though. My little sister made sure of that. When she comes to stay, she likes to cook. I'm afraid I don't have very many groceries, though."

"Then point me toward the nearest grocery store, and we'll stop on the way to your apartment."

Later, as they made their way through the store, Ashlyn dubiously eyed some of his choices. She didn't say anything, though. He figured it was because she didn't cook very often, so she wasn't sure exactly what he was doing.

She threw in a package of Oreos on the way to the checkout, then when he looked at her quizzically, she said, "Dessert."

That was fine with him. He loved cookies. He grabbed some milk on the way past dairy. If she was going with Oreos, they had to have milk to dip them in.

She hesitated, then grabbed a bottle of chilled wine.

"Who did the cooking when you were growing up?" he asked as they drove back to her apartment.

"We had a housekeeper. She did all the cooking. When

we went to live with Grandmother, our housekeeper, Betty, retired. We still exchange cards at Christmas and on birthdays. After my mother died, she became more than just a housekeeper. Sometimes, I think she was the glue that held us together."

"And did your grandmother have a housekeeper as well?"

She laughed. "She had a cook, a housekeeper, and a couple of maids. Grandmother liked to entertain, so she had a full staff. Her house was huge. I remember we found lots of hiding places."

"It must've been difficult to move into her home."

"We adjusted. What about you?" She easily changed the subject.

He didn't think it was that easy to adjust, but he wouldn't press the issue. "My mother did all the cooking, but she made sure her sons knew how to stock a kitchen and fix meals. My brothers weren't interested in cooking, but I enjoyed it."

He put his turn signal on and pulled up to the guard shack. You had to get past the man inside to get into the garage. He touched the button that lowered his window as Ashlyn leaned across him.

He drew in a deep breath, inhaling the heady fragrance of her shampoo. He'd noticed it earlier when she'd rested her head against his shoulder. It was a combination of sweet and spicy. It kind of reminded him of her. A little sweet and a whole lot spicy.

"It's me, John. We're going up to my apartment," Ashlyn told him.

He looked surprised, and Dylan knew not very many men had ever been in her apartment. He was glad. He wasn't sure why. He just was.

John studied Dylan for a moment before he nodded. "Have a good evening, Miss Pillar."

When he raised the mechanical arm, Dylan drove through. "I like your security," he told her.

"I researched different ones before I leased this apartment. I did the same with Mindy and my father's."

He had to wonder why she was the one who researched her father's apartment. If he even lived in an apartment. He was beginning to wonder. Ethan still hadn't been able to find out much about him. Only that he was no longer practicing law.

When Ashlyn pointed to a parking spot, he pulled in and shut off the engine. They both grabbed bags of food to take upstairs. They were quiet on the ride up until her stomach growled. It sounded like an angry lioness. She kept looking straight ahead but glanced toward him the second time it happened. He was trying to be polite, but he couldn't stop his smile from forming. She snickered.

"I guess that was very unladylike," she said as the elevator doors opened.

He forced a straight face. "Not at all. It just tells me you'll love my omelet."

Her forehead wrinkled. "How do you figure that?"

"Because you're going to be so hungry you won't care what you're eating."

That brought a smile to her face. He liked that she was more relaxed since their trip to Colorado. She'd finally faced her past. He had a feeling she was coming to terms with it. Maybe her nightmares would stop, and she would begin to heal.

Ashlyn unlocked the apartment door, and they went inside, taking the groceries to the kitchen and setting them on the counter.

"What do you want me to do?" she asked.

"Cutting board? And a knife," he told her.

She nodded, looked confused for a moment, then opened a cabinet on the bottom. She closed it and then moved to another one. When she brought out the cutting board, she was smiling as if she'd just found a lost treasure.

"You really don't know how to cook, do you?"

She laughed. "Is that going to be a problem?"

"Not at all. Knife?"

"Oh yeah, a knife." She nibbled her bottom lip and then moved to a drawer. She opened it, then turned with a smug expression.

"Do you realize just how beautiful you are?"

She suddenly turned serious. "I only offered dinner. Nothing more."

"That's all I'm expecting. It was just a compliment. No more than that."

She met his gaze for a moment. "Okay, but no more compliments."

"Why not? You're a beautiful woman, and I don't mind telling you."

"Can you just cook dinner? I'm starving."

"Of course. Want to pour us some of the wine?"

She paused for a moment. "Does wine go with omelets?"

"Absolutely. Wine is made from grapes. My mother always told me to have fruit with my meal."

She crossed her arms and tilted her head as she looked at him. "I kind of doubt wine is what your mother meant."

"I'm compromising."

He wondered if she would argue with him, but she went to the refrigerator and brought out the bottle of wine. After taking down a couple of glasses, she poured them some, handing him a glass. He took a drink, savoring the taste. Beer would've been better, but he hadn't thought to grab a six-pack. Wine would have to do. He set his glass on the counter next to where he was working and went back to making the omelets.

"Now what?" she asked.

"We start cooking."

"Since I can't help much here, I'm going to get out of these boots and put on something more comfortable."

"Sure, go ahead. I've got this."

As she left the room, he added just a little olive oil and a pat of butter to the skillet. While it was heating, he finished chopping the jalapeno, red pepper, and onion. He dropped a bit of pepper in the skillet, and when it sizzled, he added the rest and lowered the heat. While that cooked, he shredded the cheese and began to slice mushrooms and tomatoes.

"That smells good," she said.

"My mother always says it's not a meal if you don't have onion somewhere in one of the dishes."

"I think I'd like your mother. I love onions."

When the peppers and onions started to brown, he added mushrooms and tomatoes, then stirred for a few seconds.

"Eggs?" he asked, looking around.

She hurried to the refrigerator and brought them out. He started to ask why she'd put them away when he was going to use them but decided she'd only been trying to help.

He cracked six eggs into a bowl, then beat them with a whisk. Still, he couldn't help asking. "How did you survive not knowing how to cook?"

"I make a mean peanut butter and jelly sandwich and buy

microwaveable meals."

That's what he liked about her. She was unpredictable and resourceful.

He returned his focus to what he was doing. "Since we're both starved, I'm going to make one humongous omelet, and we'll split it." He looked around. "Toaster?"

She got it out, put two slices of bread in it, and then pushed the lever down. When she looked up, she smiled again. "I can make toast, too."

"Well, there you go. I was wrong. You can cook."

She casually leaned against the counter, taking a drink of her wine. "Thank you. I'm glad we cleared that up."

He poured the eggs into the skillet, waited a few seconds for it to cook just a little, then spread the cheese on top.

"Cooking an omelet doesn't look that difficult," she commented.

"There's nothing to it."

"Maybe I'll surprise Mindy and make her an omelet when she comes for a visit next time. Won't she be shocked?"

"I bet you could do a lot of things if you set your mind to it."

"Probably, but I would have to enjoy doing it. I'm just not that crazy about cooking."

"You'd rather catch bad guys and lock them away."

She thought about his words. "That's exactly what I enjoy doing. I like feeling that I'm making a difference."

He flipped the omelet and, after a moment, flipped it again. She'd already brought two plates down from the cabinet and handed him one. Very carefully, he moved the omelet from the skillet to the plate.

"Perfection," he said, breathing in all the flavors.

"What? You mean you're not going to flip it up in the air and let it land on the plate?"

"I'm saving that for next time."

She grabbed the bottle of wine out of the refrigerator and carried it to the table, throwing over her shoulder, "Who says there's even going to be a next time? I haven't tasted your omelet yet. I might not like it."

He liked this side of her—teasing, relaxed. He grabbed the salt and pepper and brought the food to the table. Now for the important part—the taste test. They took a seat across from each other. He waited until she took a bite, then watched her expression of pure delight as she closed her eyes and slowly chewed.

"I'm going to assume you like it," he said.

She opened her eyes and looked at him. "You would assume right. It's delicious. I've missed home cooking. Maybe I should hire you to be my cook."

"As long as it's live-in, I'd be agreeable," he joked.

Her fork stopped halfway to her mouth as she stared at him. She brought it the rest of the way and slowly chewed.

He had a feeling she was about to throw him out. Sometimes his mouth spoke before his brain was engaged.

"Do you think we can get a confession out of Elijah if we find him?" she finally asked.

He wondered what she was really thinking right now. He was pretty sure it wasn't the case or Elijah.

Chapter Sixteen

He had to watch from down the street, but he carried his binoculars with him all the time now. Had Dylan thought to catch him by putting cameras in the alleyway? Fool! He was more intelligent than all of them.

It was rather funny. He'd stopped and talked with one of the workers installing them—a friendly guy who'd been full of useless information. God, people could be such idiots.

Elijah parked just down the street instead, rather than moving to the alleyway, he stayed close to the car. He could still see her when she sat at the table. Dylan had accomplished nothing except to irritate him. If Dylan knew how easy it would be to take him out, he would think twice before messing with him. He was already pushing his luck.

When Ashlyn didn't return that first night, he reasoned that she might've gone out of town for work. He hadn't liked the idea Dylan was with her, but there was nothing he could do.

Now Elijah was back, sitting in his car, looking up at her window, and wishing she was home. He worried about her when she was gone. The light suddenly came on. His heart skipped a beat and then began to pound inside his chest. She was home! His angel! He knew she would return.

She would go to the bedroom and change into her nightclothes. He began to relax. When she was more comfortable, she would go to the kitchen, get a salad out of the refrigerator, and pour herself a glass of wine. He knew her so well.

He laughed lightly. She didn't like to cook. It hadn't taken him long to figure that one out. She would either have a microwave dinner or a salad and always a glass of wine to relax after a long day at work.

He waited patiently, getting agitated when she didn't appear after about ten minutes. Had she already gone to bed?

Without eating? He glanced at his watch. It wasn't early, but it wasn't that late either.

He was beginning to get worried as the minutes passed. What if she'd slipped in the shower? She could be lying there, unconscious, bleeding, maybe even dying.

No, she can't be dying. Not his angel. They were meant to be together. He began to pace on the sidewalk beside the car. Should he call 911? He could do it anonymously. Dammit, he didn't know what to do.

He raised the binoculars one more time before making any decision, then sighed with relief. There she was, framed by the window. His beautiful angel. He laughed. She had a bottle of wine and a glass. Was she planning to drink the whole bottle? So many things he needed to teach her, but he had no doubt that she would learn under his gentle guidance.

He leaned against the trunk of the car and stared at her. She was the most beautiful woman he'd ever seen. She was smiling. He liked when she smiled. He frowned as she began to talk to someone. He hadn't seen her phone when she sat down. Who was she talking to? Had Mindy come for a visit? It wasn't a school holiday. That was still a few days away, and then she would be out for the summer.

He moved his binoculars to look at the other side of the table. He froze when Dylan came into his line of vision, taking a chair opposite her. What was he doing there? Ashlyn never had anyone in her apartment except her little sister.

No! No! No! This couldn't be happening. He tossed his binoculars into the front seat, then scraped his fingers through his hair, pulling on the roots. Not happening! Can't be happening!

When his scalp began to burn, he released his hair. God, he was going to be sick. He raised his fist to the heavens above. "You promised that she was mine!"

He crawled back into the front seat on the passenger side

and brought his feet up to the seat. He hugged his knees close to his body. This wasn't happening. It couldn't be. He knew he didn't have it wrong—she was supposed to be his.

He looked up toward the window, but he couldn't see anything without the binoculars, and he didn't want to pick them up because he was afraid of what he might see.

Would Dylan pull her into his arms and kiss her? Would they make love? Surely she would send him away. They weren't right for each other. Not at all. Dylan was messing up all his plans. This could change everything. He might have to act sooner than he'd planned.

Elijah would give her the benefit of the doubt. Dylan was just having dinner with her and would leave soon. He'd wait just to make sure.

Except Dylan didn't leave. Someone turned off the kitchen light. Elijah waited for Dylan to come out of the garage. He had a sick feeling in his gut that Dylan wasn't going to leave.

Could he be wrong? Was Ashlyn meant to be his?

God, now he was starting to doubt himself. She *was* his! His sweet angel. Soon they would be together.

Chapter Seventeen

"Why don't we go into the living room," Ashlyn suggested after they cleaned the kitchen, then wondered why she had invited him to stay longer. This was a night of firsts for her. She'd never had a man in her apartment until tonight and would've never imagined him cooking dinner for them. It was odd how comfortable she felt with Dylan.

"More wine?" he asked, holding up the bottle.

"Sure," she reached her glass toward him, and he poured her some more.

She sat on one end of the sofa, and he took the other, leaning against the arms so they faced each other. "Do you like going on missions?" she suddenly asked, trying to keep the conversation neutral. She enjoyed his company and didn't want him to leave, but she didn't want to get too personal either.

He looked down into his glass of wine as if he was thinking over her question. "Most of the time. I like knowing I'm helping people."

"Have you ever thought about walking away? You know, finding a job with less drama and danger."

"Every time something goes wrong." He took a drink. "It can be a helluva guilt trip if an operation goes south. I try to focus on the people we've helped and not let the others get to me. What about you? Have you ever thought about changing your profession?"

"Sometimes."

"Yet, you're still working."

"I guess we're a lot alike in that respect. More than once, I've thought about quitting. Just walking away."

"Why do you change your mind?"

"I had to testify when Albert went to trial. I was terrified and refused to look at him. I was there the day the judge handed down the sentence, even though my grandmother hadn't wanted me to go. It was just something I needed to do. I was sitting in the back of the courtroom, so I couldn't see his face when the judge gave him twenty-five years. It wasn't enough for what he did, but it made him furious. He began to curse and yell. It's hard to describe, but I felt so much satisfaction that someone as evil as him would be taken off the streets. That was when I started looking into law enforcement. I wanted to keep putting them away."

"Were you there when he got a life sentence for killing those two men?"

"No, but I wished I could've been."

"And your father? Was he relieved?"

She ran her thumb around the top of the glass, then raised her gaze to his. "I usually drop by and see my father once a week. Would you like to meet him?"

"I would."

"Tomorrow, after work." Why was she doing this? It was almost as if she was baring her soul to him tonight. Maybe it was time she talked to someone, and Dylan was a good listener. "Now, are you curious about anything else in my life?"

He thought about her question for a moment. She wondered if he was going to say anything. She didn't even know why it was so important to her to tell him things she'd never told anyone. Even Mindy didn't know everything about what happened that day.

"There is one other thing," he said.

"Really?" She couldn't fathom what it might be.

"What did you whisper to Albert before we left the prison that sent him into a rage?"

Her hand trembled just a fraction. She quickly brought up her other hand to hold the glass and then decided it might be best to set it on the coffee table.

"What happened that day?" he asked.

"You said you read the transcript of the trial," she said, not quite meeting his eyes.

"But what happened that you didn't tell anyone about?"

"Why do you think I didn't?"

"Just a gut feeling. Something that you keep bottled up inside of yourself. I know from experience that it helps to talk about it."

She raised her gaze to his. "Did something happen to you?"

"We all have things we'd rather forget about." He took a drink of his wine and then set his glass near hers.

"Tell me about it."

He hesitated, then began to talk. "It was a long time ago. We were on a mission. A human trafficking ring we were trying to break up. We were doing surveillance on a house, and I was up on the rooftop. It was down in Mexico. I was looking at the house through my rifle's scope into an upstairs window. Their leader grabbed a young girl and held her in front of him when the others stormed in. I still remember the terror on her face." He closed his eyes tight, running a hand across his forehead.

"What happened?"

He opened his eyes and looked at her. For a moment, he looked far away, as though he might be looking through the lens of his scope again. He blinked past the fog and came back to the present.

"I was getting ready to take the shot, but my superior told me to stand down, that the others had him. I still wanted to take him out. When I hesitated, the man drew a knife and killed the young girl. It's something I've had to live with."

"But it wasn't your fault."

"Wasn't it? If I had taken the shot, the young girl might be alive right now. Because of that, I don't hesitate anymore. If I think someone's in danger, I *will* take the shot. Period."

No one could blame him for what he did, but she knew all about the guilt you could feel when something went sideways. He was right. It didn't even matter if it was your fault or not. The guilt was still there. He came to his feet and went to the table, bringing the bottle of wine back with him. He poured some into his glass and then added more to hers. He sat down again and took a drink of his wine.

"Funny, but I've never told anyone about that day before now. Not everything, at least."

She reached for her glass and took a long drink before setting it back down. "He forced me to put the zip tie on my father," she said, looking down at her hands. She hesitated.

"And then what happened?"

She drew in a deep breath, then exhaled. "I was terrified of what he would do to us, but I was too afraid not to follow his orders. I stupidly thought he would rob us and leave the house with both of us tied up. But that didn't happen. He pulled me into the kitchen. I thought he was going to rip my arm off. He found a thin cup towel and tested the cloth's strength to ensure it was sturdy. Then he dragged me back into the dining room. He was yelling and screaming obscenities the whole time. That's when I started to be afraid he would kill us. You don't think about dying when you're only fourteen."

For a moment, she returned to the house that day. She'd been shaking all over with tears running down her cheeks. She remembered calling out to her father and asking what she should do. When she looked at him, she saw that he was crying, too. He told her to do as Albert said, and he would let them go.

She drew in a ragged breath and continued. "He forced me into the chair, then tied my hands behind my back. I was sobbing hysterically, but I still thought he would leave. But no, he had other plans. I'd been sheltered all my life."

Ashlyn took a deep breath, then exhaled. She'd pushed this part to the back of her mind. She didn't tell the officers or her grandmother what else Albert planned to do.

"He ripped my blouse open and…and began touching me. My father yelled at him to stop, but Albert only laughed. He pressed his lips against mine while he touched me. Through all the fear and degradation, I heard my father's voice. He kept telling me to close my eyes. Close your eyes and let your mind take you somewhere safe, sweetheart, he kept repeating over and over. I did as he said."

"Ashlyn," Dylan quietly said her name. "You don't have to say anything else."

"I need to." She reached for her wine, took a drink, and then set it back down. "I still remember his foul breath. I thought I would throw up. Then he reached for the waistband of my shorts. I think it was then that I knew he was going to rape me, except it didn't happen. A car door closed, and a dog started barking. I guess he was more afraid of getting caught and his master plan not being executed because he straightened, cursing his bad luck. Then he explained what was going to happen with the fire and the bombs. He said it would be beautiful. My father begged him to let me go, but Albert ignored him and started the fires. He left us there to die."

"But you didn't die," Dylan said.

She looked at him. "No, I didn't, but I knew we would if I didn't do something. I started running toward the kitchen when I finally got out of my restraints. The downstairs had already begun to fill with smoke. My father told me to get out of the house, but I couldn't leave him."

"I made my way to the kitchen. I couldn't see through the dense smoke, but I knew where the knives were kept. I grabbed a knife and ran back, choking and coughing, then cut the zip tie. The first bomb exploded, knocking us to the ground. My father shielded me from the flying debris. We were getting close to the front door when a heavy wooden beam struck him in the head. He stumbled and fell, losing consciousness."

"The beam was still burning. I don't know where I found the strength, but I put my shoulder against it, pushed as hard as possible, and finally got it off. I dragged him the rest of the way out just as the fire department pulled up. Our neighbor had called when she saw the smoke and was hurrying over. I warned the fire department about the other bombs when they arrived."

"And the scars you hide?"

She met his gaze. "I knew my arms were burned, but I didn't realize how bad until they put me in the ambulance. The pain was excruciating. Even after Albert went to prison, I still had nightmares. All the therapy in the world wasn't going to stop them. I allowed him space in my head all these years."

"And now?"

"When I saw him in prison, it was the first time I'd looked into his eyes since the day he broke into our house. I no longer saw a monster. The years in prison made him haggard and weak. He was still evil, but I took away his power over me."

"What did you say to him that sent him into a rage?"

"I told him that I thought he would've remembered me. I was the prosecuting attorney's daughter, and I was the one who testified against him in court. I told him to enjoy prison life because he'd never get out. I think he was angry because we survived. I'm glad I faced him."

"I'm glad you did, too. You were strong back then, and

you're strong now."

"I don't know how strong I am, but I want to catch this serial killer and close the case. I don't want him to hurt anyone else."

"As soon as we can get a composite of what he would look like now, we'll put out an APB on him. Somebody knows him. It's only a matter of time before we catch him."

Suddenly nervous, she glanced at her watch. "I didn't know it was so late," she said. Why had she spilled her guts? He was probably bored to tears. "You're easy to talk to."

They came to their feet at the same time.

"I'll pick you up in the morning," he said.

"Let me know when you're downstairs, and I'll come down."

"I enjoyed dinner, and the conversation." He said as he stopped at the door, turning to face her.

"Me, too. You're a great cook."

"I have a confession to make. I can make breakfast, mostly sandwiches for lunch, but dinner, not so much."

"I like breakfast."

She knew he was going to kiss her again. She should step back and tell him goodnight, but her feet wouldn't move. His lips brushed across hers, and a shudder of need swept over her. Her arms automatically wrapped around his neck, pulling him in closer. He tasted like the wine they'd been drinking, intoxicating and with so much heat.

She could barely catch her breath when the kiss ended. One kiss and she wanted so much more that her body ached. She rested her head against his chest for a moment and heard the erratic beating of his heart.

"I guess I should leave before something more happens," he said but didn't make a move to open the door.

"Probably," she agreed, looking up into his face and taking a half step back.

"I don't want to leave," he admitted.

"I don't want you to leave either," she said.

He pulled her into his arms again and once more lowered his lips to hers. God, she couldn't get enough of this man. She felt as though she would incinerate at any moment.

Ashlyn knew what she wanted, and right now, that was Dylan. She took his hand and pulled him toward the bedroom.

She'd only forgotten one thing—her scars.

The first time she'd undressed in front of a man, there'd been such a look of disgust on his face. She'd grabbed her clothes, pulled them on, and ran out of his apartment. She'd been so embarrassed. After that, she only made love in the dark.

And, of course, she'd left the lamp on when she changed shoes. "Just a minute," she walked toward the bedside lamp to switch it off.

"No, leave it on."

She didn't say anything for a moment, only closed her eyes tightly. "I have scars," she whispered.

He came up behind her, pulling her into his arms. "Everyone has scars. Sometimes they're on the inside, sometimes the outside. I've seen scars before. Scars don't define a person, don't let yours define you."

That's what he said now, but when she removed her shirt, would he think the same thing? There was only one way to find out. She stepped out of his arms and unbuttoned her shirt. Taking a deep breath, she let it fall to the floor. She knew what he was seeing. She saw it every time she looked in the mirror.

The puckered skin that never healed from the burns. There were two rough patches on both arms. The one she got when she shoved the beam off her father stretched from her shoulder almost to her elbow. The one on her other arm, from flying debris after the explosion, wasn't quite as bad because they were able to do skin grafts. Still, they weren't a pretty sight. She held her breath and waited for him to say something.

When she felt his lips on the burns, gently kissing, her eyes filled with tears.

"I think you're beautiful," he said. He turned her to face him, then gently brushed away her tears. He raised her chin so that she looked him in the eyes. "People can be cruel sometimes. Don't let them control who you are."

"I wish you would've come into my life years ago."

"Me, too, but I'm glad I'm here now."

"I am, too."

He kissed her again. Gentle at first, but he couldn't hold back the heat of his passion, and his kiss became more intense. She didn't want him to hold back. She wanted to know his body as well as he would know hers.

When the kiss ended, she began to unbutton his shirt, but her hands were trembling, so he brushed them away and unbuttoned it the rest of the way. She pushed it off his shoulders, and it floated to the ground.

"You're beautiful," she said as she ran her hands over his chest. She wanted to feel every ridge, every muscle.

"I don't think I've ever been called beautiful." He reached behind her back and unsnapped her bra, pulling it off her shoulders and tossing it to the side.

She drew in a sharp breath when he cupped one breast, running his thumb over the tight nipple. Heat spiraled down to settle between her legs. She'd never wanted a man as much as she wanted Dylan right now.

He must've felt the same way because he stepped back and began removing his pants. She reached for the button on hers and pushed it through, sliding the zipper down. They were both kicking out of their pants at the same time. She only paused to stare at him for a moment. The black and gray boxer briefs fit snug to his skin, and he was more than ready to make love.

She pushed her blue bikini panties down, then kicked out of them. He was in the process of pushing his boxers down but stopped to stare at her.

"No, you're wrong. You're the beautiful one." His words were husky with emotion.

She could feel the heat moving up her cheeks. Funny, she wasn't embarrassed to be standing in front of him naked. She was embarrassed that he'd complimented her.

He must've noticed her rosy cheeks because he laughed lightly. "You better get used to compliments, or you'll be embarrassed a lot."

She sighed. "Shut up, and make love to me," she said as she walked closer, pressing her naked body against his. It felt good to rub against him. When he groaned, she knew he enjoyed it just as much.

In one swift movement, he scooped her into his arms and laid her on the bed as if she weighed nothing at all. But he didn't join her. Instead, he began kissing her as he traveled toward the head of the bed.

He took her ankle, lightly massaging the bottom of her foot as he kissed it. He kissed her knee, massaging the back. She closed her eyes for a moment as she tried to keep control of her body, but it betrayed her. She got lost in his touch and the sensations he stirred inside her. He came to the juncture of her legs and lightly brushed through the curls.

"Damned beautiful," he said as he lowered his mouth and began to kiss and stroke her with his tongue.

She gasped as the fire of passion quickly spread over her body. A delicious heat that touched every inch of her. She gripped the bedspread. No one had ever done this to her. It was exquisite, and she didn't want him to stop. When he inserted a finger inside her and began to move in and out, she lost it. She began to moan until her body tightened and she began to pant.

"Now," she said as she rocked her hips. "Oh God, now!" Her thighs quivered as she reached climax.

He slowed his movements and then stopped but pressed his hand against her sex as spasms wracked her body. She whimpered as she slowly came back to earth. Closing her eyes tightly, she tried to take in what had just happened. She'd never had an orgasm that strong.

He crawled farther up in the bed, lying beside her and pulling her close.

"No one has ever done that before," she breathed as she looked at him.

"Good, I like knowing I'm the first."

She lay next to him for a moment, letting everything come back into focus as they faced each other. He lightly drew circles on her back, dipping lower, squeezing her butt.

"That feels good," she said after a moment when she could breathe normally again.

"I'm glad you like it."

She frowned. "I did all the taking, and you still haven't gotten release."

He kissed the top of her head. "That's not exactly right—about you doing all the taking. I had just as much pleasure tasting you. I loved watching you come. There's something very erotic about a woman when she has an orgasm."

She'd never had a man talk to her like this, so open. Kind of dirty, but sexy, too. While she was thinking about it, his hand slipped around the front between their bodies. He began to massage her breast, tugging the nipple, lightly squeezing. She sucked in a breath.

"Not hurting you am I?" he asked.

"You know damn well you're not."

The gentle rumble of his laughter wrapped around her. She liked the sound. But when his hand slid over her hip and then moved between her legs, massaging and tugging, she couldn't stop her gasp of pleasure.

When she began to move against his hand, he gently rolled her to her back and spread her legs a little wider. He grabbed the condom he'd laid on the bedside table and ripped it open with his teeth before sliding it down his cock.

He was so big she wondered if she'd be able to take him inside her. But when he entered her, she only thought about the pleasure he was giving. He moved slowly at first, and she knew it cost him to hold back. She brought her legs up and wrapped them around his waist, pulling him in closer, and as he sank deeper inside her, he groaned his pleasure.

She rocked her hips against his as he picked up the pace, moving deeper, in and out. Plunging inside her. She clutched his back wanting…needing…

She met him thrust for agonizingly sweet thrust. Her hands moved over his back, caressing, holding, never wanting to let go.

She strained toward release until her body felt as though it exploded into tiny pieces of pure bliss. A moment later, he stiffened and cried out. He lowered himself to the bed, rolling to his side, taking her with him. For a moment, they lay there, holding each other close.

"God, that was beautiful," he breathed, breaking the silence. "I don't think I've ever felt anything like this before."

His words pleased her. Usually, when she was with someone, and they'd just finished having sex, he'd roll off the bed and go straight to the bathroom to clean up. That was always fine with her. She was usually already dressed by the time he returned. She wanted to shower in her bathroom.

But this was different, and suddenly, it scared the hell out of her.

Chapter Eighteen

Ashlyn scared the hell out of him. Dylan had never felt anything like what he'd felt last night when they'd made love. But damn, he loved waking up with her snuggled against him. There was just something about her that he couldn't quite put his finger on. Whatever it was, he liked it. He liked it a lot.

He raised just enough to look over her shoulder at the clock on the bedside table. It wouldn't be long before they had to get ready for work. They'd showered earlier. He smiled. And made love again, then showered again.

He dropped a kiss on her bare shoulder and inhaled her scent. They'd both used peaches and cream bath wash. He'd put on some cologne this morning so that no one looked at him funny. Not that it ever bothered him how anyone looked at him.

Ashlyn stretched next to him, then slowly opened her eyes. "Good morning," she mumbled. "What time is it?"

He almost came unglued when she rested her hand on his arm and then lightly stroked. All he could think about was making love to her again. But a bad guy out there wanted to hurt unsuspecting women, and they needed to stop him.

"It's almost seven," he said.

"This is the first time I don't want to go to work. I would much rather lay in bed and make love all day long. We could eat Oreos dipped in milk when we got hungry."

He laughed. "We ate all the Oreos last night, remember?"

Her eyes twinkled. "Oh yeah, that's right. I think you ate more than I did."

"Probably, but they were good."

"Everything was good about last night."

"Agreed."

"If we stay here much longer, we're going to make love again. Then we're going to be late for work."

"It's tempting, but I want to catch this guy."

"I do, too."

With a sigh, she rolled out of bed, taking most of the cover. She stood for a moment, looking down at him in all his nakedness.

"I think you did that on purpose," he said.

"Of course I did." She laughed as she grabbed a robe and started toward the kitchen. "I'm going to turn on the coffee pot. I'm in desperate need of caffeine."

"You and me both." He watched her until she was covered up. Damn, she was sexy, and now he had an ache that wasn't about to go away anytime soon.

Since time hadn't stopped, he started hunting for his clothes, getting dressed as he did. They would have to stop by his apartment so he could change. Coffee first, though.

When he joined her, she'd brought two cups out of the cabinet and set them near the coffee pot. She glanced in his direction when he came in. It was all he could not carry to her back to bed when he saw the hungry look in her eyes.

"You're killing me," he said.

Her expression turned to confusion. "How am I killing you?"

"When you look at me like you want to make love again. It's all I can do to keep from carrying you back to bed."

She didn't say anything as she poured the coffee and carried the cups to the table. He wondered if he should've kept his thoughts to himself. He didn't want to scare her off, thinking he had sex on the brain.

They each took a seat. She added cream and sugar to her coffee and slowly stirred.

"We can always do a sleepover tonight," she said, not meeting his gaze as she took a drink of coffee.

He almost choked on the drink he was taking. When he began to cough, she looked at him with concern.

"Are you okay?" she asked.

"You're supposed to wait until after I swallow before you spring that on me."

"Do you think it's a good idea or a bad one? Am I too forward?"

"I think it's an excellent idea."

"We'll have to buy more Oreos," she said.

"And wine. Maybe a six-pack of beer."

"We can order pizza tonight."

"I like pizza," he said.

"I know. So do I."

She glanced at her watch. "I guess I'd better get dressed so we'll have time to run by your apartment." She took her coffee with her.

By the time he finished his coffee, she was coming out of the bedroom with her empty cup.

"I guess I'm ready."

They locked up, then went down to the garage. He was thankful that all four tires were intact on his pickup. But then, Ashlyn had better security. If the perp had been watching from somewhere and saw them going into her complex together, he would be furious when Dylan hadn't left.

"Do you think he saw us going into the parking garage

together?" she asked as if she'd read his mind.

"Probably."

"We'll have to be more careful. He'll be furious."

"I was thinking the same thing," he told her.

They were quiet the rest of the way to his apartment. They rode the elevator up and then went inside. She stayed in the living area while he went and changed clothes, then gathered what he would need for the next morning since he'd be spending the night with Ashlyn.

Ashlyn was wandering around the room when he came back out. She turned and looked at him. "It's very generic," she said. "No pictures of home?"

"I always travel light."

"I guess I do when we're on a case where we have to go out of town. It's easier to walk away when you don't leave anything behind. Are you ready?"

He wondered if she was referring to their relationship. He wanted to tell her it wouldn't be easy walking away from her, but he didn't know what the future might bring. "Yes, I'm ready."

Before they went inside the office, they each grabbed another cup of coffee from Abe. He watched as she closed her eyes and took a drink. "Abe, you make the best coffee in the world."

He grinned. "I think that's the reason my wife married me. She does love her coffee."

Dylan laughed. "I bet it was more than that."

"You may be right. I was a ladies' man in my younger days, but once I saw Lily, I didn't see any of those other women. Every time I looked at her, she made my heart skip a beat. It wasn't that she was prettier than any of those other girls, but something about her was different. It's hard to describe, but I still feel the same way forty years later."

"Congratulations," they told him.

"Nothing to it. My daddy said always treat the one you love like your best friend and cherish the gift you've been given."

"It makes sense," Ashlyn said as they went inside the main room.

Nolan was the only one there. "How long have you been here?" Dylan asked.

Nolan turned from his computer, glancing at the clock on the wall. "About an hour. I uploaded the sketch the librarian was able to give us and sent it to the guy who was aging Elijah's school picture. When he finishes, he'll compare the two and see if we've got the same man.

"Good work," Ashlyn said.

"He said he could have it back to us before the end of the day."

The others began coming in over the next ten minutes. Dylan could feel the excitement in the air. Everyone knew they were getting close to catching this guy. It was a good feeling. He only hoped they were right about Elijah.

But if they weren't, everyone returned to their regular duties of piecing together what they'd already found and searching for new information.

Dylan and Ashlyn studied the crime scene pictures, but they didn't yield much more than they already had. Nolan and Leah were back to checking the victims' social media pages. Brad and Ginny were going over the statements of those they had interviewed.

Dylan and Ashlyn returned to inspecting the bombs, at least what they'd recovered. "So far, most of the parts have been generic. He could have bought his supplies anywhere." He felt as if they were running into a brick wall.

"Exactly," she said. "According to the lab analysis, he used a combination of bleach and drain cleaner as the accelerant to produce more fire. The part that blew out the walls was very intricate. He had to know where each one would go off and what damage it would do."

"You're right about him being smart. He's experienced enough that he was able to improve upon his technique for the last crime scene."

Dylan picked up one of the metal pieces they'd brought from the evidence room and began to study it, but he couldn't find anything out of the ordinary about the part. The perp could've bought the supplies at any hardware store and then assembled everything at home.

He was still looking at it when Ashlyn's phone rang. She reached across the desk to answer it. When she did, her arm brushed his. She glanced his way as she brought the phone to her ear. They both smiled before turning serious again. It wouldn't do for everyone to know they were sleeping together. Not that there were any rules against it.

"Hello?"

Some of the color drained from her face. Dylan whistled to the others as he reached across and hit the speaker button.

"Are they all listening now?" The man asked. "I'm assuming you've put my call on the speaker."

She looked at Dylan and nodded that this was the guy. "You know I did."

"I'm very angry with you," he said.

"Why would you be angry with me?"

"Oh, you know why I'm angry. You let him into your apartment last night. You laughed and talked and flirted with him! You see, I know everything about you, Ashlyn. I'm the only one who can make you happy. You need to realize that."

"How do I know we'll be right for each other? I've never even met you. Why don't we meet somewhere and talk it over."

He laughed. "Oh, you'd like that, wouldn't you? Then I suppose your boyfriend would jump out and put me in handcuffs. That won't happen. I know he had the cameras installed in the alleyway. But you see, I'm smarter than all of you. You'll never catch me. You might as well get used to the fact that we're meant to be together."

"What's your connection to me?" she asked.

"Do you want another woman to die because you can't figure it out?"

"Take me, but don't kill anyone else."

"Patience, it won't be long now."

A click came over the speaker. She slammed the phone down.

"He hung up."

"He doesn't want to give us too much information. He's afraid we might start connecting the dots. He doesn't know we already have," Dylan said.

"We weren't online long enough to get a trace, were we?" she asked.

He shook his head. "No, but we were getting close. That's why he hung up."

"What about the cameras? Anyone suspicious?"

"No, he's smart enough to stay out of range."

"I should've asked if he was Albert's son."

"No, it was too soon. If he uses a burner phone, we might've lost him." Waylon stood at the rail. He came down the stairs. "I don't want you left alone," he told her.

"I won't be," she said without further explanation.

Waylon and Dylan exchanged a look. He nodded. "Good, if Elijah is our perp, he'll show his hand sooner rather than later." He looked at Nolan. "How's the sketch coming along?"

"Anytime now."

By late afternoon, they had the sketch. They made their way to the conference room, and Nolan put both sketches on the board.

He pointed to the first one. "This is the one the librarian and the sketch artist came up with." He pointed to the second sketch. "This is the one that was taken from Elijah Moore's school picture and what he might look like now." Nolan faced them once again. "The boot print also suggests he's around five feet, nine or ten inches tall, small to medium build, which matches with the guy who Kimberly befriended."

"I can't see much difference between the two pictures. At least, very little," Dylan said.

Waylon rested his hands on the back of one of the chairs and looked at each of them. "It's not all good news. My sources haven't found anything on Elijah. If he moved here from Maryland, he didn't change his driver's license address and he has no arrests. Not even a parking ticket. They couldn't find a record of him even being in Texas."

"So, what do we do now?" Ginny asked.

"We put an APB out on him. We'll have all the local stations post his picture. We'll just say he's a person of interest and we need to talk to him. Someone will recognize him." He glanced at his watch. "We can't do much more here today. Go home, and we'll see what happens tomorrow."

Once they were in the pickup, Dylan turned to Ashlyn. "Don't worry about what the perp said on the phone today. I won't let you out of my sight."

"I kind of wish he would meet with me. I know that's never going to happen because he's a coward. Just like his father. He'll try to strike when I'm not looking and catch me off guard, but I'm ready for him."

"This guy is crazy," he warned. "You can't trust him. He'll do whatever it takes to get you in his clutches, and he'll do it in a way you won't be ready for him. Promise me that you won't go off anywhere alone."

She hesitated for a fraction of a second. "I promise."

"Good. Now where to?"

"To meet my father." She gave him the directions.

Her father didn't live very far from her. He knew she was trying to protect him, just like she had when she pulled him from the house without thinking of her own safety. But he might be able to shed some light on the people Albert associated with, the ones they didn't know about. Did he have another son besides Elijah? Or maybe a daughter. Women weren't normally serial killers, but they couldn't rule one out.

There was a tall, wrought iron fence around the property. To get in, you had to stop at the guard shack. He pushed the button to roll down the window.

The guard glanced inside the vehicle after he came out. As soon as he recognized Ashlyn, he smiled. "Hello, Miss Pillar."

She returned his smile with one of her own. "Hello, Leonard. How's the wife and kids?"

"Just fine. June-bug is getting ready for college in the fall. It seems like just the other day I was changing her diapers. They grow up fast. Let me get that gate for you." He went back inside the small building and pushed the button. When he did, the gate slowly opened, and Dylan drove through.

As he pulled into a parking space, Dylan noticed the lawns were well manicured. There was a sign that said they'd arrived at The Meadows. Everything spoke of money. He was pretty sure it wasn't cheap to live here.

He shut off the engine, and they got out. As they went inside, he looked around. There was a large, comfortable sitting area on one side with shelves of books and a long hallway with lots of windows and sun streaming inside. He immediately knew this wasn't an apartment complex.

"They take good care of him here," she said. "I researched this place, not just for their security, but for their resources. He's made some progress since he's been here."

"What's wrong with him?"

"My father was a very proud man. He wouldn't want anyone to know he had a disability. When you first meet him, you won't know there's anything wrong unless you're looking for the signs. When the beam dropped on his head, it rendered him unconscious. When he came to, he had no recollection of what happened the day Albert came into our home. The doctors explained that it traumatized him so badly, combined with the head injury, it put him in a sort of limbo. He's watched us grow up but doesn't quite comprehend everything."

He could only guess how much it cost her to tell him this. "I'm sorry."

"This is his room," she stopped outside the door, then knocked.

"Come in," the man on the other side said.

Her father wore gray slacks and a button-down, white shirt, and black dress shoes. There was a dusting of gray at his temples, but few wrinkles lined his face. Joseph looked like the prominent lawyer he used to be as he sat in a tall, winged-back chair, a floor lamp casting enough light that he could read the open book in his lap. If he had scars, they were hidden by his clothes.

"Hi, Daddy," Ashlyn said. She walked over to the chair he was sitting in and kissed him on the forehead.

His face broke out into a wide smile. "Hello, darling. I was hoping you would drop by."

"Is everything going okay with you?" she asked.

"Busy as always. I've got a new case going to trial next week, and I was doing a little research." He looked over at Dylan. "And who's your new friend?"

Ashlyn turned to him. "This is Dylan. I work with him. Dylan, this is my father, Joseph Pillar."

Dylan stepped forward and reached out his hand. Joseph immediately took it and gave him a firm handshake.

"It's good to meet you, sir." Ashlyn was right. He looked fine.

"Oh, there are no sirs here. I'm just Joseph. Please, have a seat. We could go out on the patio and have the housekeeper bring us a glass of tea, but it's too darn hot. Would you like something to drink, though?"

"No, Daddy, we're fine. We can't stay long. Dylan wanted to ask you about a case you worked on a long time ago."

"That may be tough. I've tried a lot of cases. Tell me which one it was and maybe I'll remember something helpful."

Dylan met Ashlyn's eyes. She gave a slight nod.

"It was the robbery of an elderly couple," he said. "The man used a gun. I wanted to know if you remembered anything about his family. We think his son might be up to no good. His name was Albert Duncan."

"Albert Duncan, the name sounds familiar." He rubbed his forehead. After a moment, he looked up. "No, I can't say as I remember this man. And this is a case you're working on now?"

"Yes, it is," Dylan said.

"Tell you what, I'll call my office and tell them to go through my papers. I always take excellent notes on every case I handle." He chuckled. "It drives my assistant crazy trying to keep up with them. She'll have everything you need. I'll give her a call after you leave, so she'll be expecting you."

"Thank you. I'm very appreciative that you could help."

"Don't think anything about it," Joseph said and then turned to Ashlyn. "And who are you again?"

Her smile wavered just a fraction. "I'm Ashlyn."

"Well, it's nice to meet you. You're a beautiful young woman."

"Thank you. We have to go now, but I'll see you again soon."

"That's nice." He picked up the dictionary he'd been looking at and opened it.

They stepped out, and Ashlyn closed the door behind them. He saw the tears in her eyes before she quickly blinked them away.

She cleared her throat. "This was one of his good days. He remembered me for a little while. Sometimes I don't get that much."

"I'm sorry," he said, not knowing the right words to say.

"I can't say I'll ever get used to his condition, but at least I have him some of the time. I want to stop by the nurses' station for a moment."

"I'll meet you at the pickup."

She nodded as she turned and walked in the opposite direction. He couldn't imagine what she had gone through since

Albert broke into their home and destroyed their lives. It would be difficult to suddenly have a once robust father change to a man who didn't always recognize her. It took a strong person to deal with something like that.

He was sitting in the pickup when she came out a few minutes later. She got in on the passenger side and fastened her seatbelt.

"He's had a good week," she said. "Sometimes, that's all I can ask for."

"Is there any hope that he'll regain what he lost?"

"The doctors can't say for sure, but they're working on a new treatment to regain his memory. Much of it has to do with Albert breaking into our house and the trauma of knowing his daughter was about to die. My father was very close to both me and Mindy."

Dylan's family was close, too. He couldn't imagine his mom or dad going through something like that. "So, you think it was a protective mechanism inside the brain that kicked in?"

"The doctors seem to think that was a part of it. The thought that I might die because of a case he'd tried was too much for him. When the beam struck him on the head, it caused something to go haywire inside his brain. It's complicated."

"You don't think mentioning Albert Duncan's name might cause him some distress?"

"It's not the first time I've mentioned his name. Once, I tried to get him to remember. I wanted him to return to us so badly that I was willing to try anything. He had no memory of that day. Much like today."

"What about his papers. He said he took meticulous notes. Would those still happen to be around?"

She shook her head. "No, they would've all been destroyed." She suddenly smiled. "Hey, let's not be all gloom and doom. Besides, I think we're about to solve this case. Weren't you the one who said don't take your work home with you?"

"I was. Where to?"

"The grocery store, and there's a pizza place closer to my house. We'll go ahead and order it and pick it up on the way to my apartment."

"Sounds good to me. I'm starved."

But he noticed that Ashlyn was still stressed. Not that he blamed her.

While they were in the grocery store, Dylan saw that Ashlyn kept looking around, then again, when they picked up the pizza they'd ordered. Not that he didn't do the same thing. The perp was watching them, but he was careful not to let himself be seen.

Ashlyn didn't start to relax until they were inside her apartment. She dropped her keys on the table by the door, but when she turned around, she caught him staring at her.

"I'm fine," she reassured him. "If he wasn't targeting me specifically, I probably wouldn't be on edge quite this much. I've handled cases almost as bad as this one. Sometimes I wonder if I'm not more angry than anything." She carried the pizza box to the table and set it down, then followed him into the kitchen to put away what they'd bought at the store.

"You have every right to be on edge and every right to be angry. This guy is crazy. It's hard to know what he'll do next."

"Exactly. By the way, I like having you with me."

He set the cookies down rather than putting them in the cabinet and sauntered over to her. Waiting until now had been a bitch. He took her into his arms and lowered his lips to hers. She tasted sweet and spicy. He kept the kiss gentle, but it wasn't easy when she pressed her body closer to his.

When he ended the kiss, she rested her head against his chest. He could feel the trembles that ran over her body. He didn't think it had anything to do with this case.

"The pizza is getting cold," she said, but she didn't make any move to step away from him.

"I like cold pizza," he said.

"So do I."

That was all he needed. He scooped her into his arms and headed toward the bedroom while she laughed.

"You do know I can walk," she said.

"But then I wouldn't get to hold you."

Once they were in the bedroom, he set her on her feet. Passion flared in her eyes as she stepped away and unbuttoned her shirt. Yeah, he wasn't about to wait much longer either. He'd been thinking about making love to her all day.

He pulled his shirt over his head, kicking out of his boots at the same time and almost losing his balance. When she giggled, he scowled at her. That only made her laugh more. He loved her laugh. She needed to do it more often, not that she had much reason to laugh in her lifetime.

He finally got his boots off, followed by his socks. He'd just reached for the button on his jeans when she pushed her pants over her hips and then kicked out of them. She stood before him wearing a lacy red bra and matching bikini panties.

His breath caught in his throat and all he could do was stare. "Damn, you're sexy."

She reached behind her back and unhooked her bra. "You make me feel sexy." She tossed her bra toward her other clothes.

Her breasts fit perfectly in his hands. He loved everything about her body and planned to show her how much. While he quickly divested himself of his remaining clothes, she removed her panties.

"You know, you're not so bad looking yourself." She stroked her fingers across his chest.

A shiver ran over him. He couldn't resist cupping her breasts in his hands, tweaking the tight nipples before leaning forward and taking one into his mouth. He teased her nipple with his tongue. She ran her hands through his hair, down his back, cupping his ass, moving in closer. The sensations of her naked flesh rubbing against him was almost too much. He didn't know how long he could wait.

"I've been thinking about this all day," she said in a breathy whisper. "All I could think about was touching and caressing your body, but right now, I want to feel you inside me."

He didn't need for her to say anymore. He grabbed a condom out of his pocket and rolled it on. She'd already moved to the bed, her legs open and inviting. He entered her slowly, then paused.

She began to rock her hips. Silently begging for more. He watched her face, saw the strain, and began to move but kept his movements slow and easy. Her breathing became more rapid as he took her higher and higher.

"You're trying to kill me, right," she gasped. "I need you...now."

He drove into her.

"Oh damn, yes."

She met each thrust, wrapping her legs around his waist and pulling him in deeper, then she did something unexpected. She tightened her inner muscles. He drew in a sharp breath as her body hugged his cock. Contract, release. Erotic pleasure swept over him. He couldn't hold back much longer.

She cried out. He followed right behind her. Damn, it had never been like this...never.

"Have I told you that you're good at this?" she asked when their breathing returned to normal.

"You're not so bad yourself," he said. He rolled to his side, taking her with him. "In fact, you're pretty damn good." He liked her pleased smile. He didn't think her past experiences with men were anything to brag about. It was their loss. He'd had good sex before, but nothing compared to making love with Ashlyn. He wondered if it would wane with time.

"I'm hungry," she suddenly said.

He smiled. "At least we can say we worked up an appetite."

She laughed as she crawled over him, her naked body rubbing against him, and climbed out of bed. He groaned.

She turned around and faced him. "Did I hurt you?" Her expression was too innocent to be true.

He threw a pillow at her. She only laughed as she hurried to the bathroom. When she came out a few minutes later, she was wearing a robe. He liked naked better.

"Beer or wine?" she asked.

"Beer. I'll be in there in a moment." He rolled out of bed and went to the bathroom to clean up. He didn't bother with shoes or a shirt, just slipped on a pair of jogging pants.

She already had two beers sitting on the table and two saucers for their pizza. She'd also closed the curtains. That was smart. She was already taking a bite of a slice of pizza.

"It's still kind of warm," she said. "And delicious. I was starved."

He grinned. "Yet you chose me over food. Now that's a compliment."

"It is. I take my hunger very seriously."

"And the lady can tease. I wonder what other talents you've hidden from me."

"Maybe I'll show them to you someday," she replied with a saucy wink.

"I like the sound of that."

She took another bite of her pizza, casually glancing at her watch. Her expression turned serious. He wondered what she was thinking. He had a feeling it was something to do with the case.

"Let's turn on the TV and see if they will say anything about Elijah and the sketch."

He had to admit, he was curious to know if it would be on tonight's news.

"Bring your pizza and beer with you. We can sit on the sofa."

She set hers on the coffee table, grabbed the remote, and turned on the television.

Dylan knew this could escalate everything. Elijah might go off the deep end, and that wouldn't be good. Or it could bring him to justice. He hoped for the latter.

The news had been on for a few minutes when the camera turned to the main newscaster. His expression was serious.

"We need to ask for the public's help right now. Law enforcement gave us a sketch earlier today. They need to talk to Elijah Moore. He's considered a person of interest. If you know his whereabouts, contact the FBI at this number."

The camera switched from the reporter to the sketch. With a split-screen, the camera went back to the reporter.

"Again, please give the FBI a call." He called off the number once more.

The news turned to sports, and Ashlyn turned off the television and looked his way.

Dylan drew in a deep breath and then exhaled. He knew they were thinking the same thing. Would this end soon, or were their troubles only beginning.

Chapter Nineteen

Ashlyn passed on getting one of Abe's coffees this morning. She'd dropped her keys twice after leaving the apartment, so she finally stuffed them into her pocket. This was ridiculous. The man they thought might be their perp could be somewhere in Maryland and oblivious to what was happening in Texas. As much as she kept telling herself that, she knew in her gut this had to be their guy.

The others were already there. "Anything?" she asked.

"Not a thing," Brad said. "They showed his sketch on TV last night."

"We saw it," Dylan said. "We were hoping that someone would've called in about him."

"This still might not be our guy." Ginny commented.

Everyone turned to look at her.

"Hey, don't condemn me for saying what everyone else is thinking. I want him to be the same guy as much as everyone else, but that doesn't mean we can stop checking every lead."

"She's right," Nolan said.

"Maybe we should get to work," Leah quietly suggested.

"You're right." Ashlyn went to her desk and pulled out the chair.

Dylan went to the desk he'd used since arriving and took a seat. He smiled briefly at her and went to work.

They were checking for people in the area that might've used explosives in their crimes. There were more than she thought possible. Dylan had taken one section of the list, and she'd taken the other. It was tedious going through each name, and they'd come up empty so far.

An hour passed, then two and three. Morning turned to

afternoon. Every time the phone rang, Ashlyn jumped. Everyone was on edge. She tried to concentrate on her list of possible suspects, but her mind kept wandering.

She looked up when Waylon came out of his office. She had a feeling something was up as he hurried down the stairs.

"Our guy is at the police station," he said.

"Someone recognized him?" Dylan asked.

Waylon shook his head. "Believe it or not, he walked into the station of his own free will. When he saw them mention him on the noon news, and then call him by name, he went to the station to find out what was going on. They have him in an interrogation room right now. Dylan, you, Ginny, and Ashlyn, come with me." He turned back to the others. "Brad, Nolan, and Leah, stay here in case we need you here. We'll let you know something as soon as possible."

The drive to the police station seemed to take forever, but it wasn't that far. Waylon talked the whole way.

"Dylan, I want you to go in first and question him. It might shake him up that it's not Ashlyn. If this is our guy, of course. As far as I know, he hasn't confessed to anything."

"But you think it is," Ashlyn said.

"I can't make that assumption, but everything points in his direction." He glanced in his rearview mirror. "Ginny, there'll be a two-way mirror in the interrogation room. I want you to watch this guy's every move and see if you can get a profile on him."

"And me?" Ashlyn asked.

He gave her a crooked smile. "You're our ace in the hole. If things aren't going our way, I'll send you in. But when you take a seat, look at Dylan and smile as if he's someone special to you. If he's as obsessed with you as much as we think he is, he might lose his cool.

Waylon parked, and they went inside. Their team worked with the local law enforcement, so the desk sergeant recognized them and took them to the detective in charge. As soon as they walked into his office, he looked up, then came to his feet.

"You're not going to believe this, but he walked in pretty as you please. He does have a limp, but it isn't that noticeable at first."

"First impression?" Waylon asked.

He grimaced, already knowing why they wanted to interview Elijah. "I don't know. He's a difficult one to figure out. Maybe you'll have better luck. I'll take you to him."

Dylan and Ashlyn looked at each other. She could almost hear him telling her to wait and see what he could learn. Holding back wouldn't be easy, though.

They followed the detective down a long hall and into a room. A man sat in a chair on the other side of the mirror. He wasn't beefy like Albert. Elijah had a smaller frame. His sandy brown hair fell forward, and he brushed it back. His nails were trimmed and clean. His face looked almost boyish.

He wasn't at all what she'd expected. She reminded herself neither Bundy nor Dahmer had been grotesque. Somehow, the sketch had shown harder planes and a more rigid appearance. Suddenly she wasn't quite so sure. She looked at Ginny. The other woman stepped closer.

"He seems calm," she said after a moment, seemingly just as surprised. "I might be able to tell more during the interview."

"Let's hope we get a confession." Dylan left the room and went inside the room with Elijah. He took a chair, his gaze meeting Elijah's, which didn't waver.

"Why exactly am I here?" Elijah asked.

His voice was soft. He wasn't demanding, just asking. Ashlyn tried not to make an early judgment call. Maybe this was his game. Had he lured the women into his murderous web using that same soft voice? She concentrated on Dylan's next question.

"Have you been watching the news?" Dylan countered.

Elijah shrugged. "Most of the time, it's too depressing to watch. I watched it today at noon, though. That's when I heard my name and saw the sketch that resembled me. I didn't know what was happening, so I came to the police station."

"And you have no idea why we wanted to talk to you?"

"No, I don't. I've tried to think if I might have witnessed a crime being committed, but I spend most of my days in my home working on a computer program. That's what I do. I design programs."

"You're originally from Maryland, aren't you?"

He looked confused for a moment. "Yes, I moved here a few years ago." His face turned red. "I've been meaning to get the address changed on my driver's license. Is that what this is all about? If I need to pay a fine, I will. I'll get it taken care of immediately."

"That's not why you're here."

Elijah frowned. "Then do you mind telling me why I *am* here?"

"Have you heard about the three women who were murdered over the last few months?"

His eyes widened. "Yes, but surely you don't think I had anything to do with them."

"Your father had a special mark that he stamped on every one of his bombs. After our current serial killer murdered the three women, he set bombs to go off. We found that same mark on those bombs. Now, do you want to explain how that happened?"

"You know about my father." He rubbed a hand across his

forehead. "I've been trying to outrun the shame of having him for my father all my life. It was one of the reasons I moved to Texas. To try to get away from the disgrace. No one forgets what he did, not that I blame them, but I'm not like him. I was one of his victims, too, when he tested a bomb. That's why I limp."

"Okay, I understand you don't care for your father. Why move to Texas, though?"

He clasped his hands on the table. "Someone I knew moved to Texas and started a software company. He was doing pretty well. He knew about the problems I was having because of my father and offered me a job. I took it."

Dylan leaned back in his chair and studied Elijah. He looked as confused as Ashlyn felt right now. This man was not checking off any boxes that pointed toward him as a serial killer, except that his father was Albert Duncan. That wasn't enough to hold him. He had a pat answer for every question Dylan asked him.

"Maybe it's time I go in," she said.

"Give them a few more minutes," Waylon said.

"You knew one of the victims, Kimberly Braddock. You talked at length with her when you would go to the library."

He downed his head. "I liked her. She was kind and nice. I stopped going to the library after she was murdered. It does something to a person when someone they know is killed. We weren't close or anything, but she always spoke to me. I hated to hear what happened. She didn't deserve that."

"Maybe you thought she should be more than just a friend. You wanted to take the relationship further, and she said no. Did you kill her?"

His head jerked up. "No, I didn't. She was friendly to a lot of people. Are you questioning them?"

"They don't have a father like yours or leave the same

mark on their bombs as he did."

"It wasn't me."

Ten minutes passed. The questioning continued. Then fifteen minutes, and still Dylan wasn't getting anywhere. Waylon turned to Ashlyn. "Go in and see if you can shake him up."

She nodded, then left, knocking on the door to the interrogation room. She didn't wait for Dylan to tell her to come in but opened the door and walked inside. She knew Ginny was watching Elijah closely for any outward signs of recognition.

From her standpoint, there weren't any. She touched Dylan's shoulder, letting her hand linger longer than necessary before sitting in the chair across from Elijah. He didn't say anything, only nodded politely.

She saw no recognition in his eyes, no hint of anger or jealousy when she'd lightly touched Dylan's shoulder. If this was their serial killer, he was damned good at hiding his emotions.

"This is Ashlyn Pillar, another agent."

Elijah's expression was confused for a moment, then his eyes widened. He opened his mouth, then closed it. "You're the one my father tried to..." His voice cracked, and he had to take a deep breath. "Oh God, I'm so sorry for what he did."

She watched all his reactions. He seemed on the level, but it could still be a game to him.

"That's why you think I had something to do with the murders."

"You're the only one that would've known about his signature," she said.

"You're right. My brother and I are the only ones who would've seen it."

They both sat straighter.

"Your brother?" Dylan asked. "Where's your brother now?"

He shook his head, looking down at his hands. "I don't know. I was hoping he would stay in Maryland. We never got along. He was too much like my father." He met their gazes. "He showed up one day at my house not long ago. He never stays in one place very long." He looked between them. "You don't think he had anything to do with the murders, do you? He's not all bad. Not that much like our father. Sure, he can be mean sometimes, but deep down, he has a good heart."

"What's your brother's name?" Ashlyn asked. Why hadn't Albert mentioned him, too?

"David Lewis. We had different mothers." His laugh was bitter. "Like my mother, his never married Albert either. Our father was good about not marrying women. I wouldn't doubt that I have other siblings besides David."

"So you were raised together?" Ashlyn asked.

"No, our father brought him around a few times. Occasionally, he'd dump him on my mother and then take off. We might not see my father for weeks, which didn't bother us. I know my brother and his mother didn't live in Maryland. I'm not sure exactly where they did live. She moved around a lot."

"We want to search your place," Dylan said. "Would you have a problem with that?"

"No, of course not. Do whatever you have to do."

"Excuse us for a moment," Dylan said, and they left the room.

"That throws a wrench into our plans," Ashlyn commented as soon as he closed the door.

"But why didn't Albert mention another son by name?"

"Elijah is probably the one he most dislikes. Maybe in his

sick way, he was trying to protect David, or he's trying to throw us off his scent."

"Yeah, you're probably right." She opened the door, and they joined the others. "What did you take from the interview?" she asked Ginny.

"I don't know. He's not easy to read. He comes across as sincere and looked genuinely upset when he found out who you were, Ashlyn. His remorse seemed real. I think we're going to have to give him the benefit of the doubt, especially if we can find his brother."

"I've already called the others," Waylon said. "I've got them searching through all our databases for a David Lewis. Elijah said his brother is mean. He's bound to have an arrest at some time or other."

"I hope you're right," Ashlyn said. "What do we do now?"

"We search his house." Waylon turned toward the detective. "Do you have some men you can spare?"

"I do, and I'll come along as well. I still don't know about this guy. I don't completely trust him. Maybe he's just too sincere."

Elijah rode in the SUV with Waylon, Dylan, and Ashlyn. Ginny rode with the detective. A police car with two officers followed.

"What about my car?" Elijah asked as they were on the way to his house.

Dylan was sitting in the back with him. "Don't worry about it. We'll bring you back to your vehicle if everything checks out."

They were quiet the rest of the way. Ashlyn noted that the yards were well maintained when they pulled into his neighborhood. Although the ranch-style houses looked older, they were still in good condition.

Waylon pulled into the driveway and the detective parked behind them. The police unit parked on the street. The neighbor next door stepped out of her house and walked toward them. She was older, maybe late sixties, with salt and pepper hair.

"Elijah? Is everything okay?"

"Yes, Mildred." Elijah smiled.

"Everything is fine, ma'am," Ginny told her. "He's helping us with a case. I'm sure he'll explain everything later."

She visibly sighed with relief. "Oh, I feel better now. He's such a good man. Once, when my Fluffy refused to come out of the tree, he immediately came to our rescue and brought her down for me."

As Ashlyn walked toward the house, she knew it looked less likely that Elijah was their suspect. Not that she would rule him out just yet.

They waited for him to unlock the door and then followed him inside. The two officers quickly went through all the rooms and then reported that it was all clear.

"Do what you have to do," Elijah told them. "There are two bedrooms, the kitchen, a small dining room I currently use as my office, and the living room. I have a washroom and, of course, the garage. You're welcome to search anywhere you want, but please, try not to disturb anything on my desk. I'm currently working on a new program."

Ashlyn waited with Elijah. She still wanted to spend more time with him to see if she could figure him out.

"You know, I *am* sorry for what my father did." He looked down at his feet, then back up. "I was the one who called the police and told them where he was. He'd come in after the fact, bragging about what he did. By the time I could call in his whereabouts, he'd already left the house."

So maybe they were judging the wrong man. "No one can

blame you for what your father did," she said. "It's not your fault. He was an evil man."

"You won't get any argument out of me. If David is involved in this, and I pray to God he's not, he was abused, too. Even though our father preferred him over me, he still wasn't kind to David. I hope you'll take that into consideration."

"If it is him, he's killed three women. We'll do whatever it takes to bring him in, alive if at all possible."

He closed his eyes tight, took a deep breath, then opened them. "Sometimes, he scares me, too. I don't know what he'll do to me if I make him mad."

She hesitated, then reached into her pocket and pulled out her card. "If he turns up, give me a call. I'll make sure you're protected."

He nodded. "You're a nice person."

She might have screwed up by giving him her cell number, but she wanted to catch this guy.

They searched the house and the garage and still came up empty-handed. Ashlyn felt as if they were still running around in circles.

"What's the password for your computer?" Dylan asked.

Without hesitation, Elijah gave it to him.

Elijah grimaced. "I hope he'll be careful."

"I'm sure he will. What are you working on?"

Elijah's eyes sparkled. "A game for teens. There are too many violent ones on the market. I'm creating something that will still make them competitive but still fun."

"No guns or bombs going off at every corner?"

He shook his head. "I had enough of that growing up. I'd like kids to have a better childhood experience."

"We need more people who think like you."

He blushed.

He was hard to read, other than what she saw on the surface. His brother David might be a different story.

They returned to the station with nothing concrete. Once inside, Elijah turned to them. "What else do I need to do?"

"Don't leave town," Waylon said. "If your brother gets in touch with you, call us immediately."

"Of course. Am I free to go?"

"For now," Waylon told him.

After he left the station, Dylan turned to them. "He was too damn calm, maybe too nice. Have we just let our perp go?"

"Maybe," Waylon said. "We have nothing to hold him on, but we'll keep an eye on him."

Chapter Twenty

"I told you they couldn't prove anything," David said.

"You've got to stop this madness," Elijah told him. "They're going to catch you," he warned.

David laughed. "If they catch me, they catch you, too. What do you think about that?"

"I've done nothing wrong!"

"Haven't you? Have you forgotten about your mother?"

Elijah began to pace. "You know I had to do it. The men who came to her just wanted her for sex. They used her, and they hurt all of us. Just like Albert hurt us, too."

"It doesn't change the fact you murdered your mother."

"No, no, no! I was helping her. She's in a better place now. What you're doing is wrong."

David's eyes glittered. "What was it like talking to her?"

"Who?"

David snorted. "Who? You know damn well who—your angel. Isn't that how you think of her? Like she's some kind of celestial being or something. She's a woman, nothing more. You know as well as I do that she's screwing Dylan. Can't keep her hands off him."

Elijah stood straighter. "Ashlyn has needs but she'll come to me when the time is right."

"God, I can't believe you're still telling yourself that crap. She's not coming to you. We're going to have to take her just like we planned."

"No, that was your plan, not mine."

"Do you want her or not?"

"You know I do. We're meant to be together, but the time

isn't right."

"So I'll ask you again, what was it like talking to her?"

Elijah sat on the sofa, leaning his head back against it. For a moment, he closed his eyes. "It was everything I imagined. Her voice was soft, almost musical. It floated on the air. I know why she stayed with me when they searched the house. She wanted to be near me. I know she felt the connection between us. Of course, she couldn't say anything. The house was full of officers searching here and there."

"We have to take her. The sooner, the better."

"No, not yet."

"Then I'm going to sacrifice another woman."

"No! Why did you even have to kill Kimberly? I liked her. She was nice to me."

"Because it was easy to take her. She trusted you." He flopped down on the other end of the sofa, stretching his legs out in front of him and crossing his feet at the ankles. "Don't feel too bad for her. I gave her enough drugs that she didn't feel any pain. Remember? She went right to sleep. I even waited until she stopped breathing before dousing her in gasoline."

"I just wanted to take her home. I didn't want her to die."

"We had to make sure everything would work when we take Ashlyn. Kimberly had to die." He sighed. "It went off perfectly, too. Even Dad couldn't have pulled off the explosion as well as I did. He would've been so jealous."

"I don't like bombs," Elijah said. "And I don't like you either."

David chuckled. "But you need me. If I remember correctly, I saved your ass on more than one occasion."

Elijah looked at his arms and the burned marks. He still remembered the beatings with the belt, too. "Not always," he whispered.

"Hey, we're not all perfect, but I have a plan. It's beyond brilliant," David said.

Elijah eyed him warily. "What kind of plan?

With a demented glitter in his eyes, David smiled. That scared the hell out of Elijah.

"You'll see, you'll see."

Chapter Twenty-One

"Three days and still nothing," Dylan said. "I'm beginning to think this David guy doesn't exist."

"Agreed," Brad said as he came to his feet and stretched.

Dylan looked around the room. Long days with lots of hours, and still, they had come up empty-handed. They were exhausted and getting close to being declared brain-dead.

He glanced over at Ashlyn. She'd been pushing herself harder than everyone else. After they went to bed, she would toss and turn. No wonder she was starting to look like she would fall over any second.

"What about your contact in the government?" Leah asked.

"Ethan? Nothing yet. David has no record of any kind. He's still searching for something on him."

"That doesn't mean he doesn't exist," Ashlyn said. "Maybe he just hasn't gotten caught yet."

"Possibly, but not likely," Nolan said.

"Elijah might have tipped him off." Ginny came to her feet, carrying a Styrofoam cup to the trach and tossing it in. "David could've been scared enough to go underground for a while. Once everything dies down, he'll probably start up again."

"Do we still have a tail on Elijah?" Dylan asked.

"Twenty-four hours a day," Ashlyn said. "And we have his phone tapped. There have been no calls in or out, and he's only gone out for fast food a couple of times."

Brad leaned against his desk. "Elijah could've used a burner phone to warn his brother. It would've been untraceable. One phone call and David goes into hiding."

"I hate to admit it," Ashlyn said. "But you're probably

right. Elijah is scared of his brother, but I could tell he still cares for him. He doesn't want to see him hurt. He might've had a moment of weakness and warned him."

Everyone looked up when Waylon came out of his office and stood at the railing above them. "I want everyone to take off tomorrow."

When Ashlyn began to protest, he raised a hand to stop her.

"We're not getting anywhere, and everyone is exhausted. Get some rest and come back Monday. No arguments." He turned and went back into his office.

"He's right," Dylan said. "We keep going over the same things and coming up with nothing new. We still have people searching for anything on David. We'll start fresh Monday."

"Yeah, okay," Ashlyn finally agreed.

He leaned down so that only she heard him. "Good, I'd hate to throw you over my shoulder and carry you out of here."

She sighed deeply. "Maybe I should have argued just a little bit longer." She gave him a saucy wink as she stood.

Maybe she wasn't *that* tired, he thought to himself as he followed her to his pickup. Once they were inside and on the road, she turned to him.

"I'm guessing David was homeschooled, and that's why we can't find any school records on him."

"Probably, now, no more talk about work. We'll go in with a clean slate on Monday and see if we can figure it all out."

"You're right. Besides, David hasn't called to taunt us, so he's probably not going to hurt anyone immediately." She rolled her shoulders. "All I want is food and a hot shower. Not necessarily in that order."

"I can help you on both counts," he said. "Why don't I

drop you off at the apartment, and I'll grab a pizza? While I'm gone, you can take your shower."

"That sounds tempting, but you're just as tired as I am. We could both pick up the pizza."

"You're tempted," he said.

"I am."

"Then it's settled. I'll drop you off at the apartment and be back before you know it."

"Okay, you've talked me into it."

Once inside the garage, he pulled into a parking space and turned the key.

"What are you doing?"

"Walking you to the elevator."

She quirked an eyebrow. "I'm quite capable of riding an elevator alone. I mastered that feat some time ago."

"Humor me."

They got on without another word and rode it to her floor. When they both stepped off and began walking to her door, she gave him a sideways look but didn't comment. Once she'd unlocked her door, he did a quick walk-through.

"All clear. Now I'll go get the pizza."

Except he couldn't resist the temptation as he walked by her. His lips met hers in a fierce kiss. He couldn't get enough of this woman. She tasted like everything he needed in his life.

"Pizza," he mumbled and stepped away.

She nodded. "Pizza," she said but didn't sound quite as sure about what she wanted as she had a moment ago.

Dylan was tempted to stay and eat later, but he saw the exhaustion in her eyes. "I'll hurry."

She nodded.

"Lock up." He stepped out of the apartment and waited until he heard the locks turn. Satisfied she would be safe, he left to grab a pizza.

He liked the idea that she would be a little more relaxed by the time he brought their food back, then sleep. No sex until after she rested. She needed to sleep. This case was starting to get to her. He knew how badly she wanted to catch this guy.

Ashlyn thought she was somehow connected to all of it. That was nonsense, of course, but he didn't think he would be able to convince her of that. She carried the guilt that she might somehow be responsible for the murdered women. There was nothing she could've done. She was doing all she could now to stop him.

Dylan had just pulled in at the pizza place when his phone rang. He glanced at the caller and saw that it was Ethan. "What have you found out?"

"I'm afraid not much. I've searched all the surrounding states' databases for a David Lewis, and nothing. If this guy existed, he's low-key, making sure he stays off the radar. Nothing in Texas either."

"Damn, I was hoping you'd be able to find something that we couldn't."

"Sorry to disappoint you. How's everything else going?"

"Everyone's on edge here. Every time a phone rings, we jump. The time between now and the last murder is getting longer."

"He went underground, waiting for everything to cool down before showing his face again."

"That's what we're thinking, too."

"If he's that obsessed with Ashlyn, she could be in more

danger."

"I'm keeping a close eye on her."

"Is she there now?"

"No, I dropped her off at the apartment complex. It's as secure as Fort Knox. She argued the whole time I walked her up to the apartment. I made sure the rooms were clear and the door locked before I picked up a pizza."

"So, when you say you're keeping a close eye on her, does that mean you're staying in the apartment with her? That's a new development you didn't mention."

Dylan grimaced. "She has a two-bedroom apartment," he finally told Ethan.

Ethan chuckled. "And which bedroom are you using?"

"Screw you," Dylan muttered.

"Be careful you don't get caught like the others."

"Me? Settle down? Not happening. At least, not for another ten years. I like my lifestyle the way it is now."

"So, how is Ashlyn?"

"I'm worried about her," Dylan said, turning serious. "She feels guilty that these women were murdered. This guy told her that she needed to figure out the clues, and then she would understand. After we discovered it was all related to Albert Duncan and when he tried to murder her and her father, Ashlyn feels as if she's partly to blame."

"That's crazy," Ethan told him.

"I know, but I can't get the notion out of her head."

"Maybe something will turn up soon. I'll keep looking for David Lewis, and if I find anything, I'll let you know."

The call ended, and Dylan quickly checked his text messages before he went in to order the pizza. There was one from Ashlyn. He opened it.

On phone with Elijah. Said David has my father. Must meet or he'll kill him. Will keep sending texts as he gives directions.

Dylan slammed the palm of his hand down on the steering wheel. He quickly called her number. Busy signal. He started the pickup as he sent a quick text.

On my way. Stay put.

She immediately texted back.

Can't. Driving. West on Dakota.

She had at least a twenty-minute head start on him. He called Waylon as he took off in her direction. As soon as Waylon answered, he began to talk.

"I left Ashlyn secure in the apartment, but Elijah called and told her that David has her father, and if she doesn't meet him, David will kill Joseph. She took off. Elijah's giving her directions over the phone."

"It's a trap. Call her and tell her to pull over right now and wait till you get there."

"He has her on the phone giving her directions so she won't hang up. All I can do is follow when she texts them to me. I'll pass them on to you."

"I guess that's all we can do. Stubborn, hardheaded." He blew out a breath. "I'll call the team and get them together, then call you back."

Dylan checked his text messages again.

South on Lincoln. East again on Buchanan.

It was another five minutes before he got to Lincoln. He was right behind her and should catch up soon. When Waylon called, he updated Dylan on the directions.

"As soon as the team arrives, I'll get everyone in route. I checked with the facility, and her father has gone missing, so Elijah's not lying about that. The facility where her father stayed tried calling Ashlyn, but her line was busy, so the director sent her a text."

His lips compressed to a thin line. "Damn! She knows Elijah isn't lying about David having her father." He gripped the steering wheel. "Okay, there's nothing we can do about it now. We'll have to keep each other updated. I'll try to get a visual on her car and let you know when I do."

He ended the call and concentrated on his driving. He was going faster than usual and barely made it through a light before it turned red.

Dylan dodged a car that pulled out in front of him, causing the vehicle behind him to slam on his brakes and hit his horn. His heart skipped a beat, but he kept driving.

He turned south on Lincoln. "Soon now, and we'll do this together," he spoke his thoughts aloud. He watched each street sign, slamming on his brakes and leaving rubber when he came to Buchanan. He quickly turned down the street.

He glanced at his text messages. Nothing new. He quickly typed ?'s. Still nothing. After seven minutes, he texted again. No answer. His gut told him something had gone wrong.

Chapter Twenty-Two

Ashland's heart pounded. All she could think about was saving her father. Why the hell had David involved him? It didn't matter. She would get her father back unharmed.

Another text came in from Elijah:

Turn down Walter Street. We're not too far from where David has your father. I've pulled to the side. Get in, and we'll go the rest of the way together.

He'll be suspicious if there's an unfamiliar vehicle with me, and I don't know what he would do.

The hairs on the back of her neck stood up. She realized this could all be a trap, an elaborate hoax to get her away from Dylan. Did she have a choice?

Are you armed? Elijah texted.

Yes

Good, I don't carry a gun. I didn't even think about getting one. I'm still hoping he'll give himself up, but that might not happen.

And then again, maybe he was on the level. She would have to be careful. She couldn't take a chance that Elijah was lying to her. Not when her father's life was at stake.

She turned down Walter Street. Elijah stepped on his brakes so that she would know he was there. She quickly scanned the area. It was a quiet, residential street. Nothing moved. She pulled over, stopped behind him, turned off the engine, and quickly texted Dylan.

Walter Street. With Elijah now. I'm armed. Will keep you updated on directions.

She got out of her car and hurried to Elijah's, getting in on the passenger side.

"We've got to hurry," Elijah said. "I don't know what David is going to do. He's gone off the deep end."

"Let's go." She turned slightly to fasten her seatbelt.

When she turned back around, Elijah shoved a cloth over her nose and mouth, putting all his weight on it to hold it secure. She struck out with her fist and made a solid connection, but his hold didn't loosen.

A setup! Damn it!

Elijah was stronger than he looked. She continued to fight, reaching for her gun, but had to take a breath, and when she did, she inhaled the noxious fumes on the cloth. Her head began to swim, and everything faded in and out. Her last thought before passing out was that she should've waited for Dylan.

Ashlyn didn't know how long she was unconscious, but her head pounded as she returned to awareness. Her hands were tied behind the back of the chair she sat on. She kept her breathing even, and her eyes closed, listening to what was happening around her.

"Why is she still asleep," Elijah whined. "You said the stuff on the cloth wouldn't hurt her."

"She's still breathing, isn't she? She'll wake up soon enough and probably have a headache. Then you'll have your angel." His voice was harder and had more of an edge.

Ashlyn figured this was David, Elijah's brother. She peeked from lowered lids. It was difficult to keep her breathing even when she saw her father tied in a chair. There was blood on the side of his head where they might have knocked him unconscious. His eyes were open, and he was looking around. His confusion apparent.

She wanted to tell him everything would be okay, but she needed to get a fix on her surroundings first. They were in a dining room, positioned at a marble table: beige walls, wainscoting, chandelier—quiet elegance. There was something vaguely familiar about the room.

Then it hit her.

Oh God, they were setting it up just like when Albert tried to kill them. She pulled against her restraints, but the ropes were too tight.

"See, I told you she'd wake up," David told him.

Elijah came into her line of vision. She glared at him. His eye was already swelling where she'd connected with her fist. Good, she wanted him to hurt.

"Why?" she asked. "I was trying to help you." When Elijah brushed her hair away from her face, she jerked her head away. "Don't touch me!"

He frowned. "It had to be this way. You never got the connection between us. We both survived bombs that my father constructed. We were supposed to die, but we didn't. God saved us because he knew we were meant to be together."

"You're wrong. We aren't meant to be together. We survived because we're strong."

His face darkened. "No! We're supposed to be together. You're my angel." He slammed his mouth against hers.

Nausea rose inside her. Dammit, she wouldn't go down without a fight. She bit his lip. He jerked back, blood running down his chin. His hand shot out, connecting with her cheek. It felt as if her head exploded.

Elijah stepped back in horror. "I'm sorry."

"Leave her be!" Her father yelled.

"It's okay, Daddy. I'm fine."

"See, I told you she would only hurt us! She's as bad as our father."

Ashlyn stared at Elijah, except it hadn't been Elijah talking. David had spoken the words, but they came out of Elijah's mouth.

David wasn't in any of the databases. They couldn't find anything on him. It was as though he didn't exist. No record of his mother, no schools...

He wasn't real. Elijah and David were the same person. Had he created David to protect him when his father abused him? Probably. She'd heard of that happening when the abuse was horrific.

"Elijah, you need help," she softly told him. "I can get you that help."

David knelt in front of her. "She's lying," he tossed over his shoulder, then turned back to face her. "If I remember correctly, you said you were going to take me in dead or alive. Not your exact words, but close enough. Well, I blew that plan all the hell."

"Look at me, Elijah. David doesn't exist. He's someone you created in your mind."

Anger turned to confusion. and Elijah jumped up. "No, you're wrong. David has always been there for me. He protected me. He took the abuse for me."

"Then why are your arms scarred from the burns where they put out their cigarettes on you. You're the one they abused, not David, because he doesn't exist. Look at your arms."

"She's only trying to confuse you," David snarled. "Look at my arms. All of the burns that I took for you." He pulled his T-shirt over his head and tossed it away. "Look at my back where he beat me with the belt buckle. The time he used the knife on me. Remember that? You hid in the corner crying like a baby the entire time he beat me. Over and over again. I did this all for you."

Ashlyn swallowed against the nausea rising inside her as she stared at his back. A crisscross of scars from burns, the belt buckle, and knife wounds lacerated his back. The skin puckered where the injuries hadn't healed right. No wonder he'd created David. How could anyone hurt their child like that?

"I'm sorry this happened to you," she said. "What they did was wrong."

David grabbed the shirt, jerking it over his head. When he turned around, his features had softened. Elijah was back.

"I told you David was a good person. He did all that for me and he didn't have to." Elijah smiled. "I have scars as well. My father set off a bomb too soon, and I caught shrapnel in one of my legs. That's why I walk with a limp. I'm proud of my scars because I survived. I knew I had to find you. Be proud of your scars, too."

When he reached into his pocket and pulled a knife, she flinched. He began to cut off her shirt. Dread washed over her as another time haunted her.

"Close your eyes, Ashlyn. Let your mind go somewhere safe where he can't hurt you, sweetheart," her father whispered the same thing he'd told her when Albert invaded their home.

Was that what happened to her father? Had he let his mind take him somewhere safe, and he forgot how to return?

Elijah ran his knuckles down the side of her face. "You really are beautiful. My scarred angel. That's why you kept your arms covered. You knew I was the only one who would accept you."

There was no reasoning with Elijah. He was too far gone. She tried a different tactic. "What are you planning to do with us?"

He looked confused for a moment. "You still haven't figured it out? I thought you were smarter than that. We were supposed to die from an explosion, but we must be together for it to work." He waved his arm. "You see, I've re-created that day when my father went to your home. Soon, we'll be together forever."

"And my father? Why have you brought him here?"

"Because we have to re-create the scene. Your father hasn't been right since the explosion. I'll make him better. He won't ever have to hurt or worry about anything else again. We'll make a family in Heaven. It'll be perfect."

Oh God, he was going to kill them. "How will we be together if you're still on earth?"

He laughed. "But I'll be with you." He looked toward the chair opposite hers. "I left an empty chair. I wasn't going to let you go without me."

She had to stall for time and pray to God that Dylan found them. "But I don't want to die."

"I know what you're going through. I feel it, too. You think it will hurt, but it won't. I'll give us something before the bombs go off, so it'll be like we're taking a nap. When we wake up, we'll all be together in Heaven."

"Why did you kill those other women?"

"I had to practice." His forehead creased. "No, David had to practice. You see, he's helping us. He wanted to make sure we wouldn't be in any pain when it happened. Remember, I told you he took the brunt of most of the beatings. He's very protective."

"Kimberly befriended you. She was going to get married, and you murdered her."

"No, David did. I told him it was wrong. She'd been nice to me." His forehead creased. "He made me watch. Kimberly pleaded and cried, even after I told her everything would be okay because she would go to Heaven. I was sad David used her."

"David doesn't exist," she mumbled.

He met her gaze. "I'm sorry, but I've got to go to the storage shed and get the supplies. I'll be back."

He kissed her on top of the head. She closed her eyes tight as a shiver of disgust threatened to consume her.

She frantically began pulling at the ropes around her wrist as soon as he walked away. She heard him moving around in the house, then a door closed. They were alone.

"The ropes are too tight. I don't know if I can get mine loose. What about yours?" her father asked.

Her head jerked up. Was it just wishful thinking, or had her father sounded lucid? "Dad?"

He met her gaze. "What?" He shook his head. "It doesn't matter. We need to get free before Albert returns."

"Dad, Albert is in prison. He's been there since he broke into our home and tried to murder us. Elijah is his son and he's trying to re-create that day."

He stopped for a moment and looked around the room. "This isn't our house."

"No, it isn't. Remember? Albert set the house on fire. He had bombs that were heat activated. I was able to get loose. I ran to the kitchen and grabbed a knife to cut your ties. You shielded me as we ran out of the house, but there was an explosion. One of the beams overhead fell, knocking you unconscious. I pulled you the rest of the way free." She pulled against her ropes, wrists raw and burning, but she didn't think she was gaining anything.

"No, that can't be right," Joseph said. "I was in my study last night. Looking over papers for a case I'm going to try." He frowned. "His name was Albert, too. He robbed an elderly couple. I swear this man was crazy."

She knew she'd lost him again, but Ashlyn felt sure she'd

had him back for just a little while. "It doesn't matter, Dad. We just have to get the ropes off."

"Of course. Maybe I can tip my chair over and wiggle away from it." He grinned. "I saw it in a movie once."

That was a good idea since she wasn't making headway loosening her ropes. "Let me try. I might be a little more limber."

He nodded. "You can do this."

She smiled. Maybe some of his memory was returning. She only hoped it wasn't coming back in time to realize he was about to die. No! She wasn't going to let that happen. She didn't last time. She wasn't going to this time.

She pushed her chair away from the table so there would be nothing in her way and began to rock her body from side to side. When the chair tilted, she braced for impact. Even though she landed on carpeted floor, it knocked the wind out of her for a moment.

"You did it. I'm proud of you, baby girl."

She sucked in a breath as she tried to wiggle away from the chair. Her father hadn't called her that in a very long time. As soon as she was free from the chair, she rolled to her back and brought her knees to her chest.

She was never so glad for yoga classes as she was right now. She wiggled her hands down and then began to raise them forward, squeezing past her shoes as she strained to bring her arms in front of her. Her labored breathing broke the silence in the room, but she managed to get her arms in front.

There was no time to catch her breath. She jumped to her feet and hurried to the kitchen, grabbing a knife and running back to her father.

"Save yourself. Don't worry about me."

"No way in hell am I leaving you behind. Not last time.

Not this time. We'll leave together." She began to saw through his ropes.

As soon as he was free, they hurried to the front door. She wouldn't worry about her ropes until they were away from the house. As soon as she opened it, her heart sank to her feet. They were in the country. Trees lined the drive leading up to the house. More trees dotted the landscape.

She had no idea how far away the next house might be, but they needed to get out of the open. "The trees," she said, and they took off at a run. She matched her father's stride so she could stay right with him. Still, he was breathing hard by the time they reached the first tree lining the drive.

"Next one," he said after only a moment.

She nodded. They were almost to the road that turned into the property. Once there, they could flag someone down, even though she hadn't seen any vehicles pass.

"Ashlyn!"

She flinched. Elijah stood in the doorway. He held her gun in his hand. She had a feeling David had taken over his mind again. She gauged the distance from where they were to the road. There was a swirl of dust in the distance. A car? Maybe. There was a full moon but it was still hard to see distance.

Her father took the knife from her, quickly cut her ropes, and then handed the knife back. He studied her face in the light of the full moon. "I've been lost for a long time, haven't I?"

"You remember?"

He reached up and lightly touched the side of his head. "Bits and pieces. You and Mindy grew up. I missed a lot. I'm sorry for that."

"It's okay. We'll make up for it."

Her father smiled and shook his head. "Don't let this be

for nothing." He brushed his lips across her forehead and held her tight before stepping away. "I love you both."

"Dad?"

"Run as fast as you can." He stepped from behind the tree and began running back toward the house.

She froze. "No!"

"Run," he yelled.

Tears ran down her face as she took off in the opposite direction. None of this felt right. She could get help, she told herself. Everything would be okay. Don't let this be for nothing, he'd said.

The gunshot echoed over the stillness of the countryside.

She stumbled but quickly righted herself. No! This couldn't be happening. Not now. She sucked back a sob for the time lost, the short time it was found again, and the future they wouldn't share.

Revenge suddenly burned inside her for what Elijah stole. He'd aim his next bullet at her. No, damn it, she wasn't going to die today. She would be an easy target in the open like this. She plowed into the brush at the side of the road, thorns scratching her arms. They would slow her down, but at least she had some cover now.

"Ashlyn!" Elijah yelled. "We belong together!"

Chapter Twenty-Three

Dylan turned down Walters and almost immediately spotted her car. He pulled behind it and jumped out of the pickup. There was no sign of Ashlyn. He looked around the residential neighborhood. All was quiet.

"Where are you, Ashlyn?" he muttered, feeling raw inside.

"Are you looking for the woman that was in that car?"

He whirled around. The older woman had a small dog on a leash and was just leaving her house. "Yes, did you happen to see which direction they left in and what kind of vehicle it was?"

She pointed down the street. "They went in that direction. It was a small blue car, but I can't tell you what make. I'm not good at all with brands."

"That's okay, I think I know the vehicle." He reached for his phone to call Waylon.

"You know, I called 911 about this," she continued.

His head jerked up. "Why?"

"Well, it looked as though they were struggling. I couldn't be sure, of course. Anyway, they said since the car had left, there probably wasn't anything they could do, but they would keep an eye out for a blue car with a man and woman."

"It's a good thing there's a concerned citizen in the neighborhood. You've helped tremendously."

"Is the young woman in danger?" She picked up her dog and held it close.

"I hope not." He raised the phone to his ear.

Waylon answered immediately. "What have you got?"

"I found her car." He continued, explaining what the neighbor had seen. "They're in his car. I know which direction they went, but I'm guessing he made several turns before they arrived wherever he was going."

"I'll get an APB out on Elijah's car. If they're still in it, we'll catch him. Leah and Brad went to his house. No one was there."

"And if they're not in his car, we won't find them. I don't think he would've stayed in it very long. He could've taken her anywhere."

"She's smart, and she can take care of herself. Don't worry, we'll find her."

Dylan wasn't so sure about that. There was a sick feeling in the pit of his stomach. Where would he have taken her? He needed to think.

Something Elijah had said was right there, just out of his reach. He replayed everything that happened the day they interviewed him. Nothing came to mind.

He talked about his brother. The brother no one could find any information on.

There'd been nothing at his house that stood out. He'd told him to search every room and didn't seem bothered they were there. He only had one request. Don't bother the stuff around his computer.

Cold chills swept over him.

"Are Leah and Brad still at Elijah's house?"

"They're just about to leave and join me."

"No, have them stay there. Leah needs to check his computer."

"They didn't find anything suspicious the last time."

"It still may give us a clue where he took Ashlyn and her father. I'll meet them there."

"I'm on it," Waylon told him.

Dylan jumped into his pickup and made a U-turn, heading toward Elijah's house. He arrived at the same time Waylon pulled up. He grimaced when the neighbor lady hurried out of her house. Waylon hurried inside.

"Elijah's okay, isn't he?"

"As far as we know," he said, brushing her off as he hurried toward the house. He stepped onto the porch but turned back around at the last minute. "Mildred, right?"

"Yes." She preened.

"Do you happen to know where he might have gone?"

The woman relaxed and smiled. "Well, I couldn't say for sure."

Dylan stepped off the porch and walked toward her, keeping his smile friendly. "We need to find him. It's very important. Any help you could give us would be appreciated."

She fluttered her eyelashes and raised her hand to her face, giggling like a young schoolgirl. "As I said, I don't know for sure, but he left the front door open a couple of days ago. A package had been left on my doorstep by mistake. I was going to set it inside and then leave, but I thought it could be important, so I took it to his study. I'm afraid I might have scared him because he jumped when I spoke. He had his back to me."

"He was working on his computer?"

She frowned thoughtfully. "I don't think so. He was looking at houses online. I asked him if he was planning on moving because I would hate to see him go. He smiled and said, only wishful thinking. The house was stunning and out in the country. I couldn't blame him for wanting to live on such a beautiful estate."

"Thank you so much. You've been a great help." He

turned and hurried into the house. He stopped in the study. "Have you found anything yet?"

Leah turned. "Only a bunch of houses that he's been looking at."

"Is one of them in the country? It would be an expensive property."

Leah turned back to the computer. "I think there was one."

"Vacant?"

"Checking. Partially furnished. In contract. Yes, it's vacant at the moment."

"Do we have a buyer name?"

"Looking. Holy crap." She turned in her chair. "Elijah Moore. He must've put a hefty down payment to hold it so it would go off the market."

"Just long enough to take Ashlyn," Dylan said. He didn't want to think about what he was planning. "Address?"

She'd already faced the computer. "I'm getting it now." She pushed some keys. "It's about twenty minutes from here. I sent the address to your phone."

"Let's go."

"I'll drive," Waylon said. "The rest of you follow in the SUV.

"I've got my laptop. I'll see if there's another entrance onto the property so we won't be barging in the front door."

"Good idea." Dylan prayed they would get to her in time. Elijah wasn't known for keeping his victims alive very long. They jumped into their vehicles.

"He's planning on blowing up the house," Dylan spoke his thoughts aloud. "That's why he put the big down payment on it.

He didn't want anyone else looking at the property."

The tires screamed as Waylon made the corner. Dylan grabbed the dash to keep from sliding across the seat. He trusted Waylon not to get them killed.

"He's re-creating the scene like his father did fourteen years ago. I just don't know what he hopes to prove," Waylon said.

"Maybe that he's better than his father. He might want him to know that he accomplished what his father couldn't."

"This is one sick family."

"I agree. I'm going to alert the local police. I'll tell them to hang back for now."

Dylan called the area Sheriff's office and spoke to the officer in charge, briefly telling him what was happening. He said they would block the road on both ends down from the house. After he hung up, he relayed everything to Waylon.

His phone began to ring again. "It's Leah," he said and answered the call, putting it on speaker.

"There's a back entrance that will lead up to the house. From an aerial view, it looks like we can get in close enough to park without anyone suspecting we're there." She quickly gave him the coordinates, and he put them in the GPS.

He glanced at his watch. They were still five minutes away. He knew it would be the longest five minutes of his life. They finally turned down a back road. He kept watching for the entrance.

"There!" He pointed. "Over the cattle guard."

They drove for another minute.

"House lights are on," Waylon said and turned off the lights on the vehicle, slowing down. He pulled to a stop and shut off the engine. "We'll go on foot from here."

They got out of the vehicle as the others pulled in behind them. Dylan wasn't waiting. He ran toward the house, only stopping when he was a few feet away and still behind cover. He told himself to think of it as another mission, but it didn't help. Ashlyn and her father were in there, and seconds were ticking away.

All clear outside. He crept up to the back door and eased it open. Once he slipped inside, he stopped and listened. There were no sounds. He didn't like it.

Waylon came in behind him, but Dylan didn't wait. He moved through the house, stopping in the dining room. He took in the three empty chairs, one toppled over. If he had to guess, he would think Ashlyn and her father escaped. He only hoped they had. But if they were on the run, Elijah wouldn't be far behind.

He moved to the front door and eased it open. There were solar lights along the driveway illuminating it. He froze when he saw the body shrouded in the darkness just off the road's edge. Everything in him slowed down. It couldn't be Ashlyn.

All at once, the blood rushed to his head.

"We need an ambulance," he said as his training kicked in, and ran out the door.

He stopped at the body, checking for a pulse.

His head jerked up when he heard a shot fired. Cold chills of dread ran up and down his spine.

"Ashlyn," he whispered, taking off down the driveway at a run.

Chapter Twenty-Four

The road was flat. Ashlyn could see the tiny beads of headlights in the distance. She prayed the vehicle didn't turn off onto a side road. She had to keep moving. Her body trembled—too much adrenaline flowing through her.

A cloud drifted in front of the moon, making it nearly impossible to see. She stepped into a hole, stifling her cry as she landed in a bush full of sharp thorns. It was getting impossible to move forward. What if Elijah started searching on this side? She had to move to the road and take her chances.

Her father needed help. God wouldn't be so cruel as to take him away now. But dammit, she couldn't shake the sick feeling that her father might already be dead. He just couldn't be.

Before stepping from cover, she looked down the road. It was still too dark to see. At least Elijah wouldn't be able to see her either. No lights. The vehicle must've turned off. There would be another one.

Her ankle burned. She grit her teeth and moved as fast as she could, ignoring the pain.

"Ashlyn, stop!"

Cold chills spread over her. God, Elijah was closer than she thought. The lights of another vehicle shone in the distance.

"Ashlyn, you can't run from me. It's God's will."

Trying to reason with him wouldn't do any good. He still wasn't that close to her, and the headlights were getting nearer. She could do this.

The moon came out from the clouds.

A shot rang out.

She was slammed to the ground by the impact of the bullet when it hit her shoulder. She lay there for a moment, drawing in deep gulps of air. Her shoulder felt as if it was on fire. She had to get up. She had to move.

Take a breath.

Breathe.

She pushed to her knees, wobbling, almost losing her balance. She had to get to her feet. Sweat rolled into her eyes. She quickly blinked, looking toward the headlights. The vehicle had stopped.

Why wasn't it coming toward her anymore? Had they heard the gunshot, gotten frightened, and stopped?

She tried to push to her feet, but couldn't quite make it. If she could rest for a few seconds, she'd be okay. She sat back on her heels and reached toward her shoulder, feeling the blood running down her chest.

Staying where she was would be certain death. Ashlyn grit her teeth and forced herself to stand, stumbling forward as the headlights started toward her again. She could make it.

She looked down at every step she took, knowing that it might spell the end for her if she stumbled again.

"Where are you going, Ashlyn?" Elijah's softly spoken words came from right behind her.

She jumped and turned slightly. "Don't do this," she said. Tears formed in her eyes. She didn't want to beg. She'd once told herself that she would never beg if she was in this kind of situation. That was right after she hit the streets as a police officer. She'd been so full of piss and vinegar back then.

"Your father's dead," he said. "It's just you and me now. I told you, we were meant to be together. You're my angel." He raised the gun.

She closed her eyes tight. "I'm sorry, Dylan. I should've waited for you. I know that now. I was so afraid they would hurt my father. I became his protector when he couldn't protect himself. I love you, Dylan."

"No, you don't love him! You love me. Say it!"

She looked at him. "But I don't love you."

"It doesn't matter, we'll be together in Heaven, and you'll learn to love me."

A gun fired. Elijah stumbled into her. She wondered for a moment if he'd killed her. His eyes were wide open, and his brow creased in confusion.

"We're meant to be together," he mumbled.

She pushed against him with the arm that wasn't injured. He stumbled to the side, dropping to his knees. Blood spread across his chest.

"I won't leave without you." He raised the gun.

She took a step away. There was another shot, and Elijah was struck in the head this time. He fell to the ground, eyes still open, but no life was left in him.

The headlights coming toward her grew bigger. Flashing red and blue lights reflected a kaleidoscope of color that bounced off the trees. Just looking at them made her dizzy. She dropped to her knees again, taking in deep breaths of air as she tried to keep from passing out.

"Where are you hurt?"

She looked up, but her eyes blurred. "Dylan?" She smiled. "You found me."

"Yes, I found you, but you were lucky I did. If you ever do this to me again…"

Everything was swimming around her. She knew she wasn't thinking straight. Probably shock. The events of tonight faded in and out, but she remembered one thing clearly.

"My father? Is he… Is he…" She couldn't finish the sentence.

"I think he'll be okay. We've got an ambulance on the way, and it should be here any moment now." He took off his shirt and wrapped it around her. "Is David here, too?"

"There's no David. Elijah created him in his mind."

A man showed up in uniform, gun drawn. Dylan flashed his credentials.

"I stopped a pickup up the road, but when I heard the gunshot, I started this way." He glanced toward Elijah. "Is he the only one who needed killing?"

"Yes, the only one. We have another victim closer to the house. There's an ambulance on the way."

"I'll grab my first-aid kit out of the trunk and be right back." He was gone only a moment. When he returned, he squatted next to her and opened a small box.

"The bullet went in and out. I don't think it hit anything vital," Dylan said as they both applied a dressing to the wound and then wrapped it with gauze.

"I just want to go home," she mumbled. "I'm tired." Exhaustion washed over her. She closed her eyes. She felt someone's fingers checking the carotid pulse at her neck. "I'm not dead, just tired."

Dylan's lips brushed her forehead. "Then rest."

"You took the shot," she mumbled.

"Damn right I did," he said, words thick with emotion.

The next time Ashlyn opened her eyes, she was in the back of an ambulance. She groaned when one of the tires hit a pothole.

"We're not too far away," Dylan said, squeezing her hand.

She pulled at the nasal cannula that tickled her nose. He grabbed her other hand.

"You need to leave the oxygen on," he said.

"Not sick."

"No, you were just shot. Then you went into shock."

"I'm okay now." She opened her eyes and looked at him. He wasn't as blurry as he had been earlier. She glanced up at the IV bag hanging from the ceiling. The fluids going into her vein probably helped.

"We'll let the doctor decide if you're okay or not."

The events of the night came back to her in a rush. "My father?"

"He was in the first ambulance."

"And?"

"Elijah shot him. The bullet grazed his temple, and he lost consciousness. Leah stayed with him and rode in the ambulance. When I spoke to her last, she said he was starting to come around."

She closed her eyes tight. "I was so afraid I'd lost him," she said. "He saved my life."

"Tell me what happened?" Dylan asked.

"I had just started toward my bedroom so I could take a shower when Elijah called. He said David had my father and wasn't sure what he would do. He was afraid he was going to kill him. I should've waited for you."

"That doesn't matter right now. I know he was giving you directions over the phone."

"Yes, and I was trying to get them to you as fast as possible. When I turned on Walter, I saw his car and pulled to the curb. He told me it would be better if we went in his car. Elijah said David might get jumpy if a vehicle pulled up that he didn't recognize."

She drew in a shaky breath. How could she have been so stupid to fall for his story?

Dylan squeezed her hand. "It's over now."

"I need to tell you everything. He pushed a cloth over my nose and mouth as I turned to fasten my seatbelt. I fought back until I had to take a breath. I breathed in whatever was on the cloth and lost consciousness. When I came to, I was tied to a chair. My father was tied to the chair at the end of the table. At first, I thought David was in the room, but I couldn't see him. It didn't take me long to figure out they were the same man. I think it was a way to cope with the abuse."

"I've seen it before in trauma victims. They create someone stronger who can survive."

"When Elijah went outside to the shed so he could set up the bombs, I was able to get loose and set my father free."

"But he came back in before you could get away," Dylan guessed.

"No, we got away from the house. I had my father back for just a little while. He remembered. Elijah had struck him on the head, and I guess that triggered something inside him. Some of his memories returned and what Albert had done that day. When Elijah came to the door and began to yell, my father told me to run, and before I could stop him, he ran back toward the house, drawing Elijah's fire on him instead of me."

She blinked past the tears, but one slipped out. Dylan gently brushed it away.

"I don't know what his condition is or if he'll remember anything."

"We're almost to the hospital. I'll check on him as soon as we get there."

She nodded. But dread filled her as the ambulance pulled under the awning. What if he was back in his own little world that had protected him all these years?

She wondered who she felt sorry for, herself or her father. Even if her father was in his own world, he was comfortable in it and happy. She would take him any way she could get him because the alternative wasn't acceptable right now.

The back doors to the ambulance opened, and her team was there, looking worried. All but Leah, who she guessed was still with her father.

"I'm okay," she told them.

"You were shot," Ginny said.

"But I'll survive."

Dylan and the medic jumped out of the back of the ambulance as the driver came around. They unloaded the stretcher and then began pushing it into the ER.

The doctor met them at the door. Gray hair, a slight paunch, glasses. His name tag said he was Dr. Adams. "I got the report over the radio from the paramedic. Let's go to trauma room three," he said. "I'll take a look and see what we have."

"I'm okay, doctor," she told him.

He raised his eyebrows. "Oh, I'm sorry, I didn't know you were a doctor. If I had known you'd already made a diagnosis, I would have sat back down and eaten the sandwich my wife packed me for dinner tonight. The one I haven't had a chance to eat."

Great, she had one of those kinds of doctors. "I apologize. Please, have a look. I'll accept your judgment over mine."

He smiled. "Good, we're on the same page then."

Once in the trauma room, they helped her move to the cot, and the ambulance crew took the stretcher back out. A nurse came in, shooed everyone out, and closed the curtain.

The doctor turned around and gathered the supplies he would need as the nurse helped Ashlyn off with her bra. She sucked in a breath and grit her teeth as pain spread over her.

"Sorry," the nurse said as she put a gown on her, leaving her left shoulder bare and tying it at the back.

"Ready, Doctor," the nurse said.

"Okay, let's have a look. Had do you feel?" he asked as he removed the bandage.

"A little queasy, a little dizzy. I hurt like hell, but nothing that will kill me. I've never been shot before."

He raised his head and looked at her. "I would imagine it hurts like a son of a bitch."

"You're right, it does."

"Let's give her something for pain. Two milligrams morphine—IV."

"Yes, Doctor." She left the room.

"How's the other guy?" he asked.

Ashlyn figured he was making conversation to help take her mind off what he was doing. "Dead," she mumbled.

"Good, I might get to that sandwich before my shift is over after all."

She couldn't stop her smile. Not that she tried.

The nurse returned and gave her the pain med. "This should work almost immediately."

"Better," she said, closing her eyes as she floated away on a cloud. At least until the doctor began to clean the wound with something that burned more than the gunshot wound. He apologized but didn't stop. X-ray came in and took a picture, and when it was ready, the doctor studied it for a moment.

"It's clean. I'll just put a few stitches in to close it."

She closed her eyes when he deadened the area and began to stitch.

"Once I get through, you'll hardly know you were even shot," he told her.

"What? No bragging rights. I won't be able to say, hey, look where I was shot."

He chuckled. "What can I say? I'm very good at putting in stitches."

He finished before she could get too uncomfortable.

"I'm going to keep you overnight. Just for observation and I want to start you on some IV antibiotics. It's just a precaution." When she started to open her mouth to speak, he continued. "No arguments."

"Fine." Kind of grumpy, but she liked him. Of course, it could be the morphine, too. She would probably like just about anyone right now.

When the nurse opened the curtain, her father was in a wheelchair looking anxious. Leah was right behind him.

"I'm sorry, but he had to see you."

"I'm okay, Dad." She studied him, but she couldn't tell how much he understood.

"He shot you," her father said, looking at the bandage.

"Are you okay?" she asked.

He smiled. "If you're asking me if I remember, the answer is yes. I remember everything. I'm not lost anymore." Leah pushed the wheelchair closer, and they held hands. "I've missed so much."

"Don't worry, we'll make up for lost time."

"They're going to admit him overnight," Leah said. "The

doctor wants to run some tests. Dylan is making sure you have rooms next to each other."

"And exactly who is this Dylan fellow?" her father asked.

She looked up as Dylan walked in. She wasn't about to tell her father they were sleeping together. What did she say, though?

Dylan stepped closer and stuck out his hand. Her father took it, and they shook. Oh God, what was he about to say?

"As soon as we realized Ashlyn was in more danger, I became her bodyguard."

His eyes narrowed on Dylan. Her father had been the best damn lawyer, and he was back.

"Bodyguard?"

"And friend," he added.

Her father thought about that for a moment. "I remember meeting you." He nodded. "I'm glad you were there for her when she needed you."

Ashlyn breathed a sigh of relief. For now, at least, she was in the clear. She wasn't exactly sure what she was going to do tomorrow.

Did it matter? No, it didn't. She had her father back, and that's all that did matter. She would deal with the rest later.

"What about Mindy," her father said. "We should call her."

Ashlyn looked at the clock on the wall. It was already after midnight. "Let's wait until morning. She'd only worry and probably drive down tonight."

His smile was wistful. "I remember her growing up, but it's as though I was surrounded by a fog that wouldn't quite part."

"She loves you very much," Ashlyn reassured him.

The nurse came back in. "We have a room for both of you. Next door to each other, as Dylan insisted. We're ready to take you up."

When her father smiled, Ashlyn returned it with one of her own. His pinched face revealed how much the stress had cost him over the last few hours. She'd caused most of it.

Two more nurses came in. Two for the cot and one for her father's wheelchair. Once they were upstairs, her father reached out and squeezed her hand.

"I'm exhausted. I think I'll go straight to bed. I'll see you in the morning. I love you."

"I love you, too."

As soon as the nurses settled her in the bed, Dylan came in, and the nurses left. He took her hand in his and brought it to his lips.

"Are you really okay?" she asked.

"When I heard the second shot, I thought the worst. I was afraid I would be too late."

"But you weren't," she reassured him.

"Just because this case is over doesn't mean that we are."

"I didn't think it did."

He nodded. "Good, I just wanted to make sure you knew that."

"I do," she mumbled. "They gave me a pain med downstairs."

"She'll need to rest now," the nurse said as she came to the door. "You look as though you're about to fall over, too. Stress will do that. Go home. Get some sleep. We have your cell number. If anything at all changes, we'll call. I promise."

When he hesitated, Ashlyn shook her head. "Go back to my apartment. Get some sleep, and I'll see you in the morning." She yawned, eyelids growing heavy.

"And there's a man outside who said he would drive you," the nurse continued.

He leaned over and kissed her on the lips. "Behave yourself."

"I will," she mumbled.

Chapter Twenty-Five

Waylon didn't say a lot on the way to Ashlyn's apartment. The night guard saw who was in the vehicle with Waylon and waved him through.

"Someone will pick you up in the morning and take you to get your pickup," Waylon said. "For now, we all need to get some rest. They'll keep a close eye on Ashlyn through the night."

"Thanks for the ride." Dylan unfastened his seatbelt and got out, but before closing the door, Waylon began to speak again.

"What you did out there was good. If not for you, I'd hate to think how everything would've turned out."

"I only did what I had to do."

"I'll never know how you got to her so fast or how you saw well enough to stop Elijah from shooting her again, but I'm glad you did."

"Full moon helped."

"Get some rest. You deserve it. I'll see you in the morning."

Dylan nodded and walked toward the elevator. His feet were dragging by the time he unlocked the door to her apartment and went inside. He went straight to the refrigerator and grabbed a beer just as his phone began to ring—Ethan.

"I didn't wake you did I?"

He began to laugh.

"What's up? You don't sound right." Worry laced his words.

"It's over." He quickly filled Ethan in on the details. "I just got back to the apartment." He took a long drink of the beer. The ice cold liquid welcome as it slid down his throat. He released a deep sigh. "So, what did you need?"

"I finally found the needle in the haystack. I just wish it had come sooner," he said. "A report from a social worker when Elijah was about seven mentioned that he had created a fictional brother he called David Lewis. I'm sorry I was too late with the information."

"You never gave up. That's what counts. Elijah is dead. Maybe he's finally found peace."

"Maybe so." He hesitated. "I'm glad you're okay and that everyone else will recover. Will you be coming home soon?"

"No, not for a while yet. I want to make sure Ashlyn is okay."

"She must be one hell of a woman."

"Why do you say that?"

Ethan laughed lightly. "Because you fell in love with her. Get some sleep. I'll talk to you later." Ethan ended the call before Dylan could say anything else.

He took another drink of his beer. Fall in love? No, that hadn't happened. He just cared a lot for Ashlyn. He'd make sure she was okay, and then he would leave and get on with doing whatever the hell he was doing before he came here.

Yeah, he needed to get some sleep. He finished his beer and put the bottle in the trash before going into the bedroom. The bed looked empty. He frowned again. Because it was empty. He quickly shed his clothes and took a quick shower before he crawled beneath the cover. He was asleep almost by the time his head hit the pillow.

Dylan groggily woke up to the smell of coffee. He felt as if he'd been hit by a ton of bricks. He'd never been an early riser. He needed coffee. Ashlyn must've already gotten up and turned on the pot. He shoved the cover away and sat on the side of the bed.

When he looked at his watch, he saw it was barely seven. He glanced toward the window and noted the sun was already up. He stumbled to the bathroom, used the facilities, and washed his hands. He still wasn't awake when he opened the bedroom door and stepped into the living room.

A dark-haired woman stepped from the kitchen with a big smile. "Good morning, sleepyhead..." Her smile slipped as her words came to an abrupt halt. "Who the hell are you, and what have you done with my sister?"

"You must be Mindy."

She disappeared for a brief moment and returned holding a long knife that he knew was razor-sharp. "Again, what have you done with my sister? She never has men in her apartment, especially one in his underwear."

"Really?" For some reason, that made him feel damned good that he'd been her first male overnighter.

"Yes, really, and in about one second, I'm going to punch in 911."

He glanced down when he realized he was still in his boxers. "Let me get some pants on, and then I'll come back."

She shook her head. "No, I want an explanation right now. You're not the first man I've seen in his underwear. Now, explain. Where is my sister?"

"She's in the hospital. She was shot."

Mindy's face drained of color.

"She's going to be okay," he hurried to tell her. "Phone and pants. Be right back." He returned to the bedroom, pulled on a clean pair of jeans and a black T-shirt, then grabbed his phone. He was already dialing the hospital number. As soon as the floor nurse answered, he put her on speaker phone and asked how Ashlyn was doing.

The nurse laughed lightly. "I believe she's ready to be dismissed from the hospital. At least, according to her. We're still closely monitoring her for any signs of infection, but she did very well during the night. We gave her something else a couple of hours after you left because she was restless and said her shoulder was bothering her. She's a very strong woman."

Dylan smiled. "I already figured that one out. How's her father?"

Mindy's eyebrows shot up.

"He'll probably be released later today. He slept like a baby all night."

Dylan knew Mindy wanted to know why her father was also in the hospital. It was time for explanations. He thanked the nurse, ended the call, and then set his phone on the coffee table.

"I could use some coffee," he told her. "Why don't we get a cup and take it to the table."

"Okay, but why is my father in the hospital?"

"Because he was with your sister when everything went down. He was shot, but his was more like a deep graze." He poured two cups of coffee, and they took them to the table, sitting opposite each other. She added cream and sugar to hers.

"I know some about the case my sister was working on," she said. "I think she left out a lot of important details, though."

He closed his eyes for a moment and took a drink of his coffee. A little weak, but it would do. When he looked up, he wondered exactly how much to tell Ashlyn's little sister.

She was pretty, with dark hair and green eyes, but there was something innocent about her, as though the dark side of life hadn't touched her. She was still pretty young, and she hadn't been home when Albert broke into their house and almost killed her father and sister.

"They're going to be okay, right?" She was gripping her cup so tightly that her fingernails blanched.

"Sorry, I'm not a morning person before I've had my coffee." He took a deep breath and began, leaving out the part about her father regaining his memories. He didn't know Joseph's condition this morning or if he'd slipped back into that other world. He didn't want to get her hopes up.

"I can't believe someone shot them," she mumbled.

"But they're survivors."

"Thank goodness for that." She took a drink of her coffee and then looked up with a frown. "Why exactly are you staying in her apartment?"

This was the tricky part.

She tilted her head and studied him.

And she wasn't stupid. She already had that sharp, lawyer-calculating look on her face.

"When we realized Elijah's interest in Ashlyn had become more of a fanatical obsession, Waylon wanted to take her off the case."

She raised her eyebrows. "I bet she didn't like that."

Mindy knew her sister very well. "Not at all. I had come in as a consultant on this case. I know my way around bombs," he explained. "I usually work government missions. I guess you could also say I became your sister's bodyguard."

"I'm glad you watched out for her."

Thank God he'd dodged that one.

"I only have one more question."

"What would that be?" He brought the cup to his mouth.

"Why were you sleeping in her bed and not in the guestroom?"

He choked on the drink of coffee he'd just taken. It took him a moment to be able to take a breath again. It was like he'd thought, she was her father's daughter. "You're going to make a great lawyer."

She smiled. "I'm my father's daughter. He was a great lawyer. I guess his blood runs in my veins when it comes to ferreting out the truth." There was a faraway look in her eyes. "I wish he remembered me, but those times are few and far between. I still like to think he knows I'm going to law school. As Ashlyn says, we take what we can get." She set her cup down and studied him for a moment. "I only have one more thing to say."

He braced himself. She was a better interrogator than some of the guys who went on covert assignments.

"If you hurt her, I'll wait until you fall asleep and then cut your balls off," she said sweetly.

He laughed outright until he saw the look in her eyes. He had a feeling she was telling the truth. For just a moment, he saw a little bit of Ashlyn in her.

"Now, let me freshen up just a bit, and we'll go see my sister and father. Ashlyn has a few questions she needs to answer."

"Better her than me," he muttered. It was Ashlyn's turn to be raked over the coals.

He smiled. He liked Mindy. He had a feeling some unsuspecting man would fall madly in love with her while she wrapped him around her little finger, then raked him over the coals. He wondered if he had any friends he could introduce her to, then laughed.

Chapter Twenty-Six

Ashlyn watched her father closely. Are you sure you should be standing? How's your head?" They'd managed to put a small bandage on it.

"I'm fine," he reassured her. "I'm tired of lying in bed."

She grimaced. "I understand where you're coming from."

Their gazes moved toward the door when it opened.

"Mindy?" What was her little sister doing here? She looked at Dylan for an explanation, but then forgot about everything. How could one man look so damned hot?

"She happened to be in the apartment this morning when I woke up," Dylan said without explaining.

"I told you a couple of weeks ago that I would come for a visit when school let out for summer, and I had everything in order." Her smile was wide. "Surprise."

From the way she said it, Ashlyn had a feeling Mindy knew exactly what was going on between her and Dylan. This could get complicated.

Mindy's voice softened. "Hello, Daddy, it's Mindy," she said as she stepped closer to him.

He grabbed her in a hug and held tight, kissing the top of her head. There were tears in his voice when he began to talk. "I don't guess I can throw you up in the air anymore. You're all grown up."

Mindy leaned back, looking between Ashlyn and her father. Ashlyn looked at Dylan again.

"I didn't know what your father's condition would be this morning. Besides, I didn't think it was my place to say anything." Dylan walked closer to the bed, going around to the far side, and taking her hand in his.

"Can someone explain?" Mindy asked, her words thick with unshed tears.

"The only good thing that came from this," Ashlyn explained, but she knew it would still come as a shock. "Was that Elijah tried to re-create the day Albert broke into the house. He posed as a worker to get father out of his facility, but then had to knock him out. When he came to, his memories were still jumbled, but things were starting to come back. The blow to his head triggered something. Then, when Elijah shot him, the trauma brought everything back to the surface."

"I've missed you, Daddy," Mindy said as she hugged him tight again.

"I've missed both my girls," he told her. He smiled as he brushed Mindy's hair behind one ear. "You look just like your mother at this age. She was so damned beautiful."

"Maybe I should go," Dylan said, suddenly feeling uncomfortable to be intruding.

Ashlyn squeezed his hand. "Don't you dare leave. I probably wouldn't be here right now if it weren't for you. You saved my life."

"I hear you're following in my footsteps," Joseph said to Mindy.

"I'm trying to, but I'll never be the lawyer that you are."

"No, you're going to be better than me."

Joseph heaved a weary sigh as he glanced between Dylan and Ashlyn. Ashlyn could've sworn she saw a slight smile before he looked serious again.

"I'm afraid I'm not used to this much activity in my life. I think I'll go back to my room and rest for a while." He looked at Mindy. "You'll come with me, won't you? I'd like to hear more about your college."

"Absolutely." Before leaving the room, she hurried over to Ashlyn, leaned down and whispered, then gave her sister a big kiss before she hurried back to her father.

"I've got my family back," Ashlyn murmured. "I think my father pulled a fast one, though. He guessed I wanted to be alone with you. I'll have to watch him in the future."

"I like Joseph. I'm glad he has his memory back." He was thoughtful for a moment. "What did Mindy whisper to you?"

She smiled. "That she liked you. I guess the cat's out of the bag."

He slowly nodded. "Pretty much. Now, I'm going to do what I wanted to do the moment I saw you."

Her heart skipped a beat. "What would that be?"

"I'm going to kiss you very soundly." He started to lean down when the door opened.

Ashlyn quickly cleared her throat. "Hello, Doctor."

The doctor looked between them.

She could feel the heat rising up her face. Better to redirect his attention. "Am I going to be released today? The staff has been great, but this is still a hospital, and I'm ready to go home. I feel fine."

"I'll just check your wound and see how it's doing before making any decisions."

Dylan stepped away from the bed as the nurse came in with supplies. She set everything on the bedside table and then moved it closer to the doctor. He cut the bandage away and examined the entrance and exit wound.

"Very clean. No signs of infection. If I do say so myself, those are great looking stitches. There won't be much of a scar. No bragging rights here." He smiled at her, and she returned it with one of her own.

"So, I get to go home today?"

"I usually like to keep my patients a couple of more days, but as long as you promise to take care of your wound and to watch for signs of infection, then your regular doctor can see you in six weeks if there are no problems before then."

"And my father?"

"As long as he's feeling fine, he can leave. I've spoken with the staff at the facility where he's been staying. Their consulting doctor wants to test his cognitive abilities and set him up with an MRI. From what little I've seen, I don't foresee any problems. He'll probably be there for another week or so, which will give you time to start looking for other arrangements that will be more comfortable. I like your father. Nice man."

"Thank you for everything."

"Of course." He looked at Dylan. "Now you can kiss her."

The nurse snickered as she gathered up the supplies and followed the doctor out of the room.

"Am I that obvious?" Dylan asked.

"Apparently, we both are."

He leaned down just as the door opened. Ashlyn was starting to feel his frustration.

Mindy came into the room. "The doctor is with Dad. I can't believe we've got him back." She looked at Dylan. "We're so grateful for what everyone did to get this killer. It could've been so much worse."

"It was a team effort," Dylan said.

They spoke for a few more minutes, then Mindy excused herself to get a soda from the machine down the hall.

As soon as the door closed, Dylan turned toward her. "Alone at last." He leaned down just as his phone began to ring.

He muttered something indistinguishable and answered. "What?"

His expression immediately grew serious. Ashlyn wondered what was going on when he ended the call.

"I have to go. Duty calls. Damn, I'm sorry about this."

"No, I understand." And she did, but that didn't mean she wasn't disappointed. "It's your job."

"I'll be back as soon as I can." He leaned down then and, very careful of her shoulder, kissed her soundly on the lips.

He was out the door before she could tell him to be careful, that she would miss him, or that she loved him…

She laughed. Love? That might be stretching it a bit. Dylan had saved her life, but that didn't mean she loved him. The pain meds must still be in her system.

"Where'd Dylan go?" her father asked as he and Mindy came into the room. "I saw him going toward the elevator. Looked to be in a hurry."

"He works for the government, and they called him to come in," she said.

"Dad's been released," Mindy said.

"It looks as though we'll both be going home today." She knew her smile was weak at best.

Except it was another two hours before they left the hospital. In between the time Dylan left, and leaving the hospital, Waylon dropped by. He'd met Dylan downstairs and given him the keys to his pickup.

"Until you get the all clear from your doctor, don't come back to work. Rest, take it easy. We have counselors on hand if you need to talk."

"I don't," she reassured him.

He nodded. She knew he was uncomfortable being in a

hospital.

"I'm glad you and your father are going to be okay. If you need anything, just let one of us know."

"I will. Thanks for stopping by."

He quickly left. Brad and Nolan dropped by next, looking as uncomfortable as Waylon had looked. They stayed about the same length of time as well. Leah and Ginny were next, bringing flowers. Before they left, they reminded her about their girls' night out as soon as she felt up to it. She told them she wouldn't miss it.

Mindy studied her for a moment after they left. "I think Dylan has been good for you."

"What do you mean?"

"Before he came along, you never went out. I think I like him more and more."

She picked at the bedspread. "Don't get too used to him. I doubt I'll see him very much."

"No, I'm pretty sure you're wrong there."

"You still believe in fairy tales and happily ever after, too. It doesn't always work out that way."

Mindy grinned. "I don't know. We never expected Dad to get better and look at him now. Speaking of which, I'll check on him."

"But Dad is the exception," she whispered, turning her face to the window.

Ashlyn was finally released, arm in a sling, which already seemed cumbersome. Without it, her shoulder ached. She supposed she could put up with it for a while.

It seemed strange to be going back to her apartment without Dylan. Both their jobs could be demanding. But that didn't mean she missed him any the less.

Neither she nor Mindy were willing to take their father back to the center. At least, not right away. He was very agreeable to visiting a while longer.

Once they were inside the apartment, Mindy fixed them a glass of tea and brought it to the living room. Her father took a long drink, closing his eyes and savoring the taste.

"Just like Betty used to make."

"She was the one who taught me," Mindy told him. "She retired when we went to live with Grandmother. We still exchange Christmas cards."

"I have something I started a long time ago," Ashlyn said. "Grandmother is the one who encouraged me to put it together. She believed that you would come back to us one day. She said this would help. I'll be right back."

"Is it something I can get?" Mindy asked with concern in her voice.

Ashlyn smiled at her little sister. "Keep your seat. I can get it."

She opened her closet when she got to the bedroom. There were six albums on a shelf. She chose the first one and carried it back to the living room, handing it to her father.

"I have five more albums. I started this first one when we realized you might not get your memory back for a while."

"I'd forgotten about the albums," Mindy said.

Ashlyn moved to sit on one side of her father, Mindy on the other. The first page was a picture of their grandmother and mother.

"I remember that my mother passed. I wish… Well, she knows." He lovingly traced the image of his wife. "See how much she looks like you, Mindy."

He turned page after page, watching his daughters grow up. The sports they'd played—the academic achievements. Ashlyn graduating high school with honors, then going to college. Mindy graduating, also with honors. His mother's tombstone. All life's memories in six albums.

"This is a wonderful gift you've given me," he told Ashlyn.

"It was grandmother's idea. Mindy and I both worked on them over the years."

"That was very thoughtful of all of you."

The day turned to evening, and they went out to eat before taking their father back to his place. The nurse and administrator greeted them, apologizing profusely. They promised nothing like that would ever happen again in one of their facilities. Ashlyn hoped not. She wanted to blame them, but she knew how determined Elijah had been. Once their father was settled, they promised to see him tomorrow.

"I can't believe everything turned out so well," Mindy said on the way home. "I know it has been a long day. How do you feel?"

"Tired, but I'm glad this case is over."

"Too tired to talk?" Mindy asked as she pulled into a parking spot at Ashlyn's apartment.

"About what?"

Mindy turned off the key and looked across the seat. "I thought we'd discuss the weather. What do you think? I want to know more about Dylan."

"I was afraid that was what you meant," she grumbled as she got out of the car. She supposed she didn't really mind.

Once they were in the apartment, Mindy poured herself a glass of wine and Ashlyn a glass of tea since she was still taking pain pills. As soon as Mindy sat down, she began to ask questions.

"Do you love him?"

"Of course not. We barely know each other."

Mindy was thoughtful for a moment. She took a drink of the wine. "So, he's just a fling?"

She frowned. "Of course he's not a fling."

"Okay, then what is he?"

"A friend."

Mindy laughed. "With benefits."

"It's not like that."

"You've fallen in love, haven't you?"

"Of course not."

Ashlyn's phone rang. She scooped it off the coffee table and quickly answered. "Hello?"

"I wanted to make sure you made it back to the apartment okay," Dylan said.

She smiled as warm tingles spread over her. "Yes, just fine. What about you? Do you know how long you'll be gone?"

"Not yet, but we're going out of the country. I can't give you any exact details. I miss you already, though."

"I miss you, too."

"Hey, I've got to go. I'm not sure when I'll be able to talk to you again."

"I understand."

He hesitated. "Bye."

There was a click on the other end. She brought the phone down to her lap.

"Wow, you have it bad for the guy," Mindy said.

Ashlyn started to tell her she was mistaken, but now, she wasn't quite so sure. "I think I'll head for bed. I'm kind of tired. I'll see you in the morning."

"Just know, I'm pretty sure he feels the same way."

Did he? She couldn't be as sure as Mindy.

But as the weeks passed, Ashlyn was even less sure. There'd been no word from him. Her father had been given the all clear. When Mindy spoke with one of her professors, he was excited to hear her father lived in San Antonio. He wanted to know if her father would be interested in doing a few guest lectures. He was thrilled with the prospect of speaking to the students. They'd left a few days ago for Austin. He would stay with Mindy at her apartment.

Ashlyn suddenly felt very alone. Going out with Ginny and Leah only made her more depressed, but she was good at pretending everything was great. She had a feeling Ginny saw through her act.

That was probably the moment she realized how much she loved Dylan.

Chapter Twenty-Seven

"It always surprises me what people will do to other human beings. I hate human traffickers," Samson said.

"We all do," Ty agreed.

"I'll be glad to get home to Macey and Rachel."

Breaker moved to the back of the plane, starting another pot of coffee. "And me Savannah. She has her hands full with the baby. Who would've ever thought two-year-olds could move so fast and cause so much damage in a short period of time." He shook his head. "Anyone call home yet?"

"No," Ty said. "I wanted to wait until we were closer to home. Damn, I've missed Raven."

Everyone looked up when Carter came to the back. "What? I've got it on autopilot. I wanted some coffee. And yes, I'm ready to get back to Alana, too."

Everyone looked at Ethan and Dylan. Dylan suddenly felt as though he had ants crawling all over him. He looked at Ethan. He rolled his eyes. Yeah, Ethan knew what was going on. They were about to get *the talk*.

"Are you going to see Ashlyn when you get home?" Carter casually asked.

"Listen, I like the woman, but that's it." Dylan wasn't about to admit to any more than that. He was already shifting in his seat. "It is not like that with us. Not what you guys have."

Ty smiled. "You know you're in love with her. I don't know why you won't admit it. I mean, we're like your brothers. You can tell us anything."

Ethan laughed outright at that. "Yeah, like the time I was dating that cute little blonde from Dallas? Remember, we met her in the bar that night, right after the mission, when we were in Mexico. You guys just knew she was the one for me. You practically shoved me down the aisle toward the preacher."

Samson frowned. "I liked her. Whatever happened to her?"

"She went back to her husband."

"She was married?" Carter asked with raised eyebrows. "I didn't know that."

"Neither did I," Ethan dryly replied. "She told me right after we had sex the first time. She wanted to get even with her husband, who just happened to be a professional wrestler. Ever hear of the Bruiser?"

"I think I saw him once. He looked like a freakin' giant," Samson said.

Carter had started back up to the front. "Bigger than you?"

"A lot bigger."

Dylan smiled to himself. Samson was the gentle giant. He wouldn't hurt anyone, unless he was on a mission or someone threatened his family. That's when the grizzly in him woke up. They were all a good bunch of guys.

Breaker, with his Cajun heritage, grew up in the swamps until he ran away from home when he was just a boy. Carter, was the son of a senator. This was his plane. His family was old money, and he inherited a shitload. Ty, the health nut who was always so serious. Then there was Ethan—lover boy. Women went a little wild when he walked into a room.

These guys were his friends, his brothers.

Ethan stretched his feet out in front of him. "I was putting my shoes on as I ran out the door. I don't mess with angry husbands. Or married women if I know they're married."

When Dylan looked at Ty, he saw the speculative gleam in his eyes. Oh God, it wasn't over yet. He was hoping they would just drop it.

"You're pink," Ty said.

"Excuse me?"

"The aura surrounding you is pink. The color that surrounds you right now means you're in love. It has to do with your chakra."

"You know I don't buy into any of that stuff. Besides, I don't see any pink anywhere."

Ethan sat forward. "Wait a minute. I think I see it, too. Yep, you're in love." He laughed at his joke.

Dylan sent him a look that should've had him quaking in his shoes. Ethan only smiled wider. "You're so full of bull. And just FYI, I'm not in love with anyone."

"How do you feel when you're away from her?" Breaker asked. "Does it make you a little queasy when you think about her?"

"And does your pulse speed up?" Samson asked.

Ty's expression turned sad for a moment. "And when he shot Ashlyn, did you feel your whole world collapsing around you?"

Dylan knew Ty was thinking about the time Raven had been shot. Was that how he'd felt?

"You guys are crazy," he muttered, but without much conviction. "I'm going to catch some shuteye before we land." He promptly closed his eyes, stopping any more conversation about his love life.

He was not in love. He had at least another five years before he settled down. As soon as he closed his eyes, he thought about Ashlyn. His pulse sped up, and yes, he felt a little queasy, but he also hadn't eaten today. It was almost lunchtime. That didn't mean he was in love.

He probably wouldn't even go to San Antonio. He might

call her to let her know he was safe and home. That would be the courteous thing to do, and he'd ask how she was doing. After all, she had been shot.

He gripped the armrest tighter as that night filled his memories. God, he'd thought he'd lost her. The light from the full moon had shown down on her and Elijah. His gun pointed at her head. One wrong move and Elijah would pull the trigger, ending Ashlyn's life. He didn't know what he would've done in a world without her.

His eyes suddenly flew open. When the hell had he fallen in love with her?

***

After the plane landed, they headed toward their parked vehicles. Before Dylan could get into his pickup and make his escape, Carter called out to him.

"Where are you headed? I thought maybe you'd like to come to the ranch and spend a few days. You know, kind of rest up."

"No, but thank you," he called over his shoulder, not slowing down.

"You could come to Louisiana," Breaker said. "We could have us a party, maybe a shrimp and crawfish boil. You haven't had good food until you eat Cajun. My grandmamma and cousins can cook us up some good food. What say you?"

When Dylan glanced over his shoulder, Breaker was grinning like an idiot. What the hell were they doing?

"No, but thank you. Before anyone else asks, I appreciate the invitations, but no thank you."

They had leaned against Breaker's pickup. All of them were grinning now.

"So, where are you going?" Samson asked.

He looked at each one of them. How the hell had they known before him? "If you must know, I'm going to see Ashlyn. Yes, I've missed her, and before you ask, my pulse speeds up, and I get a little queasy when I think about her. I hope you're satisfied."

"Take her some flowers," Samson said. "Women like that."

He shook his head. "Whatever." But he was smiling as he got in the pickup.

Although flowers were a good idea when he thought about it. He glanced at his watch. It was lunchtime. It would take him about twenty minutes to get to her apartment. The pizza place wasn't that far away either. He started his pickup and backed out of the parking space as he pulled his phone out of his pocket. He quickly called into the pizza place near her apartment complex. If he wasn't mistaken, there was a flower shop nearby.

When Dylan was in front of her apartment door, he realized that he should've called first. Maybe the flowers weren't a good idea. What if she was allergic to them?

This was ridiculous. He knocked on the door and waited.

And waited.

Was that music playing on the other side of her door? Maybe she was with someone. A man? He hadn't been gone *that* long. It could be coming from the apartment next door. Yeah, that was probably it.

He was still waiting for her to answer the door.

Had she gone back to work? It had been a month since she was shot. He could surprise her when she got home from work. Have the flowers in a vase sitting on the table. Maybe not the pizza, though. They could go out for dinner. That would be nice. Kind of romantic. Women liked that. Besides, he was so hungry he could eat the pizza by himself.

Damn, he was brilliant. He still had the key she'd given him, so he unlocked the door and went inside, closing it behind him. No, the music was coming from Ashlyn's apartment. He could hear her in the kitchen banging pots and pans and cursing. His nose wrinkled as he caught the scent of burnt eggs.

What the hell was she doing?

Dylan set the pizza and flowers on the coffee table and sauntered toward the kitchen. He stopped at the doorway. She had her back to him as she stood at the stove. There were slimy, cracked eggshells on the counter and she'd dropped one on the floor. The yolk stared back at him like a huge yellow eyeball.

She was attempting to flip what might've been an omelet at one time but just looked like a big mess. He wasn't that interested in what she was trying to cook. No, he was more intrigued by what she was wearing—or *wasn't* wearing.

His gaze slowly roamed over. She had on one of his white T-shirts that barely reached mid-thigh. When she dropped the spatula and bent to pick it up, he almost lost it. She wasn't wearing anything under the T-shirt, and he had a great glimpse of her bare ass cheeks. He could feel the front of his jeans tightening.

She quickly straightened and tore off a paper towel, wiping the spatula clean. "I'm going to make this omelet even if it kills me," she muttered.

He leaned against the door jamb, watching her. Damn, she looked cute and sexy as hell. And yes, his pulse had sped up the minute he laid eyes on her again and he felt a little queasy.

She suddenly turned, her eyes growing wide. "You're here," she said.

He straightened, looking all serious. "I'm the omelet police, ma'am. I got a call that said someone in this apartment was murdering eggs."

She dropped the spatula. It clattered to the floor as she ran toward him. "I missed you so much," she said as she threw her arms around his neck.

Dylan knew this was where she was meant to be—in his arms. He pulled her tight, grasping her ass, lowering his lips to hers. She tasted like the sweetest nectar on earth. He didn't know how he'd ever lived without her.

When the kiss ended, he continued to hold her. "I've missed you so much, too." He leaned back and looked into her eyes. "Somewhere along the way, I fell in love with you." He held his breath, waiting for her to say something.

"I love you, too."

That's what he wanted to hear. He picked her up, careful of the egg still on the floor, he turned off the burner.

"I'm afraid lunch is ruined. I'm not much of a cook. I hope you weren't hungry."

He grinned. "That's okay. I brought pizza."

She sighed. "I love cold pizza."

They were both laughing as he carried her into the bedroom.

I hope you enjoyed Explosive. Continue reading for a sneak peek at Lethal, book five in this series.

Lethal

Chapter One

Ethan raised the glass of now lukewarm beer to his lips. He'd been nursing it for over an hour and was getting restless. When was Scorpion going to show?

He and Carter had chosen a table in a dimly lit corner of the upscale club so they could observe the other patrons without being obvious. Carter looked comfortable surrounded by suits as corporate America drank their wine, highballs, martinis, and beer from a glass rather than a bottle, but then, Carter was the son of a prominent senator. He'd grown up around this stuff. Of course he'd be comfortable.

On the other hand, Ethan was from middle-class America and liked his beer in a bottle. Still, he could adapt to any situation while on a mission. It didn't hurt that he liked everyone on the team—all ex-special ops who now worked for the government. No matter their background, they were like brothers: Carter, Breaker, Samson, Dylan, Ty, and him.

"Are you sure Scorpion is going to be here tonight?" Ethan asked, keeping his words low so that only Carter heard him.

"That's the Intel I got," Carter said, his words low as well. "My contact said Scorpion would be wearing something red."

"Well, I don't see anything red."

"The night is still young. Have patience."

Patience? Yeah, he didn't have much of that. He didn't like being in the dark either. No one knew what this Scorpion looked like. He always worked deep undercover. Scorpion was a ghost. The rumors were wide and varied. All Ethan knew for sure was that Scorpion was damn good at his job. This time, Scorpion would blow his cover to some degree just to catch El Diablo, the devil. No one knew what he looked like either.

His gaze slowly scanned the room. He couldn't picture any of the men sitting at tables or at the bar as being the murderous drug lord. No sane person would tangle with him. Betray El Diablo and all they would find of your body would be pieces and parts. The man was legendary for his torture techniques. Anyone would be a fool to cross him.

But who was El Diablo? Not one man stood out to Ethan. There were two men at one table who constantly looked around. They didn't quite fit the image of the other clientele in the club. Yeah, they wore suits, but they didn't look comfortable. One guy kept tugging at his tie. These two guys had been nursing beers for about as long as he and Carter had been nursing theirs.

"What about the two men at the table near the bar?" Ethan asked.

"I've been watching them, too. Bodyguards, maybe?"

"That's what I've been thinking, but who are they guarding?"

Breaker was tending bar, but looked up and met Ethan's gaze. Ethan gave a slight nod toward the two men. Breaker smiled at a young woman just sliding onto a barstool, but pulled at the cuffs of his long-sleeved, white shirt to let Ethan know he agreed.

His gaze moved to Dylan, who casually leaned against the bar talking to a brunette. When their gazes met, Dylan's slid toward the two men, and then back to him. Ethan tugged on his ear to let him know they were in agreement.

Ty blended into the shadows, leaning against the wall, but gave an almost imperceptible nod to let Ethan know that he knew the two men didn't belong in this particular nightclub. Samson wandered through the room, acting as a bouncer. No one would mess with him. Most of the time, he was a gentle giant, but piss him off, and he became a grizzly bear ready to attack.

The whole team was here, and they would have each other's back.

As long as Scorpion showed. He was starting to doubt the man even existed. Maybe he *was* a ghost.

The door suddenly swung open. A woman stepped inside, then stood there for a moment, surveying the crowd. She wore a slight smile, as if she knew the effect she had on people—men, to be exact. Her blonde hair was piled on top of her head, with stray tendrils framing her face. Her features were delicate with pouty, full lips—the kind made for kissing.

Ethan's gaze slowly roamed over her. The red dress molded to each one of her delicious curves, the deep vee showing off the generous swell of her breasts. She had a small waist, gently rounded hips, and a dancer's legs—long, lean, and made for wrapping around a man's waist. The red stiletto heels she wore had to be at least five inches high.

Ah, hell no. He met Carter's gaze. "This can't be Scorpion," he muttered.

Carter gave a slight shake of his head. "My contact didn't say whether Scorpion was a male or female. I didn't think to ask."

They could still be wrong about this woman being the badass, deep undercover operative. Maybe she just liked wearing red.

The woman in question moved with a slow seductive sway toward one of the tables, but as she passed near theirs, she met Carter's eyes. She would've been given their identities and would know what they looked like on sight. Right now, she held his gaze for a moment longer than necessary.

A man sitting near the possible bodyguards came to his feet with a smile. She stopped in front of him, then casually placed her hand on his arm, tapping her index finger twice—her sign to let them know he was El Diablo. Before she sat down, she briefly glanced their way again.

Ethan had overlooked the man she was meeting when he first scanned the room. The guy reminded him of someone overworked and underpaid. Wearing a slightly rumpled suit as if he sat at a desk all day, he was someone you wouldn't look at twice. Maybe that was why no one had caught El Diablo until now.

Carter must've thought the same thing about Scorpion being a female because he looked surprised as hell. Then he gave the signal to move in. If they played their cards right, no one would get hurt. As Scorpion took her seat, she dropped her clutch to the floor.

When El Diablo stooped to pick it up, the team moved forward. They wanted to take him down as quietly as possible without anyone in the club getting hurt.

Like a well-oiled machine, they converged at the same time. Samson and Breaker each grabbed a bodyguard. Samson held his in a vice-like grip while Breaker wrestled his to the ground, the man's gun sliding across the floor. At the same time, Ethan lightly gripped the female's arms while Carter and Dylan grabbed El Diablo. Ty stayed in the background to make sure there weren't more men.

"What is this? I demand answers now!" El Diablo said.

"Sergio? What's happening?" the woman in red asked.

The men and women in the club began to scramble from their seats and pour out the doors. They didn't know exactly what was happening, but they weren't about to stick around to find out. Smart people.

"You're under arrest for drugs, human trafficking, murder, and whatever else we can think of to pin on you," Carter said as he fastened handcuffs on El Diablo.

Genuine concern showed in the drug lord's eyes when he looked at the woman, and then he turned back to them. "If you know what's good for you, you'll release us," he growled.

"Now, why would we do that?" Ethan asked with a smile as he fastened the handcuffs on the woman to preserve her identity. Damn, she smelled good, exotic.

"He's right, you know. We'll have bail posted within the hour," she sneered.

"Cher, did you think you'd be going to a regular jail?" Breaker asked. "No, we have a special place for the two of you."

"I'm sorry," El Diablo said to her. "I thought this was a secure meeting place. I'll find the traitor and take care of him. Don't worry. They can't keep you locked up. They have nothing on you."

Ethan looked toward the door when it opened again. The lead agent acting as their backup, came inside.

"The other agents are waiting outside—good job taking down this scumbag. We can take him off your hands. They'll both be going to separate, secure locations for questioning."

Samson and Dylan went with him as they led El Diablo out. Ethan unfastened her handcuffs as soon as they were out of the club.

"I think we kept your identity intact," he told her.

"I just wish it was over."

"Excuse me?" Carter asked. "That was El Diablo, right?"

"Oh, that was him, all right. Also known as Sergio Martinez. I'll go into more detail as soon as the other two return."

They didn't have long to wait. As soon as Samson and Dylan came back inside, she began to explain.

"It'll be easier if you know my name rather than calling

me Scorpion. I'm Stormy St. James."

And quite unexpected. What was she? Maybe twenty-eight, twenty-nine at the most. He'd expected an older agent—forties maybe. Few people surprised him. She'd shocked the hell out of him.

He quickly introduced the team, and she continued.

"Sergio has been running his whole operation from an estate in Dallas." She went behind the bar and grabbed a bottle of beer, twisting off the cap and tossing it to the side. She took a long drink before continuing. "I was acting as one of his drug buyers. We were supposed to be setting up a drop tonight." She came back around and scooted gracefully onto one of the barstools, crossing her legs.

Ethan didn't know about the rest of the team, but he couldn't take his eyes off her. How could she make going behind the bar and getting a beer, then sliding onto one of the barstools, so damned sexy? She acted as though she took down major drug lords all the time. Hell, from her reputation, she probably did.

"There are more men ready to take Sergio's place. They'll make sure everything runs smoothly until they know he's completely out of the picture. Once they know he won't be coming back anytime soon, they'll go in for the kill, and whoever comes out on top will take over the whole operation. There's no real loyalty in the drug business."

"So, what are you proposing?" Carter asked.

"I've only been on his estate a few times, but I know he keeps all his files on a computer. If we can get to them before someone has a chance to destroy them, we can shut down his entire operation. We can make it so no one will be able to take Sergio's place." She took another drink of the beer.

"And your plan?" Carter asked.

"A raid on the estate. I couldn't get deep enough into his

computers. I know he encrypts his files. If I can get to them, I think I can decode them." She shrugged. "It's one of my specialties. Computers, not so much."

Ethan closed his eyes for a moment. He had a feeling he knew what was about to happen. His month long vacation with a hot flight attendant on a private island slowly faded. How many times had he envisioned Carmen running naked along the beach? Too many times to count.

"Ethan is our computer genius," Ty spoke up.

Ethan glared at him. Ty knew about his vacation plans. Yeah, Ty looked all innocent now, but he would bet his last dollar that he was laughing on the inside.

"Then we're all set," Stormy said.

Ethan supposed it could be worse. The lady was hot.

She turned just in time to catch his speculative gleam. Her eyes narrowed.

"We'll be staying at Sergio's estate. This won't be a vacation. We'll be working." Her gaze slowly slid over him before returning to his face. "*All* we'll be doing is working."

When her phone began to ring, she reached inside her clutch and brought it out, walking away from them for privacy.

Ethan frowned. She was all business. Completely unaffected by his charm. Damn, that was a first. He looked at the others. "That sounded like a challenge to me," Ethan said with a grin. "What about you?"

Samson snorted. "Sounds like this one has your number."

Ty nodded. "I got the same impression."

Breaker grinned. "You gonna need some of my Cajun charm to win this one over."

Ethan laughed. "You think that might work?"

"Never hurt in the past."

"I think you might have met your match," Dylan agreed with the others.

"Oh, ye of little faith," Ethan said.

"You'll be there to work. Don't forget that," Carter reminded him.

"Of course I'll be there to work," he scoffed. He still couldn't help but wonder why she didn't seem to like him. That had never happened. Maybe it was the new cologne he wore. Yeah, that could be it.

***

Stormy knew Ethan's type. He was a player. He probably told women up front that he didn't do long-term relationships. Even then, he would break hearts.

If he thought she'd jump into his bed, he'd be disappointed. She'd met his kind before and wasn't about to fall for his game. They'd be going to the estate to work. She'd been undercover way too long not to end Sergio's operation.

After ending her call, she strolled over to the table where they had all gathered, grabbing a salt and a pepper shaker on the way by to use as props. "There's a guardhouse at the front gate. There will be one man on duty, and he'll be armed. Once he opens the gate, there's a short drive up to the main house." Stormy moved the saltshaker to where the house would be. "There's a guardhouse to the right and a little bit to the back of the main house. He'll have six armed guards, but not all of them will be in the house. They usually roam around the estate." She moved the pepper shaker there.

"And inside?" Ethan asked, all business now.

She met his gaze for a brief moment, then turned her attention back to the table. "He has one person on the inside— also armed. These men will shoot to kill. It's not that they're loyal to Sergio but more that they fear him. With good reason, too."

"Obstacles?" Dylan asked. "I'm good with explosives and can take care of anything that needs blowing up."

She shook her head. "No, but there's a large swimming pool behind the house." She moved another saltshaker behind the house and to the left side. "This is his guesthouse. There shouldn't be anyone staying there right now."

"Servants?" Carter asked.

She shook her head. "They won't be any trouble. They're terrified of Sergio, but not enough to fight an intruder. He brought most of them from Mexico and Honduras with promises of a better future, but Sergio forced them to work for him when they got to the United States."

She looked at each of them. "We don't have time to plan. This has to happen tonight."

"Then let's make it happen," Ethan said.

Stormy still wasn't sure about him. He seemed to be all business when he needed to be, but what would it be like working with him day in and day out. They would be the only two on the estate. She just wanted this over and done. Being undercover for almost a year had started to get to her. She'd seen too many gruesome things to ever sleep well at night.

Yeah, like she could anyway. The nightmares were getting worse. No, not really nightmares. There were more like memories. Fragments of a past she couldn't quite grasp. But were they hers or something she might've seen on television? She didn't know anymore. Sometimes, she thought she was losing her mind.

"If you're ready, we can leave now," Carter said.

She quickly brought her thoughts back to the present. Not enough sleep over the last few days. She'd known this was going down tonight and only hoped nothing went wrong. It still might.

Armed guards had a way of getting angry when someone raided the property. Not that anyone had tried before now. This would be a first, and the operation could go south fast if they didn't make each move count.

After she set her empty beer bottle on the table, she looked at the men, all ex-special ops. They were muscled, too hot for their own good, cocky as hell, but she knew they all wanted the same thing. Her gaze stopped on Ethan. Yeah, well, he might want more than the others.

She had a feeling he was going to be trouble.

If you would like to join my free newsletter group, you can find it at:

www.authorkarenkelley.com

Bound by Loyalty Honor Truth Series
Deceived
Sinner
Shadows
Explosive
Lethal

Sisters: Bound by Blood Series
Branded Book One, Savannah
Forgotten Book Two, Jade
Runaway Book Three, Rena

Not the Best Man
Not My Type

Badge of Honor Series
Broken Justice
Hidden Secrets
Fractured Lives
Shattered Souls

It's a Southern Thang Series
Bless Your Heart

Hayes Brothers Series
Dangling... Participle?
Take a Hike!
Nailed It!
Rescue Me!

Southern Series

Southern Comfort
Southern Exposure
Hell On Wheels
Southern Star

The Princes of Symtaria Series
The Jaguar Prince
The Falcon Prince
The Wolf Prince

Forbidden Series
Forbidden Magic
Forbidden Legacy
Forbidden Nights

Bachelor Series
Bachelor Party
Bachelor and the Princess
Thief of Hearts

Single Titles
Temperature's Rising
Double Dating With The Dead
How to Seduce a Texan
My Favorite Phantom
Anything You Can Do

Boxed Sets
Flocked Series
I Won't be Home for Christmas
Nerak Series Box Set

Good Girl Series
Where There's Smoke
Where There's A Will
Smoking Hot

Made in the USA
Las Vegas, NV
03 August 2022

52623369R00157